GRUMBONES

ALSO BY JENN BENNETT

Alex, Approximately
Starry Eyes
Serious Moonlight
The Lady Rogue
Chasing Lucky
Always Jane

GRUMBONES

Jenn Bennett

Simon & Schuster Books for Young Readers

NEW YORK LONDON TORONTO SYDNEY NEW DELHI

SIMON & SCHUSTER BOOKS FOR YOUNG READERS
An imprint of Simon & Schuster Children's Publishing Division
1230 Avenue of the Americas, New York, New York 10020

SIMON & SCHUSTER BOOKS FOR YOUNG READERS
and related marks are trademarks of Simon & Schuster, Inc.
For information about special discounts for bulk purchases, please contact
Simon & Schuster Special Sales at 1-866-506-1949 or business@simonandschuster.com.
The Simon & Schuster Speakers Bureau can bring authors to your live event. For more
information or to book an event, contact the Simon & Schuster Speakers Bureau at
1-866-248-3049 or visit our website at www.simonspeakers.com.
Interior design by Hilary Zarycky
The text for this book was set in Jenson.
Manufactured in the United States of America
0623 FFG
First Edition
2 4 6 8 10 9 7 5 3 1

Library of Congress Cataloging-in-Publication Data
Names: Bennett, Jenn, author.
Title: Grumbones / Jenn Bennett.
Description: First edition. | New York : Simon & Schuster Books for Young Readers, [2023] |
Audience: Ages 8–12. | Audience: Grades 4–6. | Summary: Budding sleuths Helena and her
best friend Ben hire an insufferable ghostly guide named Grumbones to track down her recently
deceased grandmother in the underworld.
Identifiers: LCCN 2022030420 (print) | LCCN 2022030421 (ebook) |
ISBN 9781665930314 (hardcover) | ISBN 9781665930338 (ebook)
Subjects: CYAC: Ghosts—Fiction. | Voyages to the otherworld—Fiction. | Grandmothers—
Fiction. | Best friends—Fiction. | Friendship—Fiction. | Fantasy. | LCGFT: Ghost stories. |
Fantasy fiction. | Novels.
Classification: LCC PZ7.1.B4538 Gr 2023 (print) |
LCC PZ7.1.B4538 (ebook) | DDC [Fic]—dc23
LC record available at https://lccn.loc.gov/2022030420
LC ebook record available at https://lccn.loc.gov/2022030421

For Hank and Charlotte

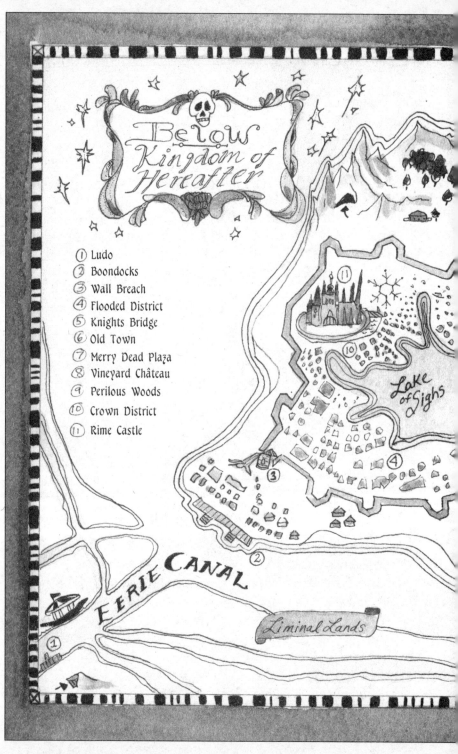

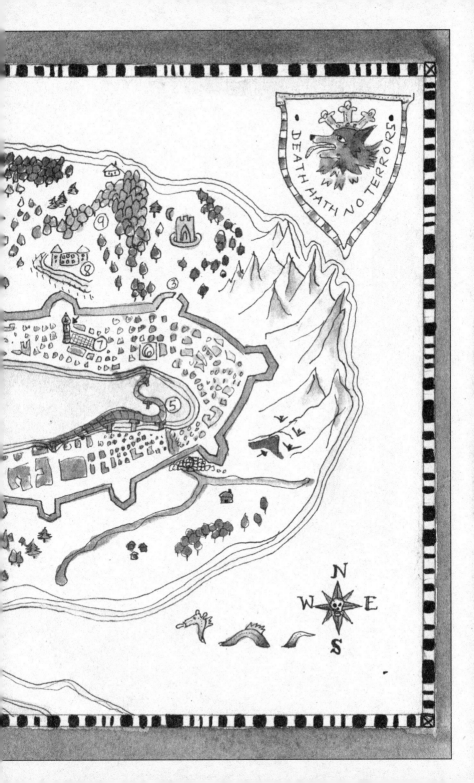

CHAPTER 1

Goth Girl

I couldn't remember how many times I'd been called "Haunted Helena."

I'd been hearing it my whole life. Practically an eternity. So it was pretty much a given that the minute I rode into town with my folks that morning, it would start up again.

Everyone in Forlorn calls me haunted. And sure, I spend a lot of time at the cemetery. I have my reasons. I also know more about the afterlife than any of my sixth-grade teachers. But I never really wanted to see an actual ghost until my grandma died. Not really.

"I think we're all ready to head into town. Jacket, glasses, keys—where are my keys?" Mom patted her heavy-duty bib overalls in her usual state of morning chaos, unaware of my plans. "Adam? Do you have the tugboat keys?"

Dad grunted from beneath his graying beard that foggy Saturday morning. He's tall, like my grandmother was, and they had the same eyes. My dad's a salvage diver, and my mom pilots their tugboat while he dives off the coast.

As he buttoned a flannel shirt over his black wet suit, he gestured toward the coffee table. "Truck keys."

He wasn't big on talking. Divers didn't need to say much underwater.

"No, the *tugboat* keys," Mom said, making a little boat shape with her hands. "Am I having a conversation with myself? Hello? Self? How are you?" Mom made talking-head shapes with her hands and answered in a goofy voice: "I'm great, but no one listens to me. How'bout you?"

"*Mom*, they're on the peg by the door," I said, standing on the toes of my red rain boots to retrieve the keys while two shaggy dogs watched. A third dog was asleep in the corner. "See? Right here, under this helpful sign that says 'Keys.' Imagine that!" I tossed them to her.

"Eww, I don't like sassy Helena." Mom scrunched up her nose as she caught the keys. "Go fetch sweet Helena, wouldya? I want to play with her instead."

"'Sweet Helena,'" I mumbled while slipping into my black storm jacket. "Sounds like a cursed porcelain doll that comes to life at night and terrifies people in their beds." I didn't feel very sweet that morning. I was too anxious about what I was going to attempt that day and hoping she didn't notice what I'd stashed inside my inner jacket pocket. If she did, I'd have to tell her what it was for, and she'd ground me. That couldn't happen today of all days.

Because here's the thing. When people call you haunted all your life, you start to wonder what's possible. Life, death, and all things supernatural . . . I thought about them a lot. And I *really* wanted to see my dead grandmother again.

Just for a moment!

And yes, I was talking about seeing her honest-to-goodness spirit from the afterworld, not some hokey vision of her face briefly appearing in the melted butter on my pancakes like some people "see" their long-lost uncle or an angel.

No, I wanted to talk to my actual grandma again. And according to everything she'd told me while she was still alive, I should've been able to do just that. . . .

"If you need me, talk to me like you've heard me talking to your grandfather," she'd told me last year. "Talking to the dead only requires a memento and a special summons."

Grandpa Novak had died before I was born, but that hadn't stopped my grandma from chatting with him every night in her bedroom using an old army photo of his. So, yeah, I guess you might say that my entire family was a little strange.

I'd been called worse.

So had my Babi—that's short for "babička," which means "grandma" in Czech—aka the best grandma in Oregon. But the truth is, not everyone loved her like I did. She'd been a florist who'd specialized in funeral arrangements and had had a reputation for being what my mom politely called "stern" but what our next-door neighbor Mrs. Whitehouse impolitely called "a holy terror." My Babi had had a rough life. I guess that had made her a little cranky sometimes.

But never to me. I was her sweet Helenka, and she was my fierce and loving protector.

We were a team. She was my "person." We shared a bond that couldn't be broken.

Not even in death.

So I did as she'd instructed: every day, I went into her bedroom, sat before a framed photo of the two of us together, and spoke the special summons out loud:

Together before, together again.

And I waited for her to appear. I waited and waited. . . . I waited to see her crooked smile (some would say "snarl") and to hear that croaky voice of hers that I loved so much.

But . . . no ghost. Ever. No cold spot in the hallway where my father was currently dragging his oxygen diving tanks. No moving shadow in the corner under the key rack near the front door. Just a sinking feeling in the pit of my stomach that something wasn't right.

But there was also something very important I needed to talk to Babi about that I hadn't gotten to tell her before she'd died. I'm talking highest level of concern. Which is why I decided to do something drastic.

Something desperate.

And because it was so extreme, I didn't dare tell my parents. Even if they had shared my enthusiasm for talking to ghosts—and they did not, I promise you—they wouldn't just have grounded me. They'd have forbidden me to ever go to the cemetery again if they knew what I had planned.

Which made me so anxious, I'd had to pee three times already.

But that morning, Mom was oblivious to the reason for my uneasy mood. "Well, daughter of mine, you're going to have to take your scary-doll routine on the road if you want a ride into town this morning. Move your buns! That goes for people *and* dogs."

Herding the dogs was my responsibility, so I called them, and we headed through the stained-glass front door. First outside was Ike the Third, my grandma's old dog, a big midnight-black mutt. She'd named all her dogs Ike. The other dogs that followed I'd named by size. Big. Little. Tiny. Those three we were only fostering until someone adopted them.

Ever since Babi had died, I kept finding shaggy stray dogs, so I kept bringing them home.

The house was getting full, but they were good company, and I didn't have many friends.

Just the one, to be honest. Ben. My best friend since forever. But things had been a little weird between us lately.

My phone buzzed with a text from him: **Ubarube yuboubu stubill cubomubing?**

That was our secret SOS code from when we were both Junior Coastal Rangers. It was really just Ubbi Dubbi, but I was nearly positive my parents didn't know what that was, so we continued to use it for texting.

I texted him back: **Ubon my wubay**

All settled. I was glad he'd agreed to do this with me. It was hard to coordinate stuff with him lately, him with all his clubs, and me with all my . . . glooming around. I pocketed my phone and herded the dogs toward the driveway.

"Let's go, Shag Pack," I told them, and they hopped into the back seat of our muddy and very dented family truck, squeezing around oxygen diving tanks while Mom started the engine. I crooked one arm over my jacket, acting natural, hoping my parents didn't notice what I was hiding inside. Then the truck rolled along the driveway, away from our two-story Victorian house, and we drove down winding, foggy streets that all sloped toward the Pacific Ocean.

It was a gray day. The anniversary of my Babi's death.

A good day to call up her spirit from the afterlife.

What I had stashed in my jacket was just part of what Ben and I would need to accomplish that task. We'd already prepared some things in secret at the cemetery. Everything was ready but the last few details, which would be handled when we met up this morning. I exhaled a long breath and tried not to think about all the things that could go wrong.

When it came to ghosts, I didn't trust that anything would be simple.

Everyone knows that my hometown of Forlorn is a historic West Coast fishing harbor, our waters once filled with whales and orcas. But local legends say it's also chockablock with old ghosts. I'm talking jam-packed, right here on our dangerously rocky shoreline. Ghosts of pirates and explorers. Ancestors of the local Chinook Indian Nation. Lost pioneers.

They don't call this area of the Oregon coast "the graveyard of the Pacific" for no reason.

Ships crash here because our fog is so thick. Locals call it the Grum: a little gray, a little glum. Grum. It's why we have not one but two lighthouses, Calamity and Blunder.

The Grum does *not* mess around. It's a ghost maker.

All these ghosts, but no Babi? How could that be right?

Mom turned onto the main road by the harbor, and though the Grum was still too thick here for us to see the ocean, I could smell the salt water, even with the windows up. Our tugboat was docked at a pier a couple of blocks from here, near Lighthouse

Blunder. When the weather's clear, I can see it from the cemetery on the hill above the harbor.

Museums and private buyers pay my parents to search underwater shipwrecks off the coast, and even though Mom and Dad claim to have never seen undersea ghosts, they've found plenty of old skeletons. Some of what they discover—skeletons not included—ends up belonging to the state or military, even other countries. Sometimes they get to keep stuff. Our attic is filled with rusted swords, a carved mermaid figurehead, and old coins. Jayne Jackson won't spend the night because she says my house smells like whale pee. Like she'd know.

At the end of the block, Mom pulled into an empty space at the curb in front of an old convenience store that was painted with black and white stripes to mimic a lighthouse. Beacon Corner Shop.

Being a two-minute jaunt from Forlorn Middle School and offering a superior imported candy selection made the Beacon a hot spot for everyone who walked to school. Being a couple of blocks down the hill from the house of Granny Booker, my best friend's grandma, also made it the perfect meet-up place for what we were planning today.

"I'm so glad you and Ben are hanging out," Mom said. "It's like the good old days."

"We see each other at school every day," I reminded her. But I knew what she meant.

"It's nice for old friends to do things together. Hey—don't buy a bunch of bubble gum in there," Mom warned me as I waited for the Shag Pack to exit the truck onto the sidewalk.

"Gum? Pfft. I've learned my lesson." I cracked my jaw to one side, causing a popping noise. A recent visit to the dentist had diagnosed me with a painful jaw condition called TMJ. That meant no chewy foods, and a night guard when I slept to stop my teeth from grinding. "So, when will you guys be back from the dive? That is, if the fearsome Forlorn Worm doesn't get you."

Dad rolled his eyes in the rearview mirror. The Forlorn Worm is our local legendary sea serpent—a big white devil that supposedly lives deep under the waves and takes down ships in the Grum. Every year, a blurry picture of the creature makes the rounds on local blogs.

"We'll be back before dinner," Mom assured me. "Forlorn Worm or not. Pick you back up here around four? Your dad promised to make us something tasty."

"In Hades?" I asked.

Dad had built a brick pizza oven in our backyard after Babi had died. He'd named it Hades because when he fired it up with wood, it got as hot as Hades. So far, we'd eaten approximately three thousand wood-fired pizzas made in Hades—no complaints from me, but Mom said she was having nightmares about us turning into flaming pizza people.

"No pizza," Mom said, and he agreed with a disappointed nod.

"Welp, see ya later, exterminators," I said. "And text me if you find any skeletons during your dive."

As I scooted across the seat, Mom peered at the bulge under my jacket. "What you got there?"

"Huh?" I felt my ears getting warm, but my dark bobbed hair was *just* long enough to cover them. Whenever I get embarrassed, my ears turn lobster red, just like my dad's. I couldn't let her see that. I was so close to freedom!

"Helena?" Mom said, reaching through the seats for my jacket collar.

"My sketchbook, nothing important," I mumbled, wiggling away. And before she could demand evidence, I pulled my jacket tight to my body, snapped my fingers to call the Shag Pack, leaving Ike the Third behind with my folks, and slipped out of the truck. "I'll be careful. Promise. See you at dinner."

Whew! That was close.

"Helena?" Mom called through the door before I could close it, a little worry in her tone. "Don't bring any cursed dolls home. Or stray dogs. Vaccination bills are bleeding us dry, hon."

"No more shaggies," Dad agreed.

"Don't forget to ask if your dog adoption flyer inside the shop has had any interest, okay? Then the two of you go straight to Granny Booker's," Mom added. "And don't go near the cemetery! Hear me? Cool it with the spooky stuff, okay?"

"It's not easy being this Goth, you know."

"Try wearing pink," Mom encouraged.

I sighed heavily. Funny that neither of my parents seemed to remember what day it was, anniversary-wise. If they had, they'd have been visiting Babi's grave themselves. For now, I was thankful for their forgetfulness.

And before they could remember that or anything else, I made like a ghost and disappeared into Beacon Corner Shop as fast as I could.

CHAPTER 2

Creepy Birds

nside the shop, the sweet scents of waxy chocolate and overripe bananas filled my nostrils. I quickly scanned the narrow shop aisles for my best friend's face, but he wasn't inside the Beacon. The clock above the door said I was a few minutes late, so that made me feel panicky.

"He was already here, Miss Helena," the gray-haired man behind the counter said, waving his hand to get my attention. Mr. Beacon himself, the shop owner.

"Ben?" I asked, stepping up to the old-fashioned register.

"He said to tell you to meet him at his grandmother's house." The shop owner gave me a little smile, his face wrinkled and kind. "Sounded like he had an errand to run. Nothing amiss. Hello there, Shag Pack," he added, peering down at the wagging tails near my legs.

I relaxed a little and checked my phone. He hadn't texted again. Maybe he'd had to run off in a hurry? It was just that I didn't want anything to go wrong today. I needed some sugary courage. A familiar display box of gum stared up at me from the counter, each red-wrapped piece printed with the word PEDRO and a tiny smiling boy in a sombrero. Babi's favorite gum, imported from Europe. "I'll take ten of these," I told Mr. Beacon.

As I gave him the last of my pocket change and asked if anyone had inquired about adopting the Shag Pack—nothing yet—a couple of boys and a girl from school walked through the shop door. I turned away, but they spotted my dogs.

The first boy was Jake, a tall, scruffy blond with a tiny red rubber ball that he bounced continually in front of him as he walked, catching it in his palm. By his side in a hoodie with a gold zipper was his dark-headed friend Dip, who used to be on the chess team—and a lot nicer—until his sister got sick. Then Dip started hanging around Jake. Trailing both boys was our school's track star, Mikki, a brown-eyed girl who moved on long legs. Her gaze caught mine, and it was filled with mistrust.

"Haunted Helena!" Jake called out, bouncing his red ball.

"Haunted Helena and her hounds from hell," Dip said. "Woof, woof!"

Mikki elbowed Jake and said, "Cut it out. She might curse you, or something. I heard she's the reason Annie Casado was in that car wreck."

What? Distress made my throat feel tight. Is that what people were saying at school? "I don't even personally know Annie Casado. Why would I do that?"

"But you *could?*" Jake challenged. "Isn't that what happened to your scary old hag of a grandmother?"

I froze.

The red ball bounced.

A terrible ache squeezed my chest.

Sure, Jake was being the lowest form of scum right now, and I knew it, but that didn't stop it from hurting. I mean, of *course* I hadn't tried to curse anyone. Wouldn't know how to start. And Babi? Why would I hurt the one person I loved more than anything else in the world?

When I didn't answer, Dip squinted at my jacket and said, "Hey now. Are you shoplifting, Haunted Helena? Mr. Beacon, I think she's shoplifting."

I glanced down to where I was holding my jacket, and felt heat spread over my ears and down my neck. "This is . . . mine. I came . . . in here with it," I explained haltingly to the shop owner, frustrated that I sounded so guilty. That I *felt* guilty.

It didn't matter now. What I had in my pocket was only a worthless household item. I just didn't want to show the entire store that I'd stolen something from my own home.

Please don't make me, I whispered inside my head like a prayer.

Mr. Beacon nodded and lifted a hand to absolve me. "You're fine."

Thank goodness! Relief loosened my grip on my jacket. But I still felt tightly wired and anxious inside.

"I don't know, Dip. Even still, I think we should call the school and report her for missing her detention," Jake said, bouncing his ball higher.

Ashamed that Mr. Beacon was hearing all this, I responded, "It's not weekend detention. It's just lunchtime. And it's completely unfair!"

Basically, I got in trouble for reading at school. About ghosts.

Not that it should matter, but tell that to fussy Ms. Lovejoy. She gave me lunchtime detention for (1) Unexcused Tardiness (I'd been reading outside school and had lost track of time). (2) Failure to Obtain a Hall Pass (I'd been rushing to get to homeroom). (3) Inappropriate Reading Material (*Death Magic for Beginners*).

An institute of education shouldn't punish me for trying to learn. I wasn't even interested in the chapter about using magic to strike down enemies. I was trying to figure out why Babi's ghost wasn't appearing to me. But whatever. All that mattered at that moment in the Beacon was that these three were trying to punish me all over again. Which was *extra* unfair. And it was three against one.

Ever since Babi had died, it had felt like the entire world was against me. Like no one understood what I was going through. Like I was more alone than I'd ever been in my entire life.

I needed my best friend. Why couldn't Ben be here? I felt heavy in my heart.

One of the Shag Pack barked at Mikki—the smallest dog, Tiny. It was enough to startle the girl. Jake jumped a little too, then shook it off and laughed at Mikki. "Now you've got me spooked. Come on, gang. Better move before Goth girl puts a spell on us."

They all chuckled and headed toward the back of the shop, Mikki careful to give the dogs a wide berth. As Mr. Beacon gave me a pitying look, I stuffed my bubble gum into my jacket pocket and quickly exited the shop with the dogs.

Outside, it took a few moments for my throat to relax and my bad feelings to shrink. But I couldn't just stand there like a lump and risk another confrontation. I needed to get away from the shop. So I hiked up the sidewalk with the dogs, huffing out quick breaths.

Hoping this wasn't a bad start to my important day.

I did my best to concentrate my thoughts on my surroundings, not the trio in the shop. When I glanced behind me, I already couldn't see the black and white stripes on the side of the building because the Grum was too thick. That made me feel better. The fog in Forlorn could be comforting, in a strange way. It clung to streetlights and swirled around tsunami evacuation signs: IN CASE OF EARTHQUAKE, GO TO HIGHER GROUND.

The last tsunami we'd had was in the 1960s, caused by an earthquake that had started in the Cascadia fault line. But we can get waves from distant earthquakes, far away under the Pacific.

Mostly we just get fog and more fog, like today. The entire block was blanketed. But the farther up the hill I hiked, the less of a comfort it was.

In fact, I had the feeling that someone was a few steps behind me on the sidewalk.

I just couldn't see them.

Were the kids from the store following me? That thought made my heart drum against my chest as a sour feeling settled in the pit of my stomach.

"Hey, Big, Little, and Tiny? You keep an eye out, all right?" I told the Shag Pack. "I know we've only been friends for a few weeks, but I've fed you pretty decently. You're living your best lives, lounging in front of our fireplace. All I ask is that you watch my back."

Tiny and Big were peeing on a bush. Little just panted up at me. So much for that.

I sped up, but I couldn't shake the feeling that I was being followed.

I was on full alert now.

In the distance, the waterfront trolley's bell dinged, and if I listened hard enough when traffic stopped, I could *just* make out the funny barks of the sea lions that huddled under Pier 13.

What else?

Huh. Not footsteps following me. Maybe it was a single voice. An animal noise? Something caught my eye. . . .

Across the street, a tufted black-and-white puffin stared at me from where it huddled near someone's mailbox, its thick orange bill moving as if it were talking. Was that my stalker?

A little relief warmed me from the inside. Not the kids from the shop. Just a bird.

And yet, it was strange to see a puffin this far up in the city streets. Forlorn has a lot of puffins that live on the harbor rocks down by the lighthouses, but they never come into the neighborhoods.

I was too far away to see its eyes, but this one's head turned to watch me as I walked, fog swirling around webbed feet that matched its brightly colored bill.

Babi had said birds were too smart. She'd always shooed them away.

Looking at this odd seabird, I understood why my Babi hadn't liked them.

"It's just lost," I whispered to myself. I was being paranoid.

Best to keep moving and not obsess over it.

Just a bird. And I was only shaken up by what had happened inside the Beacon.

So why couldn't I shake this feeling that something was . . . *off*?

Trying not to be scared, I flicked one last look at the orange-footed bird and hiked double-quick up the hill toward my destination.

The Booker mansion. Safety!

Forlorn was filled with old Victorian houses that used to be fancy but were now just drafty and creaky. Granny Booker's was yellow and had an iron gate out front. The best thing about it was that it had a huge wooded backyard that led straight into the Whispering Pines Cemetery.

If you knew the right path. My best friend, Ben, did. And he was waiting for me.

A weight lifted. I was so thankful to see his friendly face.

"High," Ben called out in greeting, one hand cupped around his mouth.

"Low," I responded to the tall and lanky shape behind the front gate.

Dark corkscrew curls stood out every which way atop his head in the fog. A T-shirt printed with a Loch Ness Monster wanted poster (HAVE YOU SEEN ME?) was half tucked into his jeans beneath a naval peacoat with three small golden letters stitched on the front, BPC, which stood for Booker Packing Company. Ben's dad ran the only Black-owned tuna cannery in North America, and his mom was a French Canadian who came from a family that owned a fleet of fishing ships.

They were all about the fish.

Ben looked behind me and counted, "Big, Little, and Tiny . . . Still got all three, huh?" His mouth lifted in amusement as I hurried toward him with my shaggy dog posse. "Whoa, Helena. You running from the law or something? Slow down."

"Don't freak, but something might be following me. I mean, maybe? I might have been followed."

"*What?*" He pushed open the front gate and glanced over my

head, a nervous gleam in his squinting brown eyes. "Where? Who?"

If I was the school weirdo for my interest in ghosts, then I was in good company. Ben Booker was a devotee of anything crypto-zoological. The yeti, the Forlorn Worm, Chupacabra, Mothman. Any unexplained creature in the woods, water, or air? He's into it.

"What do you mean, *followed?*" he whispered. "Human or beast?"

"Don't know," I whispered back.

He picked up a stick from the ground, a little terror widening his eyes as the three dogs circled us, pacing. Together we listened, peering into the Grum. Nothing.

A flock of noisy crows scattered from a nearby tree, making us jump.

"See!" I said to Ben. "Told you something is following me."

But Ben wasn't rattled anymore. His shoulders relaxed as he lowered his eyes and said flatly, "*Birds? Really?*"

"Not just any birds. What's a gathering of crows called again?" I said. "Oh, that's right, a *murder* of crows."

Ben's eyes darted from the tree to the sky to me. I knew that look. Pretty sure he was peeved I'd freaked him out for what he thought was no good reason.

"What does your *Mammoth Book of Cryptid Tales* say about crow warnings?" I asked.

He gave me a hurt look, tossed his stick aside, and said, "I agreed to do this today because I thought you were taking it seriously. But if you're just gonna fool around and make fun of me, I've got a Bigfoot Enthusiasts Club meeting to prepare for this afternoon."

"Hey," I complained, offended that he thought I was making

fun of him. Sure, some of his theories about wild crocodile men living by the river were a little . . . out there. But that was okay. Out there was good. "I always take this stuff seriously. *You* weren't at the Beacon today when I needed you. We set a meeting time."

"You got my message, right? My granny asked me to help her move some chairs for her nursing meeting—why do you think I'm covered in sweat? I wasn't lying, sheesh."

"And I wasn't lying either! You should believe me when I tell you something, and I just told you I was being followed!"

"I repeat, by *birds*?"

"There was a puffin down the street. Why would a puffin be all the way up here?"

He shrugged his shoulders high. "Doing whatever birds do, Helena. You're starting to sound like your grandmother used to, and"—he held up a single finger—"not in a good way. Babi Morana was great, but she could be . . . paranoid."

My ears got a little warm. I made sure my hair covered them so he couldn't see. I hated that he could embarrass me. I hated fighting with him. I was butt-hurt and I wanted him to feel the same way, so I snapped, "Whatever! No one can see in all this fog—it's not my fault that I got spooked. And if I'm *so* irritating to you, I can go to the cemetery by myself, you know. No one said you had to come along. You can run off to your dumb ol' Bigfooters. Just give me the booklet. I can do it all myself."

That wasn't true. I mean, I probably *could*. But I didn't want to.

Today was a big deal. We'd been planning it. Researching it in secret.

It's one thing to say you want to raise the dead by yourself. Another thing to do it.

He gave me a perturbed look and sighed. "I get that things have been gloomy for you lately. But I'm here, you know. You don't have to do it alone."

I was secretly glad he said that. I really didn't want to fight. Not with him.

"You'll help me . . . in the cemetery?" I asked.

"Friends don't let friends dabble in necromancy by themselves," he said with a hint of a smile before closing the front gate. He took something out of his pocket and dangled it just out of reach. "Besides, I'm the one who found the graveyard booklet."

"You're better at finding stuff than I am," I admitted.

"And you're better at naming things. 'Bigfooters' is a *much* better club name," he said, grinning. "Now come on. Let's get to the cemetery before your creepy puffin finds us."

Thank goodness. I was so glad to have peace between us, but there was a little worry behind his smile as he glanced toward the trees.

At least he believed me now.

CHAPTER 3
Grave Robbery

The graveyard booklet that Ben rolled up like a telescope to fit into his jacket pocket was ten pages long and bound together with red string. It looked as if someone had made it by hand—like, a hundred years ago. It was titled *How to Talk to the Dead*. No author. No publisher. No date of any kind. Just some brief old-timey instructions that had been written in neat handwriting along with a few antiquated line drawings.

Ben had spotted it in the cemetery a few days ago, left behind on a bench.

At first we thought it was just a novelty, like a Ouija board. Something that was more or less a party trick, for goofing around with friends and having fun scares. Nothing serious. But the more we looked into it, the more we became convinced that the instructions inside *How to Talk to the Dead* might actually conjure up spirits from beyond. Briefly. Possibly.

Hopefully.

If it worked, I could talk to Babi. Even for a moment, it was worth a try. After all, the special summons that she'd taught me wasn't working. Time for plan B.

Plan B just happened to involve a little dark magic among the graves.

Nerves on edge, I followed Ben on a path that led around the side of his grandmother's house and meandered through some dense pine woods. The Shag Pack trailed behind us. Granny Booker was a retired midwife, but she sometimes spoke with nursing students about her experiences delivering babies, which is what she was doing in the big yellow house that morning. That meant we were on our own until lunch. I hoped it was enough time.

The farther we walked, the more I forgot about the creepy birds, and the more anxious I became about the task ahead of us. At a fork in the path, you could go left, and it would lead you down some cliffs to the harbor. To the right, if you slipped behind a big rock, you would find an old rusty gate covered in ivy. And *that* led into the back of the cemetery.

Whispering Pines Cemetery is the oldest, largest burial ground in the state. It's so big that it would take hours to walk through it, and plenty of people come from all over to take tours of all the old graves and marble statues. That morning, however, it was quiet and foggy.

Legend says that the first body buried here was the loyal dog of a famous English explorer who, locals believe, managed to land on our rocky shores without wrecking his ship in our dangerous waters—pretty amazing, especially back then with no lighthouses to guide him. Anyway, his dog was named Winnow, and the dog's grave is near the section of the cemetery right next to Granny Booker's backyard.

Winnow the cemetery dog is one of a few popular ghosts said to haunt these grounds. But that's one more hope that I've had crushed. First of all, Ben and I have yet to see a single ghost. And we've been looking for months. And second of all, I find it hard to believe that in all the thousands of years this land has existed, and the hundreds of years the Chinook have hunted and fished here, that an English explorer was the first to bury a body in the woods.

But that's not Winnow's fault, I guess. Dogs want to be loyal and helpful. It's humans that cause all the trouble.

Whispering Pines Cemetery is divided into quadrants that spread out like a wheel. The Heights is where the rich are buried. The Flats is for regular folk. The Cliffs is where the nameless lie, like sailors who drown at sea. And the Wilds is the wooded area that Ben and I were walking through that morning, where pets were buried.

No one's allowed to bury pets anymore. Ike the First is buried there—my Babi's first dog—but ever since the 1980s, that part of the cemetery is just historical. However, rich people are still buried in the Heights.

My Babi had been buried in the Flats.

"You brought what we need for today, right?" Ben asked as we headed down gravel paths that wound around old and new graves. "Like the booklet said? Want to make sure we have it all."

I pulled out a paper tube of fireplace matches from my inner jacket pocket to show him. I'd had to sneak it when my parents weren't watching. Night before last, I had to stealth around the house like a common criminal so I could creep into my grandmother's old room to get the framed photograph of me and her. The one I'd tried to use to call her with the summons so many times without success.

Yesterday I came to the cemetery and placed the framed photo of me and Babi on her grave. It was a good photo of us. Three of us, actually, because Ike the Third is in the picture too.

Babi loved dogs. She addressed them as "Mr." and "Mrs." because she said they deserved the same respect as people— sometimes more. If she'd known there were so many stray dogs roaming the cemetery, she would have brought them home too. So along with the framed photo, I'd left a lot of drawings of Big, Little, and Tiny on Babi's gravestone. And some lily of the valley flowers that she loved.

Mementos. Tokens.

Whispering Pines was filled with tokens left behind on graves. Sometimes mourners left flowers or small crosses. A lot of military people left coins on the graves of their fellow soldiers. Some people believed rocks held the soul down or kept demons from getting inside the coffins. I kept a few good pebbles on Babi's grave, just in case.

Ben and I ducked under the sagging branches of an old tree and stopped in front of my Babi's gravestone. As far as graves went, it was fairly simple: just a headstone standing above a slab of granite on the grass with a little alcove for candles and flowers. At the moment, it was covered in fog, but I could make out the engraving on the front, just as she'd requested in her final will:

MORANA NOVÁKOVÁ

MESS WITH MY FAMILY, AND I WILL HAUNT YOU

Way to give me false hope, Babi, I said to myself.

Babi had been born in Prague after the Second World War. Some of her Czech family had had to flee the Nazis, and after the war, Babi had been orphaned. She'd bounced around Europe until an American war journalist had rescued her and brought her to the U.S. That's how she ended up in Oregon. Her dead husband had a grave next to hers. He'd been Czech American too, and his gravestone was carved with a symbol for Vietnam vets. His ship had gone down off the coast near here after his tour of duty had ended in the 1970s, when he'd been coming home for the birth of my dad . . . which he never made.

Like I said, Forlorn is the graveyard of the Pacific.

My Babi had had a rough life. I just hoped that she wasn't having a rough life in death, too. Maybe I was about to find out. Butterflies fluttered inside my stomach, a sensation that was washed away by a low unease.

"You ready?" Ben asked. "If we wait too long, someone might show up. . . ."

I let out a long exhale. He was right. Now or never.

It was time.

Even though we'd been there the day before to set everything up, it hadn't been the right date. Today was the anniversary of Babi's death. It was also gray and cloudy, which was apparently good for ghost summoning? The booklet said not to attempt this under a sunny sky.

"Tell me what the rest of the ritual says again?" I asked, even though we'd been through it a million times. I glanced around at the cemetery rows nervously, making sure we had privacy. Nobody but us and the Shag Pack.

Ben flipped through the pages and ran a light brown finger over the passage. "We need a likeness of the departed—did that yesterday when we placed your photo at the grave. And a candle, which I brought from my granny's today." He fished around in his peacoat and brought out a long taper candle, the kind that's used at a formal dinner table, or in a candelabra. "This is all I could find," he mumbled.

"A candle is a candle, right? It's wax and it'll burn with these," I said, shaking the long tube I'd nabbed from the fireplace back at home. "What's next? The symbols?"

He nodded. "Trace the summoning sigil onto the grave with a finger dipped in grave dirt."

We looked at each other, and I could see the same sinking feeling reflected in Ben's eyes. "Grave dirt," he mumbled. "Does that mean dirt from right here, on top of the grave? Or . . ."

"Dirt from inside a grave?" I finished, grimacing.

"Why would you need to dig up a body to talk to its spirit?" Ben argued. "What's the point of a magic ritual if you're just going to spend all your time shoveling contaminated dirt? No way."

"Total agreement. The drawings in the booklet don't show anyone digging up a body . . . right?" One of the shaggy dogs whined. None of us wanted to dig up a body.

Ben flipped to the next page. One twisting lock of hair fell over his eye as he concentrated on reading. Rereading. Then he looked up at me and nodded briefly. "No bodies are dug up. Just use the dirt on top of the grave. Here is the sigil we need to draw. . . ."

Not a complicated symbol. Just a circle with a triangle that overlapped it halfway, and a few lines around the outside that may have been letters from an ancient alphabet. Or maybe they were just squiggly lines; who knew? But the ground around my grandmother's grave was wet with morning dew, so it was easy enough to gather up a fingerful of clay and trace the sigil onto the stone.

"You think that's right?" I asked Ben when I was finished.

He surveyed my work and nodded. "Looks right to me. Now the next step. In order to establish a connection to the departed, the living should sit in front of the grave and hold the candle over the sigil."

I knelt on the cool granite in front of the headstone, the toes of my shoes sticking out into wet grass. My pulse was racing, and I was becoming a little dizzy. I forced myself to take a deep breath to try to relax.

"Now we light the candle," Ben said. "And when the flame is lit, you speak the summoning word in front of the photo to call up your grandmother. Ready?"

Not really. My heart felt like a trapped rabbit. Maybe we shouldn't do this. Who did I think I was, anyway, fooling around with dark magic? An image from the Beacon Corner Shop popped up inside my head, of Jake's mistrustful face when he was accusing me of cursing my grandmother.

What if I caused some irreversible damage to Babi's soul by summoning her up like this?

But . . . what if she was trapped in some terrible plane of existence, being tortured?

"Ready?" Ben asked.

That snapped me out of my thoughts. I needed to do this. If I didn't, how would I ever get a chance to talk to Babi again? To tell her what I needed to tell her?

Fumbling the candle and the fireplace matches, I awkwardly

managed to retrieve a long match. I struck it . . . and struck it . . . and finally! Fire! I lit the candle and blew out the match.

"Say the summoning!" Ben told me frantically as the wind picked up and threatened to blow out my candle flame.

Right! Oh God! I hoped for my grandmother's sake that I was saying this word correctly.

"Nostos!" I shouted while gripping the candle.

Nostos, I repeated inside my head, just in case the shouting wasn't enough.

Breath coming fast, I stared at the dancing flame, waiting for something to happen.

The candle went out.

Ben yelped.

And before I could panic fully, my eyes darted everywhere all at once as the fog briefly cleared . . . from the wisp of smoke near the snuffed-out candle, to the muddy sigil I'd drawn on the stone, to something that was *very* wrong inside the little alcove on my Babi's grave.

I squinted at what was in front of me. It wasn't a ghost. A ghost would be right.

No ghost.

No anything.

In the shifting fog, I could see now that the little alcove in Babi's grave was clean. No smooth pebbles. No framed photo, no dog drawings tucked beneath. No lily of the valley flowers. Nothing that I'd left for her.

They'd all been there yesterday.

The framed photo of me and Babi. We needed it for the summoning!

Was everything all messed up now?

"How did I not notice it was gone before we started the ritual?" I said, more to myself than to Ben. But he was panicking too.

"I could have sworn it was . . . ," he mumbled, glancing around wildly. "All your mementos? Are you sure?"

No. I wasn't sure about anything, frankly. I just felt like crying. I looked at all the other plots nearby, thinking that maybe Whispering Pines had hired a new caretaker who'd cleaned up all the graves. They aren't supposed to throw away personal mementos—only wilted flowers or things that get in the way of mowing the grass. But all the graves around my Babi's were filled with the normal trinkets.

No wind could have blown them away: Babi's grave had a little sheltered place in the front where I stashed the mementos.

Ben was just as puzzled as I was for a moment. We split up and raced up and down the rows of graves to see if my mementos had been moved, checking a couple dozen nearby graves. Maybe some shrimpy toddler had been fooling around while their parent wasn't paying attention.

Nope. Not in the nearest trash can, either.

"They've been taken!" I told Ben. "Stolen!"

He didn't answer, but his silence said everything. What else could it be?

We walked back to Babi's grave together in disbelief.

"Why would someone do this?" I asked, feeling panicked. Angry. "They weren't even worth anything." But the photo was irreplaceable. It was a printout—the original file had been accidently deleted!

Plenty of graves in the Heights had expensive flowers, sometimes jewelry. I didn't even keep coins on Babi's grave. Why would someone steal my stuff?

Grave theft was the lowest of crimes. Wormy. Slimy. This was sacred ground. What kind of scum steals from the dead? From the people mourning them? I blinked at the headstone.

Where I'd drawn the sigil in mud on the granite . . .

It was gone. In its place, written in dried clay in an unusual, old-fashioned script, were three words:

Follow The Bird.

A prickling sensation raced up my spine.

Ben made a low noise. "Do you see that?"

"I see it," I whispered. "I told you that I had a bad feeling, but you didn't believe me."

"I believe you now," he said. "I just don't understand."

I didn't either. We both looked around but didn't see anyone. No people. No birds.

My first thought was that we'd made those words appear with our magic ritual. But then I wondered if someone had written them on the grave while we were momentarily distracted, running up and down the rows, looking for the stolen mementos. If so, that someone would've had to have been waiting for a chance to scribble those words . . . watching us.

Just like I'd thought earlier.

Who would be trying to scare us?

The kids from the corner shop?

But if it were them, why hadn't the Shag Pack noticed? None of them had barked. They acted as if nothing were wrong. That made me worry more.

Ben snapped a photo of the vandalism, and then I quickly

wiped it away with the edge of my jacket sleeve. It felt wrong, disrespectful to Babi. But when I stood up from the grave, there was that same odd feeling I'd had earlier on the walk to Granny Booker's house. Now I was convinced.

Someone really was watching us.

Ben felt it too—I could see it in the small line of worry that grew between his eyebrows. "Helena . . . ? What's happening?" he said nervously.

I wanted to tell him that Jake, Dip, and Mikki must have followed us here through the secret shortcut from Granny Booker's house. If that were true, though, then how come it was so quiet? I'm talking *silent*. By all appearances, there was no one around this part of the cemetery. No tourists. No mourners. No people at all.

"I don't understand," I whispered to Ben. "It seems like we're alone here."

Or maybe I spoke too soon.

Something rustled in the tree branches jutting above the row of graves. We both peered into the swirling fog to see something that made all the hairs on my arms stand on end.

A giant vulture with a bright red head was staring down at us. A vulture . . .

With empty sockets where the eyes should have been.

We did the only sensible thing you could do in that situation. We got the ever-loving heck out of there.

CHAPTER 4
Gift Shop

We didn't have to run far. A haven was nearby.

"Help!" Ben and I shouted as we raced through the front door of the only public building inside the cemetery.

A lot of people are surprised to discover that Whispering Pines has a gift shop. But almost everyone who's surprised ends up being delighted. I know I was. It's also the cemetery's information center, as well as the place where folks line up for tours.

The cemetery souvenirs cramming the shop are one of a kind. I'd purchased nearly everything they sell with my allowance money, except for the porcelain tea set and the gold memorial plates—out of my price range. However, I *do* own the Whispering Pines stationery set, magnets, all the postcards, both books, three mugs, earrings, a hoodie, the plush version of Winnow the cemetery dog, the tarot cards . . . plus ceramic replicas of major historic Whispering Pines graves and crypts.

And it was all these things that I raced past as Ben and I sought shelter from the spooky vulture outside. A little assistance would have been nice. There was usually someone here: the shop owner and cemetery historian, Miss Neja Einarsson. I'd known her since I was a baby.

My Babi used to take me to the cemetery when she delivered funeral flowers for the gravesites. She would talk to Miss Neja while I played outside in the crypts.

"Miss Neja!" I called out as we jogged around the gift shop in a panic, bumping into each other and nearly knocking over a stand of postcards.

No one answered. Big, Little, and Tiny padded around the display shelves in silence.

I checked the board behind the counter that listed the times of Miss Neja's cemetery tours. The first one started at 9:00 a.m., in ten minutes.

Usually there was a handful of people in here, wasting time while they waited for the tour. There was a lot to look at on the walls: the history of burials, embalming tools, and paintings and photographs of local historical figures who'd been buried in the cemetery.

"Hola, children!" a pleasantly cheerful voice called from the back room, light and airy, like wind chimes. "A fine day to have your feet on the ground, wouldn't you say? The Grum is thick this morning. Perfect for a brisk walk among the gravestones."

A middle-aged woman stepped out of the shadows of the short hallway.

Miss Neja was a former nun, and I guess she was about my mom's age? It was hard to tell. She had messy salt-and-pepper-colored hair and had immigrated from Europe, like my Babi. Also like Babi—and Ben—she could write and speak multiple languages, which I wish I could do; I only know a few Czech words that Babi taught me.

But the best thing about Miss Neja was that she knew everything about the cemetery, about graveyard history and folklore. Oh, and she also wore a wolf's tooth on a necklace. That was pretty fierce. Right then I could have used someone fierce to protect us from that vulture.

"Miss Neja!" we said.

"Oh, my dears," she said, one hand untangling her wild hair. "What's the matter?"

Ben and I started talking at the same time. She hushed us, and we tried again.

I went first. "My grandmother's grave has been robbed."

"The body is gone?" she asked.

I wrinkled my nose. "No. The *mementos* I left on her grave yesterday. They were taken."

"Oh," the graveyard historian said. "Well, you know the rules." She pointed to a sign on the door:

WHISPERING PINES IS NOT RESPONSIBLE FOR STOLEN OR LOST PROPERTY. ANY ITEMS LEFT ON THE GRAVES ARE CONSIDERED FORFEIT AND MAY BE THROWN AWAY OR DESTROYED BY THE MAINTENANCE CREW AT ANY TIME.
REMEMBER: POSSESSIONS ARE MEANINGLESS AND DEATH IS PART OF LIFE. ENJOY THE GRUM!

That did *not* make me feel better.

"I know, but—" I tried to explain, and Ben helped. We told her what had been stolen. Useless items, worthless to anyone but me. We told her about the vandalism.

We did not tell her about the secret ritual to summon up my grandmother's ghost. That was need-to-know information.

But! We did tell her about the vulture.

"Many different bird species make their homes in the cemetery," Miss Neja said.

"*Eyeless* birds?" Ben said, sounding far too indignant and freaked out for someone who was wearing a monster T-shirt. "What about those?"

Something changed in her face. She was either frightened or thought we'd lost our minds. But all she said in a cool voice was, "The Grum can play tricks on your senses, Mr. Booker. We've had this discussion before when you've inquired about ghosts."

"You said it wasn't wise to rule out the possibility of ghosts!" he said, waving his arms.

She closed one eye. "Did I? Ah, well." She shrugged as if it were no big deal.

"What about the vandalism on my Babi's grave?" I argued. "Show her the picture, Ben."

He dug out his phone. She squinted at the screen and made a low noise. "I see. . . . I must admit, this *is* rather concerning. I'll definitely take a look at it—after my first tour, of course."

I gritted my teeth. "Um . . ."

"Is that a problem?" she asked.

I didn't want to tell her I'd wiped away *FOLLOW THE BIRD*, not when she was looking at me like that. As if she didn't believe me. And of course when I *did* explain, her disbelief only deepened.

"Miss Novak," she told me in a voice that wasn't quite patient.

"I'm not sure what you want me to do about any of this. You already cleaned up the vandalism yourselves, and it doesn't sound like it was a threat, exactly. Some might even say it was an inspirational message. And the stolen items are, as you've said, of no real worth. You knew when you placed them on the grave that you forfeited your right to ownership of these trinkets . . . so what can I do for you?"

Now I was indignant along with Ben. "Seriously? You aren't the least bit concerned that there's a thief roaming the cemetery? You're out here all alone." She lived in a tiny caretaker house on the property, just outside the gift shop.

"My dear," she said patiently, "if I were concerned about every little frightful thing that folks believed roamed this cemetery, I would have fled in fear many years ago. People are afraid of the cemetery because it is associated with death. They are afraid of dying because it is the Great Unknown. But that is silly. We know plenty about dying. For one, everyone does it."

"Everyone dies?" Ben said. "That's no comfort, Miss Neja."

"It should be. We're all in the same boat."

"That's a bunch of bunk," I complained. "We may all die, but we aren't in the same boat. The cemetery is separated into different parts. If you're rich, do you go to a different place when you die? What about all those unmarked graves? What happens to them? And who stole my mementos? These are all unknowns."

Miss Neja wasn't fazed. "See that picture next to the tour schedule behind the counter?"

She pointed to an old-timey print of a boy walking in front of a giant onion and this poem:

Billy knows his onions.
He is not troubled with corns or bunions.
He travels along at a good, fair gait;
Unless the roads are bad, he is never late.

"Know your onions," she said. "You know what you know, and that's what you know until you know more. When I face something intimidating, I think of Billy, who may not know the meaning of life, or what's on the road ahead, but he knows all about onions."

"Why onions? And where is he taking them?"

She lifted her shoulders. "Let's say . . . Detroit. That kid is an onion expert. He believes in onions. Dreams about them. He will not stop until he gets to Detroit and tells the good people there what he knows about onions."

"Billy is one weird kid," Ben mumbled.

"Hope he doesn't run into any onion burglars or eyeless birds," I added.

"Burglars only break into houses," she pointed out.

"Then I hope he doesn't run into any highway bandits obsessed with French onion soup."

Ben groaned impatiently.

"The point is," she said with a small smile, "the unknown is less scary when you simply concentrate on what you *do* know, keep going, and don't panic. Know your onions."

Onions. Whatever. She was so calm about all this. I'd bet if it had been her grandmother's grave, she wouldn't have been shrugging it off. If she'd seen what we'd seen . . .

"Tell you what, why don't you two onionheads stay inside the gift shop and let me conduct the morning tour?" she suggested. "While I'm working, I'll keep an eye out for thieves."

"We'll come with you," I volunteered.

"Nope. I'm good," Ben said, shaking his head. "I'll stay in here with the Shag Pack."

"Good idea, Mr. Booker. You don't have to worry about eyeless birds in here," Miss Neja said, patting him on the shoulder. When she did, the wolf's tooth necklace dangled free from the folds of her dress for a moment. But she tucked it away and it was hidden again.

"I didn't see any tourists out there this morning," I told her.

She smiled. "Stay put. There's warm cider and muffins on the table. I'll be back in a jiff."

With that, she grabbed a hooded jacket and glided out the shop door into the fog.

I sighed heavily and glanced at Ben. He looked worried. Nothing felt right about this. He knew it. I knew it. Even the pacing Shag Pack knew it.

"I think she's yanking our chain about the tour," Ben finally said, peering out the shop's only window. There wasn't much to see in the heavy fog. "There's something she's not saying."

"We didn't tell her about the ghost-summoning ritual, so maybe we're all keeping secrets."

Ben pushed a twist of hair off his forehead. "I don't like it."

Me neither. "What if the grave robber is dangerous? Like Jack the Ripper?" I said. "There could be someone lying in wait for her."

"Yeah, like that vulture," he agreed with a shudder.

Follow the bird.

An inspirational message, she'd suggested. Pfft. Give me a break. If only Miss Neja understood how my grandmother loathed birds. However, as I stared at the headstone-shaped magnets that said WHAT GRAVE FUN, I had second thoughts. What if Miss Neja was right? What if the message on the grave hadn't been written by a low-down stinking thief? What if—

"What if Babi was trying to communicate with me?" I blurted out to Ben.

"What?"

I scratched my head. "What if *she* left that message? Babi. It was her grave, after all." I couldn't figure out what had happened to all the mementos that had gone missing from her headstone, so that was definitely confusing. But if I put that aside and just tried to figure out one part of the puzzle at a time—just focused on the message that had been scrawled on the grave—then perhaps I could figure it out.

"What if the ritual worked?" I said. "What if it didn't summon her ghost, exactly, but she was trying to communicate with us any way she could? You know, from the beyond? Maybe that was ghostly handwriting. Maybe she rearranged the clay sigil I drew on the grave, you know, with some kind of, uh, ectoplasmic energy?"

Okay, it sounded ridiculous, even to my own ears.

Ben wasn't convinced. "I hear what you're saying, but . . . *huh?*"

"What if Babi was trying to tell us to follow the bird?" I said.

"Why would your grandmother want us to follow a zombie vulture with no eyes?"

I blinked at him. "That's . . . a very good question."

But now I wanted to find out.

I didn't know why we should follow the bird. All the same, whether it was Babi or not, *someone* was sending a message. The kids from the Beacon? If they were trying to scare us, I could understand, but why hadn't the Shag Pack noticed them hiding?

I couldn't think of anyone else it would be. The only people who came to visit Babi's grave on the regular were Ben and me. Even my dad stayed away. Cemeteries gave him the chills. Back when Babi was alive, Dad never came with her and me to Whispering Pines when she delivered funeral flowers. Mom, neither. The only other person who would come back then was Granny Booker, who sometimes would walk up here from her house to chat with Babi and Miss Neja.

That's how I had met Ben, actually, when we were both little kids.

I pressed my face to the gift shop window, searching for the vulture. "Where did it go?"

Ben moved to the side so that his body wasn't visible from outside. "Get away from the glass. That vulture was evil, Helena. It'll see you."

"With what? It had no eyes! I don't think it can break through. Didn't this use to be a chapel at one time? Let's be practical. If it *is* an evil undead bird, it probably can't cross the threshold here. Besides, I don't see anything out there. I wonder where Miss Neja went?"

"Probably abandoned us," he said glumly. "Left us to die. My last moments on earth are going to be spent in a cemetery gift shop, with nothing to defend myself with but some discounted fountain pens shaped like shovels that say 'I'm digging it' on the side!"

I rolled my eyes. "Look, we can't just sit here, doing nothing. I—"

"LEAVE A PENNY, TAKE A PENNY."

Who'd said that? I looked at Ben. Didn't sound like his voice. Was he teasing? I didn't understand. "What's that supposed to mean?" I asked.

"I didn't say anything."

Um. Okay. "But did you *hear* something?"

"I . . . heard you mumbling about pennies."

I stared at him. "That wasn't me."

Ben's eyes widened. We both glanced around the shop. The scent of cider wafted with the smell of all the fog-damp dog coats. Not a pleasant mix.

It was suddenly too warm in the cramped space. All I could hear were the sounds of Big, Little, and Tiny, their claws clicking on the ceramic tile floor as they listlessly roamed the shop.

Ben stilled. Before I could ask what was wrong, he craned his neck, took a long step, and bent to pick up something off the floor. When he held it up with shaking fingers, I felt as if the walls were closing in on us.

It was a long black feather.

Forget Billy and his dumb old onions. I was afraid!

I wasn't staying there a moment longer.

"Granny Booker's house," I told Ben. "Now!"

We raced out of the shop, barely watching where we were going. But the fog slowed us down. It was too thick to navigate. One second we were running, and the next we were tripping over a gravestone, both of us screeching like maniacs.

When we dusted ourselves off, it took me a moment to get my bearings. I thought that storm my parents were worried about was making the sky darker than it should have been, because it felt as if the fog were moving around us.

"Where are the dogs?" I asked, a little breathless.

"They stayed in the shop."

"Which way is the shop? I'm turned around," I admitted, panic creeping over me. We were exposed out here. The protection of the four shop walls was gone.

Granny Booker's place seemed miles away.

"Okay, hold on," Ben said, sounding as panicked as I felt. "We need a landmark to guide us. Look! There! The Doorless Tomb is that way. See it?"

I did. And from there, it was a straight shot back to the section that led to Granny Booker's woods. We could follow a footpath from the tomb to the woods. That would be easy to keep track of inside the fog. Hopefully.

"Stay close to me," I begged Ben. "I don't want to get stuck out here alone."

"That makes two of us!" he whispered, a little frenzy behind his words.

We clung to each other and scuttled forward, heads turning in every direction.

The Doorless Tomb was one of the main attractions in the cemetery, in the center of Whispering Pines. A wealthy Forlornean had built a mausoleum in the late 1800s for himself and his wife that had no doors or windows. Just four sides and a roof. And four simple words inscribed on each of the smooth walls: DEATH HATH NO TERRORS.

It means death can't cause fear here. Don't be afraid of death.

But as Ben and I approached the granite tomb, we were both very much afraid. Because from around the corner, a strange figure stepped out of the fog.

It was a medieval monk, wearing a brown cowl and robe with wide sleeves. A heavy rope was tied around his waist like a belt, and hanging from it was a brass ring with large, heavy keys.

Sure, his clothing was odd, but I couldn't stop staring above his neck. Because what we'd seen earlier at Babi's grave had somehow transformed. The monk standing before us had the body of a human man . . .

And the head of a vulture.

As Ben and I stood in shock, he opened his beak and spoke to us:

"Who summoned me?"

CHAPTER 5
The Tomb

Don't know how you'd feel, but when I saw a talking creature with a vulture head, my first instinct was to flee. Fast
and far away. But even though I *wanted* to run, I couldn't.
My feet just didn't work. It was as though my body decided to
have a major service interruption at the worst possible moment.
Ben's, too.

So we just stood there, dumb with disbelief.

Chump one and chump two.

Billy the onion boy would have been halfway to Detroit by
now.

"Do not be afeared," the vulture monk said. "If you summoned
me, I am but your humble helper, my lady."

Ben whimpered at my side and shrank into the collar of his
peacoat.

I was too shocked to even do that. It felt like I was dreaming
but my brain hadn't realized it yet. Any second now, I'd wake up.

But if I was dreaming, then none of this was real. Right?

At least this vulture-headed monk wasn't of the eyeless variety. That was something.

"W-who . . . ," I stuttered, too scared to speak. I took a breath and tried again. "Who are you?"

"My name is Fizzle," the vulture said, bowing his crooked neck. "I assume you summoned me. I came."

Ben and I stole a worried glance at each other.

"I tried to summon my *grandmother*," I said. "Not you." Whoever he was.

Trust me, I knew a lot of underworld myths and legends, after listening to all my Babi's funeral stories—and hanging around Miss Neja's shop. I'd never heard of a vulture monk named Fizzle.

I remembered one thing my Babi had said about birds: that sometimes they can be a special kind of spirit guide, like an angel in the afterlife. "Are you a psychopomp?" I asked.

"I'm a door guardian and an author. But I seem to have misplaced my book. Have you seen it? You must have used it to summon me."

It took me a second to realize what he was talking about. The booklet, *How to Talk to the Dead* . . . This was the anonymous author? A vulture monk?

Had he drawn all the illustrations?

The vulture muttered in a low voice, "It must be one of his minions, working on the outside. How else would it end up here without my knowledge?"

I had no idea who he was talking about. And I knew Ben didn't either, but he was busy being freaked out about other things. . . .

"But we didn't—we didn't finish the summoning," Ben argued

to me, not to the monk. He was trying his best not to look directly at him, as if the creature were an eclipse and Ben might be blinded if he gazed too long. "The mementos were stolen. The summoning required a possession of the dearly departed."

Fizzle gestured broadly with one calloused hand. "The summoning calls me. I open a door between the lands of the living and the dead. I can even lead you to the dearly departed...." He paused and cocked his head, considering this. "Or I *could* have, if the ritual had been done correctly. Something isn't right here...." His voice trailed off as a look of concern passed over his eyes.

Ben and I both made low noises at the same time. What did he mean by that? Curiosity won out over my fear. I spoke up accusingly:

"Did you steal the stuff off my grandmother's grave?"

The vulture shook his head and looked perplexed. "No, my lady."

"Who did?" I asked. "If it wasn't you, then who did? Who wrote the message on Babi's grave? If our summoning was messed up because our memento was stolen, then what do we do now?"

Fizzle answered, "I dwell in the underworld. I could not steal an object of this world. I only open doors. But I am worried . . . ahh!" The vulture grasped his feathered black head, as if in terrible pain. He squeezed his eyes closed.

Ben and I stepped back in tandem. Something seemed to be happening with the monk. We just didn't know *what*.

When Fizzle reopened his eyes, they were . . .

Gone.

Empty sockets. Like they'd been when we'd first encountered the vulture at Babi's grave. Just black holes.

"No, no, no," Ben whispered in fright, gripping my arm painfully.

I tried to back farther away, but there was nowhere to go. A grave was behind us.

The fog was everywhere.

We were trapped.

"DO NOT BE ALARMED, CHILDREN," the monk told us in a calm manner, no longer in pain. "THIS IS MERELY A CONDITION OF TRAVELING BETWEEN THE PLANES. NOTHING TO WORRY ABOUT."

That voice! The monk's speaking voice had changed. And it was the same voice from the gift shop: TAKE A PENNY. It sounded hollow and strange.

Not of this earth.

"NOW, WHAT WAS I SAYING?"

"Before you lost your eyes?" I mumbled, feeling on the verge of hysteria.

"And before your voice went all creepy?" Ben whispered.

The monk ignored us and said, "RIGHT. I WAS TELLING YOU, HELPFULLY, THAT I AM FIZZLE. I AM THE DOORKEEPER. A PORTER. A BAWAB. I OPEN DOORS AND SEND YOU WHERE YOU REQUEST. A LOVELY DAY TO SPEAK TO THE DEARLY DEPARTED, WOULDN'T YOU AGREE?"

"No," I said. "You were telling us that you were worried, and that something was wrong with our summoning!"

"WAS I?" the monk said. "AGAIN, MUST BE AN EFFECT OF INTERWORLD TRAVEL. NOTHING IS WRONG WITH YOUR SUMMONING, OR I WOULD NOT BE HERE."

"I'm so confused," Ben whispered in a dreamy voice. "I'm seeing things . . . hallucinating. Think I've hit my head or eaten bad shrimp. Take me to the hospital, Helena."

"We can't both be having the same hallucination," I whispered back. Then I cleared my throat and said to the monk, "Look, if you can't tell me who stole my mementos, then I just want to know one thing. Can you help me talk to my grandmother?"

Fizzle held up one bony finger, requesting that we both wait. From his robes, the monk took out a piece of white chalk. Then he walked up to the side of the tomb. There, he drew an arched doorway. Just one long line of chalk. Then he knocked on the tomb twice, and—

The granite swung open.

He'd created a door into the Doorless Tomb. One that went right through the stone.

Ben made a little gasping noise beside me.

My legs felt unsteady, as if they might betray me and give out at any moment.

I couldn't see anything inside but darkness and a set of steps that went downward. Nothing else. Fog swirled around the newly created entrance as Ben gripped my shoulder.

"I don't understand," I told the vulture. "Where does that lead?"

"BELOW THE GRAVES," Fizzle said, as if it were a prize. Disneyland. A golden ticket to the most marvelous place in the universe.

"Why would we want to go there?" Ben said in exasperation, finding some courage.

"YOU WANTED TO SPEAK WITH THE DEARLY DEPARTED, DID YOU NOT? THIS LEADS TO THEIR REALM. YOU MAY TRAVEL AND SPEAK TO THE DENIZENS IN THE LAND OF THE DEAD."

I stared.

Ben stared.

The land of the dead.

I had hoped for so long. Was this actually happening? I could walk into the Doorless Tomb, enter the land of the dead, and talk to Babi again?

It was that easy?

"Hold on one stinking minute," Ben said, letting go of my arm. "There's got to be a catch. If we walk down there, will we die? Will we get stuck down there with the dead?"

Fizzle tilted his head quizzically. "OF COURSE NOT. YOU ARE JUST TOURISTS, PASSING THROUGH. YOU ARE FLESH. ONLY SPIRITS STAY."

"We can leave anytime we want?" I asked.

"I've got a Bigfoot Enthusiasts Club meeting," Ben reminded me.

I wanted to punch him in his arm. Who cared about that now?

"IF YOU ARE LOST BELOW, YOU'LL NEED A GUIDE. THERE ARE EXITS TO THIS WORLD. ALL ONE NEEDS TO DO IS ASK. YOU ARE FREE TO LEAVE AT ANY TIME, UNLESS—"

"Unless what?"

The vulture shook his beaked head. "IT CAN BE DANGEROUS, SOMETIMES. NOTHING TO WORRY TOO MUCH ABOUT, BUT YOU SHOULD HIRE A GUIDE WHEN YOU ARRIVE. THAT WOULD BE BEST."

What kind of dangers? But before I could ask, the vulture said:

"IF YOU WANT TO LEAVE, THERE'S AN EXIT INSIDE THE CASTLE."

"The castle?" Ben repeated.

Fizzle nodded. "A GUIDE CAN SHOW YOU. AND THAT IS ALL YOU REALLY NEED TO KNOW. YOU ARE SMART. BEING A FLESH TOURIST IS EASY, MY LORD."

"Flesh tourist? Ew," Ben whispered, making a face.

In the distance, something that sounded like a hunting horn cut through the silence, making all of us jump. It was hard to tell in the fog, but I thought it came from the direction of the Wilds section of the cemetery.

Fizzle tensed. He spoke quickly. "TIME HAS RUN OUT. THAT IS ALL I CAN SAY. YOU MUST DECIDE NOW OR THE DOOR WILL SHUT AND THIS WAY WILL BE CLOSED FOR GOOD. THIS IS YOUR ONLY CHANCE TO SPEAK TO MORANA. WILL YOU ENTER?"

Wait. Had I told him my grandmother's first name? How did he know? Or . . . he was a magical creature that we had summoned with a spooky spell, duh. Of course he knew.

Maybe? I wasn't sure! It was hard to make rational decisions about irrational things when I was under all this pressure!

Ben whispered into my ear, "What was that hunting horn sound? I don't know if I trust this birdbrain."

I wasn't sure I did either. All of this was scary and confusing. There were too many unanswered questions floating around inside my head. But at the same time, this was the most exciting thing that had happened to me. I'd have been a fool to walk away from this chance.

There was just one thing that was still bothering me.

"How do I find out who stole the mementos I left on Babi's grave?" I asked the vulture.

He hesitated, looking into the fog. "THEY HAVE BEEN TAKEN

BELOW. HIRE A GUIDE TO HELP. YOU WILL NEED ONE, REGARD-LESS, TO FIND YOUR GRANDMOTHER. IS THAT NOT MORE IMPORTANT?"

The hunting horn blew again. This time, it sounded closer.

"NOW, MY LADY, OR NEVER. IT IS ALMOST TOO LATE," Fizzle said, gesturing for us to hurry through the door. Feathers scattered from his sleeves. He seemed to be shrinking inside his robes, and the granite door was slowly swinging shut.

I wanted to get my stolen grave mementos back.

I wanted to talk to Babi again.

I wanted to see the underworld.

My heart raced as I watched the door closing. I looked at Ben, and he was shaking his head. He wasn't coming? After all this?

"Please, Ben," I begged. "You said you'd help me today. You'd be here for me."

"I didn't mean in the land of the dead!"

The door was almost closed. . . .

Maybe I *was* destined to be Haunted Helena, the class loner.

Those kids in the Beacon were probably right to be afraid of me. It just hurt more because it was Ben. He was supposed to have my back.

"Fine. Go be with your Bigfooter friends!" I told him angrily as I ran for the door. "I guess this is where our onions separate. Bet that Detroit Billy kid would join your club."

Ben made an exasperated noise. "That's not what Miss Neja was—uughh! Wait!" His feet pounded the ground behind me as he caught up. "You owe me big-time, Helena Novak."

Thank you, thank you, thank you. I really didn't want to do this alone.

We slid in, one after the other, as the door was closing. And as we did, the vulture shouted behind us in a voice that sounded a little different: "Whatever you do, don't trust—"

His words didn't reach us. We were inside the tomb.

In an expanding darkness.

More afraid than we'd ever been before.

Without a single onion between us.

CHAPTER 6

Ferryman

B en and I had been inside most of the Whispering Pines tombs that were open to the public. Many were decades old, if not older, and they weren't that exciting. They smelled a little like our basement did after the water heater broke and leaked all over the cement floor. Dad and I mopped it up, but it reeked of dusty mildew for weeks.

That's how the narrow hallway in the Doorless Tomb smelled. Behind us, there was a sliver of gray light and fog seeping in through Fizzle's closing door, and in front of us, a skinny set of stairs descended into darkness.

Fizzle was definitely not coming inside the tomb with us. Before I could call out to him, the door shut tightly, and all the light disappeared.

Darkness surrounded us. Nothing but darkness. And the stink of a dank basement.

"High?" I whispered.

"Low," Ben whispered back. "I can't see anything!"

Panic settled in my chest. Then I remembered what was in my pocket. "I can help!"

I fumbled around inside my black storm jacket until I found the tube of fireplace matches. They were harder to light in the dark than they had been at Babi's grave. I kept trying. When I struck the long match and the flame finally caught, Ben and I sighed in relief.

"Wait a minute. Wouldn't this be easier?" he said, retrieving his phone from his peacoat and turning on the flashlight function. A slant of white light filled up the space between us.

I felt a little dumb for not thinking of my phone first, and shook out the long match. But after I got out my phone as well and shone it around with Ben's, the point was that we could see—well, that there was nothing here, only the same stone that was on the outside. No bodies entombed, not even the man who'd built the mausoleum or his wife.

There was one thing: a sign on one wall warning about tsunami evacuations. But no door leading outside. Why had someone posted a warning if you couldn't get out this way?

However, on the opposite wall from the tsunami sign, a narrow stairwell sloped downward into darkness. . . .

That was the only way out of the empty tomb. Down.

"Uh, after you, milady," Ben said, pretending to be polite like the vulture.

I snorted a laugh. "No, you, milord. I insist."

"Hey, who wanted to follow the advice of a birdbrain door-keeper? Not *this* guy," he said, pointing a thumb at his chest. "Let the record state that I think this is a terrible idea. What was the monk saying at the end? Don't trust . . . ?"

"Dunno," I said, shrugging. "Guess we should be on guard."

I held on to my phone and took a cautious step down, one hand on the smooth wall. "Let the record state that Big Bad Ben, who thinks Bigfoot is real, is scared of a couple of steps."

"Hey. *You* think Bigfoot is real too," he said, following me. "When I showed you the evidence—the footprints up at Bald Bone Lake. Then there's the Skookum Cast. Even Jane Goodall believes. *And* I invited you to join my club, for the record."

Right. His dumb club. No thank you. I secretly suspected it was just a way for him to spend time with some of the other smarter kids in class—the ones who didn't have dead grandmothers and weren't secretly reading up on scrying with bloody finger bones and weren't getting lunch detention, which completely embarrassed Ben.

Anyway, I loved getting him worked up about his favorite subject, Ye Olde Sasquatch. It never failed, even when we were walking down an impossible staircase into the unknown. He talked, I argued, and we descended. Step by step, the staircase didn't end, and I couldn't see the bottom.

How low did it go?

"Maybe we shouldn't be using our phones for lights," I told Ben, looking at the meager battery life left on mine.

"Nah, I'm okay," Ben reported. "I've got plenty of juice."

I stored my phone in my pocket. I figured I would use up the fireplace matches first. Best to save the battery for later. At least I'd have a backup light source. As my Babi liked to say, a dead mouse only has one hole. I was going to make sure I had lots of holes in case I needed an extra one for escaping. So I struck a long match, and down we went.

Treading step after step.

Passing more signs for tsunami evacuations that pointed to higher ground. "Do you think this was used by the cemetery staff at some point in the past?" I asked. "Why would these signs be here?"

"Maybe they sealed up the tomb for some reason and moved the bodies?" Ben suggested, but it didn't sound like he believed his own theory.

I didn't have a better one, and I didn't want to think about where we were going as we descended farther down the stairs; I just wanted to get there. So I shifted the conversation to safer sub-jects to pass the time.

We talked more about Sasquatch. Wendigos. The Jersey Devil. We continued to talk as the granite walls ended and turned to dirt and clay and twisted tree roots. What tree could have roots this deep, we didn't know. But trying to figure it out distracted us from the worries we shared in our eyes now and then, worries like: Where did the vulture monk go? Was Miss Neja looking for us? Were Big, Little, and Tiny okay, back in the shop?

And where exactly were we headed?

That old chestnut.

No way to know the answer, so as a distraction, I offered Ben a piece of the bubble gum I'd purchased at the Beacon.

"Mmm, good old Pedro gum," he said thankfully, taking the red-wrapped bubble gum. "I thought you weren't supposed to have this anymore because of your TMJ?"

"I'm not supposed to be inside a tomb, walking down steps that may or may not lead into the underworld, Ben, but here we are."

He snorted a soft laugh.

Tutti-frutti filled my mouth as I chewed with a tender bottom jaw.

Ben and I had known each other most of our lives. My Babi became friendly with his granny after many chats with Miss Neja in the Whispering Pines gift shop. Our parents then also became friends. But Ben and I weren't *best* friends until second grade. That's when our parents forced us to join the Junior Coastal Rangers, the outdoor scout troop in which we learned our secret text code. We both hated it until we discovered we could team up to earn the skill patches faster—and spend the rest of our free time exploring away from the troop.

Not sure if we ever thought we'd end up exploring something like this, though.

There was no skill patch for the underworld.

But I was thankful Ben was there with me.

I hoped he didn't regret it.

By the time my gum went stale, I'd burned through all the fireplace matches but one and I worried we might need it later, so I stored it in my jacket and we just used Ben's phone to light the way. But once we'd gone through half his battery, we weren't only worried about running it down; we were just so exhausted. We had to take a short break.

When we sat down, I looked back up the stairs and wondered if we'd made a huge mistake. I imagined us trapped on stairs that never ended, and a little panic took hold in my chest.

Breathing faster, I pushed up from the stairs and tried to stand but felt dizzy. When I steadied myself, my hand brushed something on the wall.

Paper. That was weird. I concentrated on the small distraction, waiting for the wave of dizziness to pass, and squinted into the darkness to see what my fingers had touched.

An old, empty matchbook. Several of them, shoved into a crack in the wall.

It took me a moment to realize what that meant.

"Ben," I whispered. "Someone else has been this way before us."

"Matches," he said, sounding a little surprised. Worried, too. Then he spotted something on the stairs and toed the object with his shoe, causing a metallic clink. "What is that?"

I bent to pick it up. An old bottle cap.

Strange. It was a metal one that came from a glass soda bottle. The only ones I'd ever seen topped expensive imported Coke bottles from Mexico that my mom would buy for special occasions.

"'Cascadia Bubbles Soda Company,'" I read around the ridged metal, bent on one side by a bottle opener. "I've never heard of that. When do you think this soda was produced?"

"Not anytime in the last fifty years, I'd bet," Ben said, tossing it back onto the ground, where it bounced down a few steps and then landed on something else. A wilted lily of the valley stem. I smelled its sweet perfume when he picked it up, and it made my chest hurt.

Babi used to grow these behind our house.

It was one of the flowers I'd put on Babi's grave yesterday.

Flowers that were stolen.

"No way," Ben said, handing it to me. "Is it one of your memento flowers?"

"It's still damp," I said, squeezing the stem and feeling anger bubbling up inside me. "It can't be a coincidence. Someone took my stuff and came down here."

Ben glanced around. "I liked it better when I thought the birdbrain was the thief."

Was it another human? Someone like us?

Confused and frantic, we scouted around for more of my mementos but only found more bottle caps. I carefully stowed the lily stem inside my jacket pocket, unsure what to make of all this, when something snagged my attention in the endless stairwell.

It was no longer black below us.

"See that?" I asked, pointing downward. "It's getting lighter!"

"Finally—the bottom! Let's hoof it," he encouraged.

We picked up the pace, pushing our aching legs down the last of the stairs toward what was clearly some kind of cross tunnel. The dirt walls were more compacted with roots here, but something had changed: the roots weren't exactly *roots*. Leaves were growing. It was humid and smelled like—

"A river!" Ben said, moving his phone above my shoulder to better see it. "An underground river."

He was right. It flowed under muddy roots and twisty vines that arched like a tunnel above it. And that wasn't all. There was fog down here.

"The Grum," I said. It felt familiar and good. Like the fog back home, but more exciting.

And there was something even better: light.

As we trod down the last few steps of the long stairwell, the humble glow from Ben's phone shone across an old stone dock. A cheerful flatboat was moored at its edge. It had a red-and-white-striped canopy on top and an old-fashioned steam boiler engine in the back. A name was painted on the side of the boat:

The Sweet By-and-By.

Lanterns hung from the boat's canopy, shining warm light in the dark tunnel, but they weren't the only source of illumination. A fire had been built in a metal drum trash can on the edge of the dock near the boat. And standing over the trash can fire, cooking what smelled like dirty, wet socks, was a small man in a dark coat and a muddy raccoon hat.

Ben turned off his phone's flashlight. The two of us stared at the boat and the strange man and the trash can fire for several moments, just taking it all in, wondering what the heck to do next.

Then Ben whispered, "Is that man by the fire wearing a raccoon hat . . . or is it his head?"

Now that Ben was questioning it, I wasn't entirely sure. After all, we'd recently talked to a vulture-headed monk.

The man by the fire heard us and looked up.

Definitely a raccoon *hat*.

That was a small relief after our experience with the monk. Only slightly odd was that this man was the color of a silvery fish, and that his eyes had a whitish film over them. But he was most assuredly human.

He had a very long face with a pencil-thin mustache that twirled up at the ends like the mustache of that famous painter Salvador Dalí. The twirls curled up tighter when he welcomed us with a wide smile.

"Salut! Good tidings, travelers," the man said in a thick French accent. "I am Ludo, the ferryman." He bowed formally, spoon in hand.

"Don't think this is the guy who stole your mementos," Ben whispered.

No. He had a wooden peg leg. Not to say that he *couldn't* make it up and down all those stairs, but it wouldn't be easy. Unless there was a secret elevator around here. I sure hoped not, because that would have meant we'd walked down all those steps for no good reason.

Best to put Ludo on the "unlikely thief" list but not rule him out completely.

"Uh, hello?" I called back. "I'm Helena and this is Ben. So you're, like, uh, the underworld ferryman? Does that mean this is the river Styx?"

He looked confused and put a hand over his chest before swinging around, teetering on his peg leg to glance at the water behind him. "This? It isn't a river. It's the Eerie Canal."

"The Erie Canal is in New York," Ben said. "I've been there with my dad."

"Wrong one. Spelled wrong, too. This is the original." Ludo pointed to a bent sign near the water's edge that read EERIE CANAL.

Ben and I looked at each other. Maybe we didn't want to know why it was named that.

The man asked, "Would you like to sup with me? Root snails from the canals are delicious this time of year with garlic and butter."

He ladled heaping spoonfuls of dark, glistening curls from his pot and mounded them in a bowl before gesturing for us to come closer. We hesitated. The smell was overwhelming. I cautiously approached to see that his "snails" were actually roly-poly pill bugs, their brown shells all boiled up into tight, little balls.

I shut my eyes and puffed out my cheeks.

"Nope," Ben said. "We're good."

I cleared my throat. "Mr. Ludo? You wouldn't happen to have seen anyone else come this way since yesterday? From those steps?"

"Since yesterday? I do not believe so, no."

Hmm. He sounded honest. "Well then, I guess we're looking to get into the land of the dead. You know anything about that?"

He smiled. "But of course. I'll take you. It is my pleasure."

"Great, thank you," Ben said.

The ferryman smiled. "I'll just need your payment."

Uh-oh.

"Which is . . . ?" Ben asked.

"One denier coin, mon ami." The ferryman smiled, then added: "Each."

I didn't know what a denier was, but I knew I didn't have any kind of coin. I had a prepaid credit card for emergencies. All my allowance had been spent on the newest Whispering Pines playing cards (yesterday) and Pedro bubble gum (just this morning). But after I tried to explain this, the ferryman just repeated himself:

"One denier coin each. No coin, no travel."

Ben signaled to the ferryman that we needed a moment to figure out our funds situation. I was alarmed to find that Ben, too, was coinless.

"Nothing?" I asked. "Not even a penny?"

He stopped digging in his jeans pocket, and we looked at each other.

Leave a penny, take a penny.

"Birdbrain's warning in the gift shop," Ben whispered.

"He was trying to tell us to take change along," I whispered. "And we didn't listen."

"We're going to be stuck down here with this guy? I can't watch him eat bugs, Helena. I will be sick," he hissed at me, frantic and angry.

Think, think . . .

I glanced back at the happy-go-lucky ferryman, who was offering a spoonful of bugs to the dead raccoon on his head. But maybe it wasn't quite as dead as I'd originally thought. The raccoon uncurled itself from around his head and took a bite from the spoon.

"For the love of Sasquatch," Ben murmured under his breath. "Why would we even want to ride on a boat with this man? He's all mixed-up. He thinks bugs are snails. And he's got a muddy raccoon buddy who's just chilling on his head!"

Mixed-up.

If the ferryman was confused about those things, maybe he didn't need an actual coin.

"Quick, Ben," I said. "Give me your phone."

Using the phone's light to guide me, I raced up a few steps to the place where we'd seen the old soda-pop bottle tops and grabbed two of them. They sounded like coins when I shook them around in my hand.

Ben sighed. "Maybe that will work," he said, not sounding all that hopeful.

I returned his phone and jogged back over to Ludo. I did my best to ignore the raccoon's shiny eyes and Ludo's crunchy chewing.

"You have my coins?" he asked, setting down his bowl.

"Sure do," I said, placing two bottle caps in his waiting hand.

He looked at them. Jingled them, weighing them out. Held them up against the light of the trash fire. My stomach turned.

He placed the bottle caps in his coat pocket and grinned. "Yes, indeed, travelers. Let us fire up the boiler and get you to the gate. Hop onboard!"

Whew! I couldn't believe that had actually worked.

I secretly fist-bumped Ben, hopeful for the first time since this whole mess had started, and we boarded *The Sweet By-and-By*.

CHAPTER 7

Eerie Canal

T hese are the rules," Ludo the ferryman said as we entered his flatboat, taking seats on a bench under the striped canopy. "Stay in the passenger area. Keep your arms and legs inside the boat at all times, and do not ask me any questions—"

"But—" I started, wanting to assure him that my mother was a tugboat operator, my father was a diver, and I had practically grown up on the water. Maybe I could even help him.

Ludo did not want to hear it. Not one word.

He held up a finger. "If you ask me questions, then I cannot concentrate on running the boiler here in the back of the boat. And if I cannot run the boiler, the boat stops. And if the boat stops, then we will be stuck. Forever."

"Forever?" Ben said, worried, looking into the water as if the Forlorn Worm itself might be down there.

"Sans cesse," the boatman said in French. "There are rules here, and they must be followed. It is different Below from Above.

You must agree, or I will refund your passage and you will exit."

Ben and I agreed. We didn't want the bottle caps back.

"Good," Ludo said, nodding. "We will depart. There is nothing to see on the journey, but you will find some reading material up front that may be useful. Now we will have silence between us. Let us begin!"

With that, he and his raccoon turned their backs on us and began heating the massive boiler engine at the stern, shoveling a pile of black coal into it. A fire burned bright inside the engine's belly, and steam poured from the pipe above. Ludo tugged a string that clanged a bell, which echoed down the tunnel's low ceiling, and then he pulled a lever.

The boat chugged forward in the dark water.

We were on our way.

Ben and I scooted closer together on the bench, peering below the canopy as we glided under knotty roots and dangling vines. They made a rustling noise like dry fingers as they brushed over the boat. There was little light ahead, and I didn't understand how Ludo could see well enough to steer. But I guess there really wasn't much to see, so maybe it didn't matter.

The tunnel was dark, the engine was loud, and all of it was boring.

A little claustrophobic, too. It made my chest feel tight.

"Wonder how long this will last?" I asked, raising my voice so that Ben could hear me over the engine.

"Don't know, but I don't like this guy. He's so weird." After tossing Ludo a look over his shoulder, Ben leaned forward to inspect a wooden rack that was attached to the front of the boat. Three brochures sat inside it, like you'd see at a hotel desk. But these were printed in odd fonts and the graphics were bizarre. They did not look modern.

The first brochure was titled "Welcome, Afterlife Tourist!" It listed a bunch of "must-see" places to visit in the underworld and included drawings and brief descriptions.

"'Explore one of four underworld kingdoms: Beyond, Rapture, Ever, and Hereafter,'" Ben read. "'Each one is unique.'"

"Wait, that's not part of any underworld mythology I know."

"Maybe everything you know is wrong," he teased in a good-natured tone.

I snorted. "Oh, please. In your dreams."

"Just saying, this piece of poorly printed paper claims there are kingdoms down here. And everyone knows that if something is printed, it must be true. No one wastes ink on lies, Helena."

"People lie every chance they get. If this brochure claims there are kingdoms down here, does that mean they have kings and queens?"

"I'd assume so," Ben said. "Oh, listen to this. 'You wouldn't want to miss the Baroque Dream Tower, where all your dreams come true, or the Timeless Banquet, where you can have dinner with anyone who's ever died . . . in all of history'? Whaaaaat?"

"Like Cleopatra?"

"In small print it says, 'Language restrictions apply.' Check this out, you can tour buildings that were destroyed in the world of the living. 'In the kingdom of Hereafter, visit Gothic cathedrals and battle medieval knights.' Dang! This is wild."

"That sounds . . ."

Ben turned the brochure over in his hands. "Yeah?"

"It sounds too good to be true."

Ben gestured around the boat. "Come on. Look where we are, Helena."

He had a point. I took the next brochure. "'Above: Not All That Interesting. 25 Reasons Why the Land of the Living Isn't Great.' What the . . . ? Here are some of the reasons—sickness. Starvation. Terrible weather. Overcrowding. And number twenty-five, 'If it's so great, then why are humans always killing each other? Sounds like they're in a hurry to get down here.'"

"Wow. Dropping truths."

"Or propaganda," I said, frowning. "This sounds like jacked-up hype to convince people that things are better down here. What's inside the last one?"

Ben unfolded the third brochure, a map. But not a very helpful one. It was the vaguest map I'd ever seen, completely unusable and mainly marked with pitfalls and things to avoid—POISONOUS! DANGER! WOE!—and a lot of symbols of knives and ghosts.

"What the heck is this?" Ben asked.

He flipped it to the back, which featured a portrait of an underworld guide named Sir Krak: a *very* white dude wearing a hat with a feather and carrying a sword, who looked as if he cosplayed in a Renaissance Faire or was part of some weekend LARPing group. He was available to hire for a small fee and would help tourists avoid all the pitfalls while getting them to where they needed to go—and the best part was, he'd get tourists back *out* of the underworld.

"This is what ol' birdbrain told us to hire," Ben said, thumping the brochure. "A guide. It says to ask for him at some place called Pokie's, after you enter the gate. What gate?"

"And which kingdom? Aren't there four different ones, according to the brochure?"

The boat took a sudden turn, and when it straightened, the tunnel opened into a vast cavern. Fog covered too much for us to see where the ceiling was, but you could just feel that it was bigger in here. No more claustrophobic tightness in my chest. Just in the distance was a massive gate.

"Hey, maybe that's it!" Ben said excitedly as he pocketed the brochure.

A giant statue stood guard on either side of the gate. They were carved from the compacted clay that lined the walls down here, both dressed in hooded robes that hid their faces. Between them, they held a sign made from twisted roots that arched over the entrance to another fog-filled cavern.

The sign read HEREAFTER.

A secondary cloth banner hung below it: LAND OF THE MARY DEAD.

"Mary dead?" I said, snorting a laugh. "Is that a typo?"

"It's painted. Someone can't spell," Ben said.

"And one corner of the banner is sagging. Guess they can't tie a knot, either."

I squinted. Was the banner covering up another sign below it? It looked like it might have said HOUSE OF . . . something. It reminded me of the cheap vinyl sign that hung over Dinky's Sandwich Shop in downtown Forlorn that said UNDER NEW MANAGEMENT.

"This is the underworld?" Ben asked, dubious.

I couldn't see past the gate, only that there were lights beyond it. But over to our left, way, *way* in the distance, there was another foggy entrance and two more giant guardian statues. The kingdom of Beyond.

"Look." Ben pointed to our right. "There's a third entrance, there. And a fourth. Rapture and Ever? One for each underworld kingdom."

We were headed toward the gate to Hereafter.

"What if your grandmother is in one of the other kingdoms?" Ben asked.

Babi wasn't all that "merry" in life. Would she be merry in the afterlife?

Panicking, I turned around and asked Ludo, "Hey? Mr. Ferryman? I'm sorry, I know you said no questions, but this is important. Are you sure this is the right gate? Because—"

The engine made a terrible noise, and the flatboat came to a jarring stop.

The ferryman shouted in French and stomped with his peg leg. "No questions!"

"But—"

"Those are the rules. You cannot break the rules!"

"Okay, but I just need to know if this is the right gate! There are three others."

The ferryman grabbed his raccoon's tail and yanked the animal off his head. It scampered away, hiding behind the boiler engine in the shadows.

Ludo's head was bald, nothing but shiny silver skin. He looked at me with sad eyes as steam trickled out of the boiler engine. "Silly, spoiled princess. I am the ferryman. I am never wrong. Yet you didn't trust Ludo, and now we are stuck," he moaned.

This was *my* fault? Because of trust issues? I glanced at Ben, who shrugged unhelpfully.

"Can't you just . . ." I motioned for the ferryman to shovel coal. "Get it going again?"

"We are stuck," Ludo repeated, sitting down to put his head in his hands. "Forever."

"Wow," Ben whispered. "Drama queen."

We couldn't be stuck forever. Not, like, *forever*-ever. Right? We were minutes away from the gate. A dock, too! I tried to make the ferryman understand this, but he just shook his head and mumbled to himself in incomprehensible sentences while the raccoon cowered.

That's when a slow-moving anxiety began spreading up my chest. Once it started, I couldn't stop panicking, like a grass fire that couldn't be stamped out.

Could we actually be stuck here?

I glanced around. Though we were relatively close to the gate, an easy jaunt for the boat, that distance was *way* too far for us to swim.

My chest felt overwarm. I was going to be sick.

"We have to do something! Talk to Ludo," I begged Ben, clicking my stiff jaw to the side painfully. Maybe I shouldn't have chewed that gum after all. "Use your language skills."

Ben gave me a look that told me he thought it would do no good. But he cleared his throat and politely addressed Ludo in French, speaking formally, pleading, and though the ferryman responded once, he mainly just shook his head.

It was hard to concentrate on what they were saying. Was the boat swaying? It felt unstable. How could that be? The lake had been serene and boring just a few minutes before. I looked over the side, peering into the dark.

Huge mistake.

The calm lake had transformed, and now it looked as though

we were sitting in the middle of the Pacific Ocean during a storm. Choppy waters rocked the boat, angry and forceful. Something sloshed up onto my rain boots.

"Oh crap! We're sinking!" I shouted, shaking Ben's shoulder.

"What?" He glanced down at the water puddling around us, utterly surprised.

"The boat's taking on water!" I said, frantic. "Storm . . . on the lake!"

Ben freaked. He shouted at the ferryman to help—even I recognized that in French. But Ludo would not move. His raccoon scurried atop the canopy.

That's when I knew we were in trouble.

Okay. Crap. We couldn't just sit there like dum-dums and wait for the boat to sink. What could I do? Try to start the engine myself? I mean, how hard could it be? I'd seen him do it: shovel the coal from the pile . . . that was . . . ? Where had all the coal gone? Was it some kind of magical coal pile that had disappeared?

Ugh! I was really hating this boat!

Never mind. I tried to pull the lever to start the engine. It wouldn't budge. Grunting, I tugged and tugged. "Why. Is. This. So. Hard?"

Ben grabbed my arm to drag me away. He was in a full-on panic now. "Forget the engine—we're tilting! This thing is going under."

How? I didn't understand. Was Ludo's boat like Cinderella's pumpkin at midnight? Freezing water streamed into my boots. Half the canopy collapsed at the bow.

We were definitely going down, and there wasn't a single life preserver in sight.

Guess a boat in the land of the dead didn't need one.

The boat rocked sideways, and Ben grabbed me around my shoulders as we toppled and slid into the railing—

And overboard.

The last thing I heard was the piercing scream of the raccoon. Then we went under.

Freezing. Darkness. Lungs bursting. Briny water.

Being pulled down into a force greater than you could ever conquer was horrifying. I couldn't trick my way out or run away from the water. I was drowning in darkness, and it happened so fast.

For some reason, in the middle of drowning, I thought about walking into the Forlorn General Hospital a year ago. Dad had picked me up from school and taken me there. When I got to Babi's room, I saw my mom's face, streaked with tears. Then I saw Babi in the hospital bed. Not my Babi, the strongest lady in Forlorn, who had no patience for racists, "buffoons," and people who thought they were too important for rules. My Babi liked bright lipstick and laughed at all the bad jokes in TV shows. Loudly.

This Babi was just a frail shell. Hollow. Empty.

Gone.

She'd left me, and I hadn't even gotten a chance to say goodbye.

The image of that hollow Babi faded as I clung to Ben in the dark water and he clung to me. How long could we survive underwater? I tried to open my eyes, and in a flash of white ahead of us, I swore I saw something serpentlike in the water. All I could think about was the Forlorn Worm. I knew that was back up top, Above—wherever *that* was compared to down here.

But then it didn't matter.

A vise grabbed my storm jacket.

Something yanked me, hard. It pulled me through the water like a tugboat.

I held on to Ben, and it dragged us and dragged us . . .

Until my shoulder hit solid wood. And I could breathe.

Ben and I lay coughing and gasping for breath until I could pick my head up and gaze into the eyes of our rescuer.

Not human. Animal.

Even if I hadn't been able to read the animal's name right there on the round, silver name tag dangling on its collar, I'd have recognized its face. I'd visited his grave in the cemetery countless times. The plush version sat on my bed, purchased from the Whispering Pines gift shop.

Winnow, the official cemetery mutt. First buried. Best of all the dogs.

Just one small detail. The Winnow up above in my world?

He didn't have three heads.

CHAPTER 8
The Boondocks

I wasn't sure if there was a proper way to thank a three-headed dog for saving your life, but when Ben saw the beast and screamed bloody murder, I knew *that* wasn't it.

"It's only Winnow!" I assured Ben as he calmed down long enough to cough up more water. "Mr. Winnow, sir. Or is it 'sirs'?" I said to the dog's heads. "Thank you for saving our lives. I don't suppose all animals talk down here, like that vulture, Fizzle?"

The dog sat and shook water out of his coat, spraying Ben and me with a fine mist that stank of salt and kelp.

"Guess not," I said, wiping my face with my hand. I was soaked from head to foot and starting to shake from the cold. Ben, too. We glanced back at the water, but any remnants of the canopied boat—and Ludo—were gone. Could a ferryman in the underworld die? I really hoped not. A twinge of guilt made my gut contract.

Out of the corner of my eye, I thought I spied a wet raccoon darting across the dock. That gave me a little hope. If Ludo's furry hat was still kicking, surely Ludo was too. My eyes followed the raccoon as it leapt between the legs of a man on the dock who was hauling a barrel, and then the raccoon disappeared.

I exhaled a long breath, relieved, then slowly became aware of our surroundings.

We had been pulled out of the water near a maze of twisty docks and sailboats, swaddled in fog. Crates and boxes and barrels were stacked on the weathered boards. Gulls swooped. Ship bells were dinging. And towering over the waterfront was a block of brightly painted row houses—ones that looked hundreds of years old. The fog was dense, so I couldn't see much farther. But everywhere I looked, there were people.

People walking. Talking. Working. In the underworld?

I thought they were all human. It was hard to tell. The fog was thick, and I was shivering in front of a three-headed dog.

I'd also just nearly drowned, so everything was shaken up inside my head.

I wasn't the only one. Ben was miserable.

"Helena," Ben begged as we helped each other up. "P-pulease find us a place to get warm. Want to be warm. Now."

Scratch that. He wasn't just miserable. He was mad at me. I could tell by the strained tone of his voice. But how was I supposed to have known that the ferryman meant the boat would *literally* stop, forever, if I asked a question?

And surely Ludo was okay.

I mean, you couldn't kill someone who was already dead . . . right?

Besides, I couldn't dwell on that now. Ben was right about one thing: we needed to dry off. And the longer we sat there, the more people stared at us. The looks we were getting weren't all that friendly, either. Maybe these people weren't used to tourists.

"Looks like there could be some shops up there," I told Ben. "Unless you want to try to find something on that map from the brochure?"

Ben tugged out the floppy folded paper from his peacoat. "This? The map that makes no sense and is now the consistency of a wet napkin?"

Guess not. I checked my pockets to make sure I still had my lily of the valley. It was wet but fine. I still had the single fireplace match left, but it needed to dry out.

"My phone is gone," Ben said weakly.

Huh. I still had mine, but it was dead. Either the dip in the waters killed it or the underworld didn't like technology. So much for hanging on to my phone as a backup.

Guess I was now a mouse with only one hole.

Ben and I squeezed as much water as we could out of our clothes and then got our bearings as we cautiously began walking down the docks. The air was strange here. It didn't quite feel right. Maybe that was because you couldn't tell if the place was indoors or outdoors.

"Are we still in a cavern?" I asked Ben in a whisper. I couldn't see the cave's rocky ceiling above. No sky, either. Just the illusion of space and misty Grum.

"Don't know if the rules of our world apply down here," Ben whispered back. "I'm having flashbacks to when my parents took me to Disneyland last year. This place is like the inside of Pirates of the Caribbean. All these docks and old buildings."

Some of the docks reminded me of Pier 13, near the twin lighthouses in Forlorn, but the colorful row houses here looked like pictures of Europe I'd seen from when Babi flew to Amsterdam every spring to visit her friend . . . only things here were a bit haphazard. There were no French balconies and palm trees in Amsterdam.

"Everything here is all mixed-up," I said. "I can't tell where it's supposed to be."

"Or when," Ben added.

People were dressed in all manners, from any number of eras and classes—seventeenth-century sailors, Victorian gentlemen, and a couple of small boys running around in jeans. So many cultures, too. It was a melting pot of people, times, and places.

"This place is wild," Ben told me under his breath as we walked past two men hauling the gigantic carcass of a pink, prickly fish— with tentacles. "Okay, *that* creature definitely doesn't exist Above. Do things from the real world get distorted down here?"

"No idea," I whispered back. I didn't understand the rules of this place. And after what had happened to the boat, I was beginning to think that we most definitely needed to.

People stared as we passed, and some moved out of our way. At first I thought it was us—because we were alive, and they were dead? Then I realized that Winnow was following us. No one wanted to get too close to him. Hey, fine by me.

I love a guardian.

"What a good dog," I told him, smiling at all three of his heads. "Thanks for having our backs. And if you have any advice for us about the underworld, feel free to let us know."

Still no response. Kind of wished the dog talked instead of the vulture monk, but then I supposed we never would have made it down here.

Ben slowed to read some flyers that had been pasted to the corner of a bright yellow row house. "Hey, check this out. These are like old broadsheets. Postings for jobs, help needed . . . and wanted posters."

They looked as if they'd been printed by hand with one of those old presses with the wheel and crank. And the broadsheets were pretty interesting, too. There were guilds down here? And a royal guard that was tracking all the criminals in the wanted posters and offering rewards for information on their whereabouts?

One criminal in particular: the Nightmare.

"'Beware the Nightmare,'" Ben read. "'Last seen in Merry Dead Plaza. Responsible for the harrowing of three denizens.' *Harrowing*. What's that?"

I shrugged. "Sounds bad. The drawing is vague. Like a ghastly ghoul in a horror movie."

"That *definitely* worries me," Ben murmured. "What the heck are dead people afraid of?"

He had a point. Best steer clear of this Nightmare.

But Ben also found something a little cheerier: a poster for Sir Krak, that knight guide for hire who was advertising in our brochure. "He must be popular," Ben said. "Maybe that place to hire him is around here. If we're lucky, we can get inside and dry off there too . . . kill two, uh, birdbrains with one stone. See what I did there?"

"Your death jokes will definitely go over super well here."

"Maybe I can do stand-up in exchange for shelter and heat."

Shivering and wary, we set out for the colorful row houses along a wide, cobbled road named Soul Street, according to a wooden sign. We walked under laundry hanging from lines that crisscrossed from windows above, looking into an odd collection of shops as we passed. There was an old-fashioned fishmonger with candles on the counter, and then a bar with a lit-up martini glass above the entrance. Next door was a candy shop selling things I'd never seen—chocolate-covered rose petals and toffee witch hats. And on the other side of that was a window, illuminated by the soft glow of a neon sign:

POKIE'S NOODLE HOUSE

"That's it!" Ben said. "Pokie's. Look. The sign under the flashing red arrow."

UNDERWORLD GUIDE FOR HIRE

If Pokie's had a place to get warm, what more could we ask for?

Scents of garlic, ginger, and broth filled my nostrils when we stepped inside. The narrow restaurant was shadowy and full of people eating at small tables scattered on two levels, the second of which was accessible from a staircase to the left. To the right was a busy counter, behind which a man with a bandana wrapped around his head was pouring steaming broth into a bowl of clear rice noodles. When he was finished, he slid the bowl down the counter, then looked up at us.

"Welcome, travelers," he said. "Can I interest you in a hot bowl of nutritious noodles? It will help you on your journey."

"Uh, hello." It was hard to tell what time of day it was down here, on account of there not being a sun or sky, but it seemed early for soup. "Are you Pokie?"

"Yes, milady."

Everyone was so strangely polite here. It made me feel uncomfortable. "You wouldn't happen to know a woman named Morana Novak, would you? Silver bobbed hair, elderly? She may use the

last name Nováková, which is how you say it in Czech, on account
of the fact that she was a woman." I was talking too much. I felt my
ears getting a little warm and clicked my jaw to the side. It was still
sore. "So, anywho . . . Everyone just called her Babi. That's who
we're looking for."

Now *he* was the one who looked uncomfortable. "Sorry,
milady. I just make the soup."

Hmm. Was he nervous? Sweaty? It was hard to tell. It was
dreadfully warm inside the noodle restaurant, which was good for
drying off my damp clothes, at least. It was also smoky, though.
There were lots of pipes—like the ones that old sailors smoked in
black-and-white movies, back before they realized tobacco caused
cancer. Were people smoking seaweed here? Yuck. That couldn't
be good for anyone's lungs. Then again, none of these people were
alive, I supposed. . . .

I wondered if Winnow the three-headed dog was allowed in
here. I turned around to locate him, but he was gone. Had he not
come inside? I wasn't sure if I should be concerned about that.
Stray dogs go where stray dogs please. Maybe the waterfront was
Winnow's territory.

"If you can't help us with that, then what about a guide? We're
looking for one," Ben said, stepping up to the counter next to me.
"The sign outside? Can we find a guide here?"

Mr. Pokie nodded. "Oh, yes, milord. Upstairs, on the balcony.
At the captain's booth. Please," he encouraged, gesturing toward
the tiny staircase. As he did, he whispered, "Long live the Rime
Queen."

That was . . . strange. Was that the queen of this kingdom?
Seemed weird for him to be whispering about her. But he with-

drew, so I just thanked him. Then Ben and I headed upstairs.

The tables weren't as packed on the second level, and the ceiling was low. Fishing nets hung from the rafters, and Ben was forced to duck as we snaked past a couple of tables. Wary eyes stared back at us full of distrust. I didn't like it up here. It was hot and stuffy, and the corners were too dark. All except one: a red lantern hung over a corner booth. And above it, carved into a plank of wood, were the words CAPTAIN'S TABLE.

A lone person sat on one side of the booth. His face was hidden in shadow cast by the short brim of a black wool fishing cap, and he wore a long tan duster coat that was the same color as his sunbaked skin. He was extremely thin, extremely tall, and to match his beard, he had the longest white hair I'd seen aside from Santa Claus.

Only, he wasn't the least bit jolly.

And when I say he was thin, I mean *deathly*. Sunken eyes. He looked like some kind of outlaw who would kill all the good guys.

Like Santa's evil skinny brother who lived alone in the California desert.

"Children," he called out in a raspy voice that sounded as if his vocal cords had been roughed up with sandpaper and then set on fire. "Y'all lookin' for a guide? Sit yourselves down. The name's Grumbones. Guide for hire. Dyin' to serve you." He grinned to show off a set of chompers that included one gleaming gold tooth.

"No, no, no," Ben whispered to me under his breath. "Not him."

"Uh, thanks, but no thanks, Mr. Grumbones," I said. "We were actually looking for, uh, a guide named Sir Krak? The knight?"

"Sir Krak? Pfft," he said. "First of all, he's as dirty as a grave-digger's shovel, and second, he's already been hired by a couple of ignoramuses. Which makes it"—he pointed two bony fingers in our direction—"your lucky day."

Funny, I sure didn't feel lucky.

"Don't worry, I'm the best," he assured us. "Just got back from a tour of the city. The last fleshies who hired me said they'd give me ten stars if they could. Beaucoup stars."

Uh . . . what?

"Sit," he encouraged, pushing white hair over his shoulder. "You don't need to be skeered of ol' Grumbones. I got all the proper identification. Here's my guide license. 'Official Underworld Guide,' see? I'm licensed in all four kingdoms, not just in Hereafter. The chump in the bulky knight armor can't offer you that."

He flashed us a yellowed card written in ink. I couldn't read it all because his finger was blocking half of it, but I did spot the words "Grumbones" and "Underworld Guide." He needed to clean under his fingernails. And were those tattoos under his sleeve?

I looked at Ben and calculated his mood to be somewhere between Despair and Angry.

Maybe Evil Santa only *looked* like a weird old coot. Babi had taught me you shouldn't judge people by how they looked, and first impressions were often wrong. He might be kind once we got to know him. Besides, Babi—or whatever remained of her after death—was somewhere in this strange land, and I desperately needed to speak with her.

How would I know where to find her? Go knocking on doors around the docks? People outside the noodle house didn't seem all that friendly, and the people inside were strange in a whole different kind of way.

The odds were not in our favor.

We needed an underworld guide to change those odds.

Gathering my courage, I slid into the booth, across from Grumbones, pulling Ben alongside me. He wasn't happy, but I tried to ignore that. I also tried to ignore the satisfied smile that was lifting the corners of Grumbones's deep-set eyes.

The old man dug something out of an old leather saddle-bag that sat next to him. When he unfolded it in front of us, it covered most of the table: a big, convoluted map, more detailed than any I'd ever seen. The lettering was so small, it would take a magnifying glass to read it. He pulled one out of his bag and smacked it down.

"Made this myself," he said. "I know these lands like the back of my hand. Where do you want to go? Dream Tower? Timeless Banquet? I'll take you."

"Those sound fake," Ben said.

"*You* sound fake," Grumbones retorted. Then he smiled. "Just joshin' you, kid. Cheer up! You're in the underworld. You can do anything you'd like. Can't kill us—we're all dead."

"Why would I want to kill anyone?" Ben asked, horrified.

"You sure dumped Ludo pretty fast," the guide mumbled with a shrug of one shoulder.

"Oh no," I whispered. "The ferryman is . . . ?"

"Dead?" Grumbones said, leaning back in his seat to reveal a richly patterned vest. "Naw. He's immortal. He's back at his post now, missing a few more marbles," he said, tapping his forehead. "But he was already short a few before you two showed up. Lots of folks don't follow the rules, but you'll learn fast. Below ain't the same as Above. You break the rules here? You pay the consequences. Laws of the underworld."

I didn't like the sound of that. "How did you even know about Ludo?" I asked, frowning.

Grumbones scratched his beard. "Word gets 'round real quick-like. I keep my ear to the ground. A good guide does, you know. Speaking of—where would you like to go?"

Straight to the point. Fine. I supposed I didn't have to like the old man.

But I did *need* him. . . .

"I want to visit my grandmother," I told him, also straight to the point. "Morana Novak. People call her Babi."

He made a long face and stroked his beard. "Malicious Morana?"

"Hey!" I said, offended, though I'd heard worse from kids in our neighborhood.

He held up a hand. "Nothing meant by it, young miss. I respect a woman with a fiery tongue, and Morana is what we'd call a Number-One Dragon, ain't she?"

He laughed.

I didn't.

Then my anger fizzled as the bigger picture came into focus. "Wait . . . you know my grandmother?"

And Ben asked the more important question: "You know where to find her down here?"

"Sure, sure," Grumbones said. "She's in the city. Quite a trek from the Boondocks—that's where we are now. This here isn't inside the kingdom proper, you understand. These are unincorporated parts."

"These are the Boondocks, and she's in the city," I repeated excitedly, my breath speeding up to race my tumbling thoughts. "What city?"

Grumbones gestured broadly. "Hereafter. It's the name of this underworld kingdom *and* its main capital—an old grand dame of a city just outside the Boondocks, with districts and a lake, and a forest."

I gave him a dark look. "Okay, hold on. I've never even heard of the kingdom of Hereafter, and I know a *lot* of chthonic mythology. What about Elysium? Or the Duat or Mag Mell, *hmm?*" As I argued my point, I sat up straighter in my seat. Babi always said that it didn't matter whether you won an argument, as long as you didn't lose your pride. I'd already lost that once today in the Beacon corner shop to those three kids.

I wasn't going to lose it a second time to some corny old dude.

"Different words for the same thing. Everyone who comes down here has their own experience . . . sees things through their own filter, so to speak. But the bones of things don't change. Four kingdoms. This one is called Hereafter. You can call it what you'd like, but that's what we all call it down here right now."

Right now? What the heck was it called before?

Grumbones opened his hands. "As I was saying, the city is a sight to see. Big and grand. The castle is hundreds of years old."

"Only hundreds?" Ben said, surprised. "That's not very old."

"Wouldn't stuff in the underworld have been around forever?" I asked.

Ben scratched his curls. "I guess this noodle house has electricity. So that's modern, huh?"

"Ding-dong, kid." Grumbones pointed at him encouragingly with one bony finger while flashing him a smile that included his gold tooth. "Down here, it's sort of like things are Above. Sometimes you see an ancient pyramid, sometimes you see a McDonald's.

The underworld is alive. It changes and grows. The oldest part of it? Well, few dead ones have seen that."

"When did you die?" I asked.

He snorted. "Not polite to ask a gentleman his death date, sassafras. Now, where was I? Oh, yes. The Boondocks. The folks who choose to stay where we are now, outside the walls of Hereafter, and spend eternity here at the Boondocks? Locals call 'em canal rats."

"Locals?" Ben said, squinting. "You aren't a local?"

"I'm from a neighboring underworld kingdom, but I do a lot of traveling—I'm a guide, remember? I like freedom. Anyway, the canal rats avoid the city. They like it here instead because it's safe and stable. Close to Above. Lots of travelers like you two come through and remind them of the good old days, when they had flesh."

I frowned. "What do you mean by 'safe and stable'? Is it not safe inside the city?"

His shoulders lifted in a slow shrug. "Depends. It can be as safe as your mama's arms . . . and as dangerous as a bear's mouth. People forget what they know in the city. There's old magic there. Old memories. Old *creatures* . . . if you catch my drift." He leaned over the table and squinted a sharp eye at us.

Ben sucked in a quick breath.

"Never fear, children," the man said, softly pounding the table with his fist several times in a reassuring way—at least, that was his intention. Nothing about Grumbones was very reassuring. "That's why you have me. I know the safe routes through the city. You wouldn't want to go alone to search for yer dear grandma—oh, no. Might drown, or fall into a monster den, or get skinned alive, pulverized, slimed, or robbed at fang-point. But ol' Grumbones will keep you safe from the danger-filled underworld. I'll get you safely to Grandma."

"Sounding less and less like the brochures," Ben muttered with wide eyes.

But at that moment, I didn't care much about the danger. All I heard was 'grandma.' And it filled me with a buoyant hope that lifted my spirits all over again. "You know where Babi is? You've seen her?" I asked, trying not to sound as desperate as I felt.

"Haven't seen her *per se*, but I do know her location. Yep." He nodded several times as if he were considering it. "Definitely. I can take you there."

"But we need to be back home in a few hours," Ben added. "A vulture doorkeeper named Fizzle told us you guides could do that."

He nodded. "Trusty Fizzle. Yep. Time runs a little different here. Two hours here is about two days Above."

"What?" Ben said, alarmed.

Grumbones waved his hand limply as if he were shooing a fly away but wasn't really all that committed to the task. "Switch that, my mistake. You got plenty o' time here, is what I'm sayin'. But sure, I can get you back home. Your grandmother is holed up here"—he tapped his finger on the northwest section of the map, above what looked to be a lake—"in the Crown District. I can have you there in a matter of minutes in the-land-of-the-living time. An hour, tops."

Ben stared at the man's map. "The castle you were talking about earlier is in the Crown District?" He glanced my way and reminded me, "That's where birdbrain told us we could go back home."

Grumbones rolled his eyes. "Yes, the castle is in the Crown

District. But you'll need my help. You two peanut heads can't just waltz into Rime Castle without permission."

"But you can lead us there?" I said, heart racing with hope.

"Didn't I just say I could?" Grumbones complained, nose flaring with frustration. Then he gestured toward Ben. "There's an exit door to Above there, so you can leave when you're ready, little lord. No exit here, though. Not in the Boondocks."

"What about through Ludo?"

Grumbones shook his head. "Sorry, kid. Ludo's a one-way ticket. There're a couple of options past the wall. The woods, Rime Castle . . ."

Ben's mouth twisted. He was worried. I understood the feeling. But there was that word again—"Rime." That must've been what Pokie was talking about, the Rime Queen. Guess there really was underworld royalty here. Towers. Castles. Queens. Crown Districts.

Sounded more glamorous than Ludo's boat and these docks.

"How much?" I said, suddenly realizing that all I had was my emergency credit card.

"Oh, I don't take money," Grumbones said. "Coin is useless down here unless you're missing marbles like Ludo. Rest of us barter for soul deeds. Here." He whipped out a card and slid it across the map. "At the end of our journey, you just mark a star rating from one to five and drop that card into any mailbox you see inside the city wall. No postage required. I'm only a few stars away from a promotion. I aim to please."

Ben picked up the card. It looked homemade. "You do this . . . for the *likes*?"

Grumbones's nose wrinkled. "Likes? I do it for the stars, son. And the noodles. Nothing I like more than a steaming bowl of noodles, yum-yum-o!"

Ben gave me a side glance that told me just how much he loathed Grumbones: like, a lot. I gave him one in return that told him how many other choices we had: like, zero.

Ben sighed.

"What you say, youngins? You follow me, I take you to the Crown District and get you to old Babi, and then you just pay up by dropping that five-star card into a mailbox."

"*And* you'll show us a door that leads back to Forlorn—no tricks," Ben said.

"Agreed," the guide said. "Sign the back of the star card to initiate the contract."

He produced a black pen stamped with POKIE'S NOODLE HOUSE in gold on the side and showed me where to sign. This was all happening so fast. But if it got me to my Babi, if I could hear her throaty laugh just one more time and tell her the one thing that I so badly needed to tell her? That would make this worth any price.

So I signed.

Grumbones held a hand over his chest. "I do hereby swear, while I'm under hire as a guide through the province of Hereafter, I will lead you away from harm, I will drink of no hard liquors, I will not use profanity, I will not quarrel or fight, and I will faithfully lead you to the Crown District. This I do swear on my good honor."

Um, wow. Quite a speech. Ben and I exchanged secret uncomfortable looks.

"All right, then," I said, clearing my throat. "I guess this is, uh, happening, Mr. Grumbones. You're hired."

He pounded his fist on the table and grinned, gold tooth gleaming. "I knew you'd come round, sassafras. Let's get you to your grandma, shall we?"

CHAPTER 9
The Wall

It didn't take us long to dry off. And while we did, Grumbones gave us something we'd need for our journey: old miner's hats with lights attached to the fronts.

"The city is dark and foggy past the wall," he explained.

"I have a question, Mr. Grumbones. Is the entire underworld below the real world?" Ben asked. "At first we were definitely in a cave, but now I can't see any cavern walls. And how does an entire city fit inside a cave?"

"Let's get one thing straight right off the bat, children. Don't call me 'mister.' And don't say 'real world.' Just because I'm dead doesn't mean I'm not real. That's insulting. I was alive just like you."

"Sorry," Ben muttered. "It's just that it looks like it might be daytime here at the Boondocks. Maybe?"

He wasn't wrong. "Yeah," I said. "How is it overcast around the docks if there isn't a sky?"

Grumbones rolled his eyes. "Just because we're Below doesn't mean we're physically *under* the living world."

"We walked down a heck of a lot of stairs below the cemetery to get here," I said.

"Did you? Were they real stairs, or did you just pass into a different realm?"

I couldn't answer that.

Grumbones said, "Technically those stairs and Ludo's canal are spaces between the worlds. We call those 'between' places the Liminal Lands."

"Liminal Lands," Ben repeated.

"The Boondocks is a mixed Liminal spot between Ludo's canal and Hereafter. It's more part of Below than part of Ludo's territory, though."

"But that doesn't answer our question about why it feels like daytime here," I said.

Grumbones groaned. "Hereafter and all the kingdoms of the underworld are called 'Below' because they slip *below* the flesh world's notice. Below as in *hidden*. You catch my meaning? All worlds exist in the same space, basically. It's like . . . an onion."

More onions? I glanced at Ben, paranoid. He was a little weirded out too. But sometimes coincidences are just that. "An onion?" I said carefully, feeling as if I were walking into a trap.

Grumbones explained, "Each layer of an onion is a different world. The living world is the outer skin. The dead world is the second layer. And I guess Ludo's canal is the space between the two layers. Get it?"

I sort of did. "Does that mean there are other layers below the dead world?"

"Sure," Grumbones said. "All kinds of worlds hidden below the living world, kid. You got your demons and angels. Monsters. Faery. Cat."

"*Cat* world?" Ben said.

Grumbones glanced around, paranoid, as if someone might be listening. "Never mind that. All you need to know is that they're all invisible to each other. You can't see the layer above you while you're here, just like you can't see Below when you're Above. But what I'm trying to tell you is that we *do* have a sky down here. It just looks a little different from your point of view. Now let's get going before word spreads that you're here."

That was a little alarming. "Why would anyone care that we're here?"

"The two of you?" he answered, sounding suspiciously innocent. "They wouldn't. But there are things out there that have a keen interest in travelers. Let's get a move on, youngins."

Ben and I were both a little miserable now. The miner's hats weren't comfortable, and I wished we'd taken more time to ask around about other guides before signing Grumbones's contract. But now I feared what might happen if we broke it, rule-wise. So when he packed his map and picked up a gnarled branch that served as his walking staff—which was as tall as he was and outfitted with a strap that allowed him to carry it on his back—we followed him out of the noodle house.

We were on our way to the city.

To see my Babi again.

"Just keep quiet and follow me," our guide instructed us as we headed through the Boondocks. I wasn't sure if this was an underworld rules thing too, so I just kept my mouth shut and stayed behind him, trailing after his tan duster coat and billowing white hair.

Ben walked alongside me.

Past the brightly colored row houses, there wasn't a lot to see. A few derelict buildings. Some creepy underworld people standing around, doing nothing. Abandoned wagons of fish bones left to rot. We made our way up a winding path that became overgrown with tall, dry grass. The light grew dimmer here, and the shadows lengthened—so I guess he wasn't wrong about that sky thing. I just couldn't see a sun when I looked up. I only had a sense that the farther we walked, the more it felt as if we were leaving Ludo's cavernous canal behind and entering a real world.

I didn't say "real" to Grumbones.

No need to offend our guide again.

After a few minutes, we marched into a wooded area. It reminded me a little of Granny Booker's backyard. Leaves crunched under our feet as the lights from our helmets shone around the slender silhouettes of tree trunks. And when wisps of fog shifted in the distance, just past the woods, an enormous stone wall came into view.

"The city's inside there?" I asked.

"Schoolin' is really teaching you logic up Above, ain't it?" Grumbones said sarcastically.

"Excuse me?"

"Cool your jets," he said. "Surprised that Morana's offspring would be so soft."

"I'm not soft," I argued. And so what if I was? Ugh. I did not like this man.

"That gate looks like it's been out of action for a while," Ben said, shining his headlamp on a massive double door in the wall that was strangled by dead vines and twisted roots from a nearby tree that had grown into the stonework.

"Decades," Grumbones agreed. "Been a bit of a power struggle in Hereafter. Access to the city was shut down. Local politics, boring stuff. We'll have to take the ramp."

Ben and I looked where he gestured. The so-called "ramp" was a massive tree that had fallen onto a crumbling watchtower, smashing a small section of the wall open.

"Nature's ramp," Grumbones proclaimed, as if that were an attractive feature or selling point.

But Ben was not sold on the idea. "You want us . . . to *scale the wall*? An actual city wall?"

"Buck up, kid. It'll be fun," Grumbones said, urging us toward the fallen tree. "It's stable, don't worry. Just go one at a time and watch your footing. If you slip . . ." He chuckled in his raspy voice. "Well, that fall would hurt a fleshie, wouldn't it?"

"This is how people who've died have to get into the afterlife? They have to sneak into the city like criminals?" I asked. "My Babi had a bad knee. How could she climb this tree?"

Grumbones adjusted his saddlebag across his chest, a look of frustration in his eyes. "The dead don't travel here like you did. They're already inside the wall. And don't ask me how or why, because I'm not supposed to reveal the mysteries of life and death to fleshies."

"What about Pokie and the people on the Boondocks?" Ben asked.

"All the canal rats chose to leave the city. They fled. That's what rats do. Not that I blame 'em. Rats are some of my best companions," he said with a flash of his gold tooth. "Now. Up with ya. More climbin', less yappin.'"

The root ball of the tree had been hacked with an axe to create a kind of step system. We used that to hoist ourselves onto the fallen trunk and carefully, slowly walked up the length of it. One step at time, mindful of my feet. I didn't want to slip on the bark.

The only time I paused was when we were most of the way across the fallen tree, straddling the smashed watchtower. My heart hammered when, in the dark below us, I thought I spotted something moving deep inside the crumbling stone. But it was probably just the fog shifting. . . .

Had to be.

When Grumbones made it to the wall, he slung his staff over his shoulder along with his saddlebag and called back, "Be careful not to slip when you're climbing down. It'll hurt your delicate baby hands." Then he grabbed a fat coiled rope that was tied to a metal post. As he turned, a soft purple light glowed from beneath his clothes. For a second, I thought I saw symbols in the air around him—symbols made of that purple light.

Then he dropped onto the other side of the wall. Gone. Into the fog.

What the heck was that purple light? I couldn't think about it because I was next.

"I can't see anything past this wall," I told Ben. "What if there are crocodiles below? Hey, maybe your wild crocodile men down by the river actually live here instead." I was trying to be a little lighthearted, to help ease the tense situation, but Ben didn't appreciate my attempt at humor.

"I hate this, I hate this," he mumbled behind me repeatedly. "I'll never forgive you for dragging me here."

His bitter tone caught me off guard. "Now this is my fault?" I said. "You're the one who volunteered!"

"You practically guilted me into coming. I wasn't going to let you run off here alone so you could get in trouble."

"Trouble?"

"You heard me," he said, fretfully glancing down the tree as he balanced. "Why *are* you always in trouble at school lately?"

"I don't *try*." I opened my mouth to stretch my painfully tight jaw.

"Right, sure. Detention just falls into your lap."

That stung a bit, coming from him.

"Maybe I got bored and lonely, waiting while you were off playing monster-in-the-woods with your smartie friends," I complained.

"I keep inviting you, but you seem to like to be alone lately— unless it's cemetery related."

Why was he needling me about this while we were here, of all places? Frustration and anxiety combined and pressurized inside my throat. "I didn't ask for this!"

"You *literally* asked for this. You wanted to raise the spirit of your grandmother."

"Sorry I'm such a burden to you. I didn't ask for her to be *dead*, Ben. And by the way, I didn't curse her, despite all the rumors around school. Why would I do that?"

"Please. No one with a brain thinks you cursed her," he said, making an impatient face. "That's just a bunch of boneheads talking."

It didn't matter who was saying it. They were saying it about Babi. And me. The rumor made my stomach curdle. It sullied Babi's memory. And the final memory I had of her was already stained. If Ben only knew! I wouldn't tell him. Couldn't.

"She was the most important thing in my life!" I said, feeling desperate and raw, as if the size of my chest were shrinking every time I took a breath, so I had to inhale harder and harder and harder. . . .

He looked at me with intense eyes. "I used to be up there too, you know."

My chest deflated all at once, painfully.

Of course he was . . . important. We were best friends. At least, we used to be. Still were. I mean, of course we still were, even though things had been strained between us since Babi had died. Friends didn't just grow apart because you didn't have pizza and Minecraft speedruns every Friday night.

So, yes, we were still best friends. And he knew that. Didn't he? It felt weird and awkward to tell him that now. You know, in the middle of the underworld. While Grumbones could be listening.

"Just . . ." He flailed his hand and made random frustrated noises. "Can we not fight when I may drop to my death? Take the dumb rope and go. Please!"

Fine. Yes. Anything but this awful conversation.

I tested the rope. Loose. So I grabbed it, turned around like Grumbones had done, and descended the wall using my feet. Down I went. Awkwardly. It was difficult to look down while holding on to the rope because I immediately felt dizzy and trapped, like I might slip and fall. I wasn't coordinated enough to do this! Why was the rope so fat? It smelled bad and was burning my "baby hands"—ugh, I *really* hated that Evil Santa was right.

How far did this rope go, anyway? I was worried that I couldn't hold on much longer. I was worried about what was at the bottom.

Secretly I was worried that Ben thought I didn't feel like he was important anymore.

Finally. My rain boot touched something solid below. Not crocodiles. I swung off the rope, shook it to signal to Ben that it was his turn, and then looked around, shining my miner's helmet into the clearing fog.

I was standing on the roof of a building that was several stories high. It was dark—twilight, or just past it. The light was that funny grayish-pink color it is right before night falls completely, and there was a sky above us, but no stars. Just slow-moving mist under a golden crescent moon. And spread out beneath that moon for miles and miles was the most amazing thing I'd ever seen.

A dark medieval city. One filled with thousands of Gothic spires, turrets, and towers. Jagged iron fences lined tight, maze-like streets that were hidden in shadow. Bridges crisscrossed each other like catwalks. Flying buttresses and arched doorways held up grand buildings.

It was a city that fancy vampires would stalk at night.

One that reminded me of my Babi's old photos of Prague.

Only this city was sort of falling apart. Beneath the building where I stood, the streets were flooded with water.

"Whoa," Ben said, swinging off the rope. "This . . . is amazing."

"Welcome to the great city of Hereafter," Grumbones said as dark birds flew through the distant fog. "Majestic, ain't it? Got the lake in the middle. Mountains all around. Some forests that you don't want to walk in alone if you want to keep your head."

"I would," I said.

"Smart girl." He gestured with one hand. "They used to call the city the Black Spire, on account of all the pointy roofs. They also called it City of a Thousand Bridges. Last few years, there've been more statues than bridges. You'll see 'em. Hope you ain't jumpy, because they can sometimes fool yer eyes." He slapped Ben on the shoulder, causing him to lurch forward. I had to grab the back of his peacoat to steady him as a clay roof tile slid off into the dark water below.

"Thanks," he mumbled to me.

I guess we weren't fighting anymore. Good. I hated fighting. I hated making up more; so awkward! Maybe we could just ignore the problem and concentrate on finding Babi.

Acting natural, I turned to Grumbones and asked, "Is that our moon in the sky? The same one we see when we're—"

"Above?" Grumbones said helpfully. "Yep, pretty sure it's the same. Looks different from here, though, don't it? Sky is pretty and purple at twilight. If you're sentimental. Which I'm not. Clearly."

"Clearly" was right. And speaking of purple . . . "I saw a purple glow beneath your clothes when you went over the wall," I noted.

"That's my passport," he said.

"Your . . . ?"

He pulled up the sleeve of his tan duster coat. He was more muscular than I'd thought he would be, but it was the kind of muscular that had no bulk to it—all lean muscle over bones with the skin pulled drum-tight. And on that skin was a network of strange symbols.

Tattoos. On every inch of his arm from his wrist up.

"My passport," he repeated. "The city has wards. That's a magical barrier, basically. Every district of the city has one. Keeps the denizens . . . safe. People like me? I'm a traveler. I can move between wards. This is my passport. Because I'm an official underworld guide. A guide. That's me."

Babi always told me that when adults explain too much, it means they're trying to hide something. Ben and I glanced at each other. I cleared my throat. "Uh, so how come we didn't need a passport?"

"The wards stay open briefly after my passport deactivates them. They'll reset any second now. . . ."

A puffing sound drew my attention behind us, and when I turned, purple light radiated where we'd dropped off the rope. Then there was nothing.

"Boosh!" Grumbones said. "Told ya."

Ben reached out where the purple light had been, and his hand pushed against an invisible wall. I tried it too. It was cold and solid, and it made me want to snatch my hand away.

"Like I explained, it's a ward," Grumbones said. "All you need to know is that you can't travel between districts without me because you need my passport to get through the wards. So we can't split up in the city, or you'll be stuck here forever."

"Forever?" Ben said, voice cracking. Reflected in his eyes were memories of our recent "stuck here forever" problem involving Ludo's boat sinking in the lake. "You couldn't have told us that?"

"Just did. Stick with me, and you'll be fine. Nothing to get upset about. It's a magical wall, not a monster. Buck up. We're just getting started." Grumbones retrieved his gnarled walking staff from his back and attached a metal lantern to the hooked top. The lantern swung gently from side to side, and its flame lit up the area around us better than our miner's helmets.

"I want one of those," Ben said, so impressed with the gadget that he temporarily forgot about the threat of being stuck in the underworld.

"This thing? My dum-dum stick? Hey, die and become an underworld guide, and then it's all yours, kid," Grumbones said, using the staff to pick his way along the roof toward the next building. "This is the Flooded District. Used to be the Lower District before the Siege."

"What siege?" I asked.

"Like, a military siege?" Ben asked. "Has there been a war here?"

"You could say that. An invasion."

"This kingdom got invaded by an army?"

"The city, mostly. And it was a naval attack from the Lake of Sighs. Navies come by water. Armies come by land. If you want to get technical."

"That's why this district is flooded," I murmured.

"Oh!" Ben said. "Did the canal rats use to live here?"

"No need to get wrapped up in local politics," Grumbones said. "Besides, it was a few decades ago. That's all you need to know. We have to jump over to the next roof. Hang on to the iron railing, and don't fall into the water. It'd be worse than Ludo's boat. There are bad things down there, and I ain't jumpin' in after you. I don't do water rescues."

He moved fast for an old man, and his legs were longer than ours. I wasn't sure how dead people stayed in such good shape, but he had an impressive kind of grace in the way he prowled the rooftops, answering our questions breezily as he went.

"Where are all the people?" Ben asked, persistent. "Did the Siege wipe them all out?"

"Naw. The Siege hit this area the hardest and folks scattered. Some are in enclaves inside the magical wards. Where there's light, there's a soul. Or a trap. Not everyone is friendly. We're fairly safe here, but when we get into some bad neighborhoods, we'll need to watch out for things."

"Like the Nightmare?" Ben asked.

Grumbones grunted. "All kinds of nasties in the city."

I should have been better prepared. All I had to defend myself was . . . a Whispering Pines Cemetery pen that I'd bought with my allowance. The pen barrel was filled with little plastic skeletons floating in blue liquid that moved when you shook it up. It was my favorite pen.

"Should Helena and I have weapons?" Ben asked our guide. "Silver bullets or stakes or something?"

"Silver? Pfft," Grumbones scoffed. "You're thinking of movies, son. Silver don't kill nothin' here. What you want is steel to put down any demonic creatures."

"Demonic?" Ben and I said together.

Then Ben said, "If we're going to run into demonic creatures, then give me a steel weapon and pronto!"

"You know how to use a weapon? No? That's the answer to your question, too," Grumbones said, hopping over an iron railing that ran along a balcony covered in night-blooming jasmine. I breathed in its sweet-smelling perfume as we passed.

"I once saw a lady take off a necklace made of steel beads and use it as a weapon against a dude who was trying to take her purse," Ben said. "You know, self-defense, like a whip—swung it at the mugger. I could do that. Pow! Right in the kisser."

Oh boy. I'd heard that story a thousand times. Some tourist passing through Forlorn. Ben started watching old kung fu movies after that incident, nonstop. He wouldn't shut up about it.

"No purses in the underworld, hero, so you just let me worry about protecting our kissers," our guide said.

"I've got a Whispering Pines Cemetery skeleton pen in my jacket pocket that I could use as a shank," I told Grumbones. "You know, if it came to that."

Grumbones huffed out a dark laugh. "I'd say your chances of ending up in a prison riot here are slim to none."

That was something, I supposed. I'd rather have kept my favorite pen blood-free. I leapt over a drainpipe capped with a stone gargoyle. "I thought once you died, it would be easy. You know. Heaven. Sunshine. Playing games and being happy. Hugging your family in the field of reeds. Drinking a mug of ale with your buddies in Valhalla."

"Been looking forward to endless nights of beer-swilling with your fellow Viking warriors, have ya?" Grumbones said dryly.

"I'm just saying, this place is all ruins. Not what I expected out of paradise."

"No one said anything about paradise. Not in my contract, anyway," Grumbones said with a rude chuckle.

"Is that a cathedral?" Ben said, pointing. "Why is it black and spooky?"

"Is this the Bad Place?" I asked.

Our guide shrugged dismissively, in a way that told me he thought my question was pointless. "Bad, good . . . Sometimes things are more complicated than that."

"My Babi always said you know in your heart what's right and wrong."

"Uh-huh," Ben agreed. "My granny says the same thing."

"Look," Grumbones said, now sounding perturbed. "Good people make bad decisions and get swindled by crooked players. Should an entire kingdom be punished because of that?"

"Huh?" I scrunched up my face. He wasn't talking about *us* being swindled, was he?

Grumbones shook his head. "All I'm sayin' is that some of the underworld is good, some of it's neutral. Some of it's chaotic. A lot of it's jumbled up."

"Oh!" Ben said brightly. "Now I get it. This place is chaotic neutral. Or evil?"

"It's chaotic none-of-your-beeswax. Now look, kids, Grumbones will not be imparting any celestial wisdom. You wanna know the meaning of life and death? Too bad. Telling you would be against the rules."

"But you know the meaning of life?" I said, peering at his wrinkled face.

"If I did, I wouldn't be here, groveling to be your guide, now, would I? Stop asking me dumb questions, for the love of . . ." He grumbled to himself, then told us, "Stay close and don't touch anything. We're going down here."

After dropping down to the next balcony, he pulled out a ring of large keys attached to his belt and unlocked a small door.

"Where did you get the keys?" I asked.

"I won them from Pokie, because I ate more bowls of noodle soup than any other patron," he said lightly.

I snorted a laugh. "That sounds unlikely. Go on, tell us."

"It's a guide secret," Grumbones said.

"If you tell us, you'd have to kill us?" Ben asked.

"Ask me again," Grumbones said, one brow raising slowly, "and we'll find out."

We declined, so he just shooed us inside.

Dust motes danced in the air as our headlamps flashed around a stone-walled room that was empty of furniture. It looked as though no one had lived here for hundreds of years. Crumbled rocks had piled up beneath a rusted shield on the wall. On a ripped oil painting of a landscape, some words had been graffitied in red:

WHEN THE DEATHLESS QUEEN FINDS LOVE

HOUSE OF RIME WILL FALL

FEAR THE WYRM

Ben shuddered.

"What the heck is this?" I asked in a low voice, a little scared too because it reminded me of the Forlorn Worm with a different spelling.

"Eh, some waste of space who thought they were a poet," Grumbones answered, unconcerned. "This house was abandoned decades ago. Down these stairs. The floodwater will've receded, but your feet'll get a little wet on the lower level. Watch for sewer meeks."

I didn't know what those were, but I didn't like anything with the word "sewer" attached to the front of it. We quietly followed Grumbones down a circular stone stairwell with broken stained-glass windows until a shuffling sound below caught our attention.

Something splashed on the floor beneath us.

We weren't alone in the house.

CHAPTER 10

Abandoned House

S tay behind me." Grumbones peered around the wall to
shine his flame staff into the room below.

We listened. Was it a sewer meek? Something worse?
How bad was a sewer meek?

But after holding our breath and watching, we realized that
whatever it was, it had gone.

There was only silence now.

"Coast is clear." Grumbones moved to the ground floor of the
building, stepping over shallow puddles of water, so I supposed it
was okay to follow.

At first, all I noticed was that it was a grand entrance hall. A
broken iron chandelier that held real candles had fallen upon a
large round table in the center, where old leather-bound books
had scattered. Over the impressive front doors hung a large
medieval banner woven with a heraldic wolf wearing a crown,
and stitched beneath it were the same words that had been

etched into the mausoleum in Whispering Pines Cemetery: DEATH HATH NO TERRORS.

I swallowed hard, my throat dry. It weirded me out that the phrase from Above was down here, too.

But I quickly forgot all about this when I spotted what Grumbones was studying next to the entrance hall doors.

A polished statue. But not the kind you'd see in a museum. This was made of something that looked like black honey: shiny, dark, and you could *almost* see through it.

That wasn't all. The statue itself was of an adult human male, and he held his arms up as if he were defending himself. An expression of terror was frozen on his face. It looked so real.

The way the man in the statue was clothed was oddly familiar. Hat with feather. Sword. Some kind of Renaissance knight or man-at-arms . . .

"Holy crap. Is this Sir Krak, the other underworld guide?" Ben said, alarmed.

Sir Krak? From the brochures. Ben was right! But I was so confused. Why would someone make a statue like this? Statues are for tributes, to honor someone. Not to capture what looked to be his last terrified moment before . . .

It looked *so very real.*

"Um, is this the *actual* Sir Krak?" Ben asked with widening eyes. "Is he . . . dead?"

A sickening feeling slid down my spine.

"Maybe it's not him," I said, really hoping it wasn't.

"It is! Look at his hat," Ben argued, sloshing through the water. "What the heck happened to him?"

"Husk," Grumbones said from behind us. "Left over from a

soul after it's been harrowed. Like the preserved shell of a cicada bug dipped in amber. Eerie, huh?"

I held my hand against my chest, as if that could protect me. "What's 'harrowed'?"

"Vvooom!" Grumbones sucked in his cheeks and thumped one side of his face. "Soul sucked out. Removed. Goodbye forever in the most painful way possible." He shivered and shook his head as if he didn't want to think about it happening to him.

My sickening feeling turned to dread. If Sir Krak was supposed to be a guide that protected tourists against the dangers of the underworld, did that mean that Grumbones was susceptible to harrowing down here too?

How dangerous was this place?

One of the doors opened. Ben and I moved behind Grumbones, who held up his staff.

Two people entered the hall. Guards, judging by their long swords and the look of their uniforms—and from the same era as the husk of the man in front of us. Their dark coats were heavily padded and embroidered with the heraldic wolf crest from the banner over the door.

Above their shoulders were brown feathered hawk heads.

More bird people?! No way. I wanted to turn around and run back up the steps we'd come down. Ben must have too, because he was moaning anxiously beside me. But Grumbones didn't react as if they were enemies.

"Halt," one of the hawk guards said. "Who goes there?"

"Sheath your swords, fellas," Grumbones said, showing them the tattoos on his arm. "My passport. Official guide, transporting two fleshies through Hereafter. I'm on your side."

The word "transporting" made us sound like prisoners. The guards looked us over with a bit of curiosity, then turned back to Grumbones. One of them said, "You don't look like one of the grand admiral's crew."

Who? I glanced at Ben, but he was too nervous to take his eyes off the hawks.

"Got no skin in your war, but if I did, I wouldn't be working for an evil tyrant," Grumbones assured the guards.

They both relaxed, and then one said, "This is no place for travelers."

"I can see that," Grumbones said. "We'll be on our way."

"Sir Krak was a guide like you," I blurted out to Grumbones. "Don't you recognize him?"

Why wasn't he as freaked out about the statue as I was?

Grumbones gave me a sharp look, then cleared his throat, covering his mouth with his fist. "Ah, yes. I believe I do. What, uh, happened here, fellows?"

One of the hawk guards cocked his head in a very birdlike manner and answered, "This here is the Nightmare's work."

"The Nightmare?" Ben and I said together.

Fear knotted up my stomach.

"Probably a day old," the hawk confirmed. "Maybe less. Caught a couple of its minions snooping around, trying to cart away the husk. Didn't catch them, but at least we chased them off."

Grumbones tsked, sympathetic. "Can't believe the Nightmare's out here in the Flooded District."

"It's on the prowl, getting bolder," the other guard confirmed. "We'd not seen a harrowed soul this far south before," he said, taking out a small glass vial with a cork stopper. Using a knife, he cracked off a sliver of the statue's elbow and carefully dropped the black shard into his vial.

"What will you do with that?" Grumbones asked.

"Sorry, that's royal army business," the guard said.

"Let's just say that all the rumors could be true," the other guard said. "You know, the rumors that say souls can't come back to Hereafter after they've been harrowed. True death."

"That's what our commander thinks, anyway," the first guard confirmed. "No one to ask since the queen—"

Grumbones signaled for the hawk to be quiet and explained, "Tender ears."

I didn't know what that was about, so when everyone was looking around awkwardly, I got up the nerve to ask, "Where do the harrowed souls go?"

Grumbones tossed me a perturbed look. "Told you not to ask questions like that." He gave a conspiratorial glance to the hawk guards and said in a low voice that I could still plainly hear, "Fleshies. So nosey."

The second hawk trained his beady black eyes on me, and I got an uncanny feeling, like breath on the back of my neck. I wished he wouldn't stare at me like that, as if he were early and I were the worm. But when Grumbones asked him another question about where they'd tracked the Nightmare's minions, and the three of them huddled to shield me and Ben from their conversation, like adults often do, I was both relieved and frustrated.

"Did you hear all that?" I whispered to Ben.

"Heard it. But are you seeing this? Sir Krak had tattooed skin like Grumbones," Ben whispered, staring at the husk's wrists. "See the symbols? Was he leading people like us through the underworld when he got attacked? He looks terrified."

"Yeah, he's backing into the corner," I agreed. "If he was guiding other tourists through Hereafter, where are those tourists now? Don't see any other husks here. Did they run away?"

"Maybe living people don't get husked?" Ben squinted at a dark shape on the floor. "What's that?"

It was a piece of paper, floating on the surface of the dirty water. Some kind of handwritten note on fancy stationery with a military insignia at the top. Ben held the damp paper by the corner as we read the message that was scrawled on it in ink.

> *Take the asset to the tower. Per our agreement,*
> *our contract will be settled upon safe delivery. I'm*
> *counting on you. Don't mess this up if you want*
> *a cushy position in my crew. If you don't, I'm sure*
> *I can find a place for your harrowed soul in my*
> *ground troops. Or maybe I'll just chop off your*
> *head.*
> *Ta-ta for now,*
> *Your friend on the inside*
> *P.S. Beware Howlers. They are getting too bold.*

I made a low noise. "Was this letter to Sir Krak? Was he involved in some kind of shady deal? Is this a warfare thing? 'Asset' makes Sir Krak sound like a spy or secret service, or something. But who would he be secretly servicing?"

"And what crew?" Ben asked, rereading the letter. "What's this business about Howlers? Are they an underworld gang?"

"Don't know, but whoever wrote this letter sounds like a jerk.

Look at the name in the fancy design at the top of the stationery. 'Grand Admiral.' Who the heck is that?" I asked.

"Harrowing, head chopping . . . What I don't understand about any of this is that I thought everyone was already dead here," Ben said. "How can you re-kill what's already dead?"

Grumbones stamped through the water and snatched the letter. "What did I tell you about touching things? This is evidence," he said, shoving it into his pocket.

"If it's evidence, shouldn't you give it to the guards?" I asked, peering behind him. They were gone, and the door was open to a city street.

"They're heading back to their post. And why would babies be interested in local politics? Clearly this nincompoop was dull enough to get caught by the Nightmare. Why would you care about his business, anyway?"

"We're not babies, we're twelve," I told him.

"Huh. That old?" he said, tugging his white beard. "Are you promised to each other, or something? Going steady? Engaged to be married?"

"What?" I said, feeling my ears get hot beneath my bobbed hair. "No! You weirdo! Ugh."

"We're friends. Ever heard of it?" Ben said, insulted.

"I can't keep up with modern trends." Grumbones shrugged as if he hadn't just embarrassed both of us. "Anyway, it doesn't matter. The Howlers are a group of . . ." He hesitated, squinting thoughtfully, as if he were searching for just the right word to describe them. "Well, you might say they're revolutionist do-gooders who live outside town. They stick their noses into people's business and may do more harm than good."

Ben's nose wrinkled. "How do they fit in with this grand admiral person who wrote this letter?"

For a moment, Grumbones looked as if he wanted to tell us more. Then he kicked the leg of the husked-out man, and the kneecap shattered like thin glass. "Do you want to see Morana again, or do you want to end up like this wasted sapper? I'd suggest you leave the city's problems to the locals. Now let's get moving before the sewer meeks catch our scent."

Wow. Talk about no respect for the dead. We had definitely irritated our guide. But I, for one, did not want to stick around and argue in front of a dead man. Dead-*er* man. So when Grumbones stomped through the standing water and out the door, Ben and I shared a look of resigned acceptance and followed.

Goodbye, Sir Krak. Not sure if you were good, bad, or chaotic neutral, but I guess we'll never know, will we?

The narrow street outside sloped upward out of the water, and though it was lined with buildings, they were all dark and abandoned: no lights in the broken windows, no signs of life. In the road itself, we had to walk around carriages that looked as if they once belonged to noblemen, but they sat with no driver or horses. Wagons had been left with their contents raided and scattered: barrels split open, boxes and wooden chests rummaged through. Some looked as if they'd been set on fire.

Glancing around, it hit me all at once. The reason I hadn't been able to talk to Babi's ghost the past year . . . all my foreboding feelings that something was wrong? Maybe it was because she was stuck down here in all this. Flooding. Fire. Abandoned buildings. I'd seen no electricity on this side of the wall. Had she traded modern conveniences for a medieval war zone?

Or worse—

"Mr. Grumbones," I said as we turned under a bridge lined with parapets. "What if my Babi has been turned into a husk?"

"Naw," he said. "She's still kickin', kid. You just got spooked because of what you just seen, and that's understandable. But the chances of that happening to your ol' grams are slim. She's as tough as they come."

"And that guy wasn't? Did you know him personally?"

"Him? He's just some loser. Back in my day, we had a name for people like that who take the cushy jobs and stay out of harm's way while the rest of us risk our necks. . . ."

"Looks like he didn't stay that far out of harm's way," I mumbled.

"Mm-hmm," Ben agreed.

Grumbones snorted. "Forget about him. He's not worth the ulcer, sassafras."

Maybe he wasn't, but the whole thing didn't feel right. "Hey," I said, "how do you know my Babi if you aren't originally from this kingdom? I mean, just how many souls are there in Hereafter? What if she's in trouble and we don't know it? There's no phone here on this side of the wall? I can't call her?"

"*Thundering tarnation*," he swore under his breath, scratching the side of his neck. "Look, kid, we're almost in the next district, right over that hill. . . ."

"I'm just trying to understand," I persisted. "By the way, someone stole all the mementos off my Babi's grave, and Fizzle said you could help me find who did it."

He grunted. "How would I know that?"

"That's what he told me."

"Birds are dumb creatures," he said.

That wasn't true. My grandmother didn't like them for just the opposite reason: Birds are extremely intelligent. *Too* smart.

I showed him the wilted lily of the valley stem that I'd found on the steps near Ludo's boat. "This is one of the mementos. There were other things too."

He squinted at it and listened to my descriptions of what I'd lost. "Fine. I'll try to put some feelers out during our trip. I know some folks who know some folks. But that wasn't part of our original deal, just for the record. You're better off just forgettin' about a bunch of trinkets. After all, you'll be seeing your actual gram-grams. Isn't that better?"

"*If* she's not a husk," I pointed out.

"Tell you what," he said. "If she's not up and about when we get to the Crown District, you get your money back."

"We didn't give you money," Ben pointed out.

Grumbones didn't say anything for several steps, but when he did, it sounded as if he were swearing. I'd heard my fair share of profanity, and most of it from my Babi, who was known to shock and awe with the best of them, and once cussed out the mayor's wife in front of the post office for nonpayment of some funerary flowers.

Right now, Grumbones was dropping a few choice words of his own.

So much for that fancy speech full of vows he made to me and Ben, back in the noodle house. Let's hope he kept his other promises better than that one.

CHAPTER 11

Knights Bridge

At the top of the steep hill we took a sharp left. When the fog drifted, golden specks of light appeared up ahead. The light was coming from lampposts. They were made from ornate iron and were taller than any I'd ever seen, and each one flickered with a flame inside glass.

Hundreds lined the sides of an enormous stone bridge.

And between them, massive gargoyles crouched on the bridge's railing.

Down below the arching stone, dozens of other giant figures stood in dark water, holding up the bridge. They were stone statues of medieval knights, some women, some men. And they all wore the same wolf crest on their armor that we'd seen inside the flooded house.

I'd never seen anything so big and impressive. Nothing in Forlorn, that was for sure.

Grumbones pointed with his staff. "Kids, this is the Knights Bridge."

"*Whoa,*" Ben murmured in an astonished voice.

I nodded, just as dazzled. "I wish our phones worked. We need a photo of this."

"Try your brain," Grumbones said. "It takes snapshots that last forever."

"Can't show my Bigfoot Enthusiasts Club a photo of my brain," Ben said, pushing a lock of curly hair out of his eyes with an exaggerated gesture.

Grumbones snorted derisively. "The problem isn't your brain. It's the fact that you're in a Bigfoot club. Is that how you two spend your time up there?"

"It's how I spend *my* time," Ben said, indignant. "She spends hers alone in her room or hiking around the lighthouses in the fog."

That was embarrassingly true. But why should I be ashamed to spend time alone? Babi had loved taking morning walks down by the lighthouses. She'd said it helped her clear her mind. That's why I tried to talk to her ghost there a million times, using her photo and the special summons she'd taught me: *Together before, together again.* But all I'd gotten for my trouble was a face full of ocean spray from all the waves crashing against the rocks, not a way to connect with my grandmother from beyond and tell her what I desperately needed to tell her.

What I couldn't talk to Ben about . . .

I was a little peeved at Ben for sharing my personal stuff with our guide, so I gave Ben a dirty look. He just shrugged it off.

Grumbones squinted at me as if he might say something, but thought better of it. Maybe this was too much personal drama for him. "Anyway, as I was saying, this bridge is the only route over the Lake of Sighs—that's the big lake in the center of the city. Since Hereafter's boats got destroyed in the Siege, this is the only way into the part of the city that hasn't been flooded. Which is good and bad. You'll need to keep your snot lockers clean once we clear this."

"Huh?" Ben and I both said.

He tapped his nose. "Snot locker. Keep it clean."

I was still confused. Why did I need to blow my nose?

Grumbones explained, "Not literally. It means don't yap your jaws at anyone. Let me do all the talking. Watch out for enemies." He shrugged his saddlebag off his shoulder. "I need to rearrange my gear. You go on, but not too far. Stay where I can see you. I'll just be a moment."

As he rustled through his bag, muttering to himself, Ben and I looked at each other. I was still a little miffed at him for saying that comment about me sitting alone in my room. But when he stuck his hands into his pockets and gave me an awkward glance, I knew he felt as weird as I did.

"Come on," I mumbled.

He nodded, and together we left Grumbones and hesitantly walked onto the big bridge.

The fog was clearer here. It was a relief to have some light, even if the flickering lamps made shadows dance spookily on the gargoyles. Better than relying on our headlamps and Grumbones's lantern stick.

A few carriages without their horses had been abandoned on the bridge. Ben peered into the open door of one that was also missing a wheel. On the bench seat inside, WYRM was cut into the leather, which made me think of the graffiti inside the abandoned house. But next to this, someone else had written in the dust OUR BELOVED NIGHTMARE.

Ben grimaced. "What's up with this? It was in that creepy graffiti on the wall of the abandoned house, too. Did the Howler revolutionists write this?"

"Don't know," I said. "But it sure sounds like somebody is really into this Nightmare creature."

"She's a monster," a tiny voice said.

Ben froze.

I swung around, looking for the source. But there was no one. Just Grumbones in the distance, who had his back to us and was taking a swig from some kind of metal flask. "Who said that?" I whispered.

"I did, milady," the voice replied. "Down here."

I squinted back into the carriage, where a small animal perched on its hind legs. It was black and had a slick pelt like a beaver, waxy-looking and shiny, but it had the long, scaled tail of a lizard . . . and no ears. Not ones that I could see. Its red-rimmed eyes were too small for its face, making it look sad and pitiful.

Was it mammal or reptile, or some kind of hybrid? The creature looked foreign yet so familiar.

"Hello?" I said, bending down.

"Milady," the strange animal said, bowing its head. "You were talking about the Nightmare. She's a monster. A feral one who will suck the very soul from your body. You must beware. She will harrow you."

"It talks," Ben murmured, utterly delighted as he crouched down.

The lizard-like animal covered its small eyes, blinded by our dueling miner hat lights. Ben switched his off and said, "My bad. Is that better, little guy?"

The cowering animal blinked, then replied, "You are flesh, milord? From Above?"

Ben nodded. "This is Helena, and I'm Ben. Nice to meet you, uh . . . What is your name?" Ben held out his index finger for the animal to shake.

The sad-looking face suddenly changed. Beady eyes narrowed and its mouth opened to display four rows of bright orange teeth covered in filth.

Quick as a snake, the creature struck Ben.

"Ahhh!" Ben screamed, jerking backward with a bloodied finger and falling onto his butt.

"Ben!"

"It bit me!" he cried, holding up his hand as proof.

"Eughh!" I grunted in sympathy.

From the end of the bridge, Grumbones shouted something I couldn't hear as he ran in our direction. I was too concerned with defending us in case the weird talking hybrid attacked again. But the horrible creature had scampered off through the carriage and burst through the door on the other side. I briefly considered chasing it down, but it was racing across the bridge on all fours, so I checked on Ben instead.

"Are you okay?"

"No, I am not! I got bit," he snapped. "It really stings."

I held his hand to inspect it and wiped away the blood with the edge of my coat. The finger didn't look *too* bad, but there were three little puncture wounds.

"What in the blazes did you nincompoops do?" Grumbones shouted as he jogged up to us.

"I got bit!" Ben said, showing him his finger. "You said you'd protect us. What *was* that thing? Am I going to need a rabies shot?"

The guide glanced at Ben's finger—as if he couldn't care less—and peered across the bridge. "I told you not to talk to anyone!"

"But—" I argued.

Grumbones fixed me with a cantankerous look. "Did I not?"

He had. "I didn't realize you meant *animals*. It talked to me first."

"Of course it did. It was a sewer meek, you ditzy cherries!"

"Sewer germs?" Ben said, completely grossed out as he squeezed fat droplets of blood from his bite marks.

Grumbones shook his head. "That don't matter none at the moment. It's just a scratch, buck up." A medicinal cough-drop scent drifted from his breath when he spoke. "Bigger problem for us right now is that it got yer blood. Sewer meeks on the bridge are friendly with the one thing down here that likes blood. We could've just waltzed over the bridge with no problems, but you had to wake it up, didn't ya?"

I didn't like the sound of that.

The bridge rumbled under us.

The stones beneath my feet felt as if they were shifting. Alive. Like I was a tiny kid, standing on my dad's stomach on the living room floor while we played Walk the Plank: he was the plank, and I tried to balance in my socked feet, laughing, while he rumbled beneath me and wiggled until I fell into the shark-infested ocean that was the rug near the fireplace.

Only now it was cobblestones shifting below me and rippling, and it was all I could do not to lose my balance. Ben swayed and bumped into me. Grumbones gripped his walking staff and held on as a dry wind whipped over us, swirling up a nasty dust that blinded me and made me cough. I had to bury my face in my arm.

Then the wind died down, and a terrible cracking drew my attention up ahead, to the center of the bridge.

Where one of the gargoyles climbed down from the railing.

It was roughly the size of my parents' truck. Only, the truck didn't have scaly wings, huge talons, and a monstrous grimace. The gargoyle shook the bridge with each step it took.

"Flesh and bone, dare to roam, enter not my sacred home," it said in a deep and elegant voice that sent chills down my arms. Bats erupted from its wings and circled its head before scattering into the purpled sky.

"Bats?" Ben whispered in a terrified voice, losing sight of the fact that there was an enormous Gothic creature approaching us.

A few fruit bats were the least of our problems right now!

"We did not mean to awaken you," Grumbones said. "Our apologies."

The gargoyle wasn't interested in apologies. "Wake you did. Now you stop. Defeat the Guardian, or . . . drop." The monster gestured with one taloned hand toward the water below, which was several stories down. Too far to survive.

Yet surviving a fight with this creature didn't seem all that viable either.

"*Really* wish we had some of those steel weapons about right now," Ben moaned.

"You don't fight a Bridge Guardian with weapons, steel or otherwise," Grumbones said in a low voice. "You fight 'em with words."

"What kind?" I whispered. "Is there a secret password I need to know?"

"No, nitwit. This is like . . . a troll. They taught you about trolls up Above, right?"

"Yes," I said shortly, unhappy about being called names.

"This bridge didn't have a ward before. *Now* it does. A different kind of ward from the ones around the city. And neither of ya have got passports. I don't think I can get all three of us through a ward made from gargoyle magic."

Grumbones's skin was emitting that soft, purplish glow beneath his clothes.

Uh-oh.

"All you had to do was keep your yaps shut," our guide said. "Hope you're pleased with yourselves. And I dang sure hope you're good at puzzles." He cleared his throat and spoke up to the gargoyle. "Go on. Give them the riddle they need in order to use the bridge."

"Why us?" Ben said, eyes wide.

"You woke it, you answer it," Grumbones told us. "Them's the rules."

My heart dropped into my stomach.

The gargoyle sunk its talons into the stone of the bridge—not good—and lifted its head, as if pondering. After several panic-inducing moments, it finally spoke again.

"The maker doesn't want me. The buyer doesn't use me. The user never sees me. What am I? Tell me and you don't die," the gargoyle said.

A riddle . . . or death. No pressure. I took a deep breath to calm my anxiety.

I looked at Ben. He looked at Grumbones, who merely shrugged. "Hey, not my job. Put your minds together. Told you already—you break it, you buy it."

"I'm going to break something, all right," I mumbled before pulling Ben aside into a private huddle.

"This is bananas," Ben said, holding his injured hand as he glanced over his shoulder at the gargoyle.

"Are you okay?" I asked. "How's your finger?"

"Sore," he admitted. "But I'll survive, I guess."

"Okay. Let's do this. Riddle."

"Right," Ben said. "Riddle. The maker doesn't want me. . . . What about bread? Like, a bread maker bakes bread and sells it to the buyer, who gives it to the user . . . who's blind?"

I wrinkled my nose. "I think Mr. Gargoyle is looking for a simpler answer than that."

"Well, I don't know, then!" he said, flustered. "I'm trying, Helena. It doesn't help that I'm bleeding to death."

He wasn't, but his injury did look pretty swollen.

"Let's think together. Think, think, think. What was the riddle again?"

"It said the maker doesn't want it, the buyer doesn't use it, and the user doesn't see it."

"Hmm . . . The buyer gives it to someone who never sees it," I said. "What kind of person wouldn't see something that was made for them?"

"A dead person? Oh! Hold on!"

Our gazes connected. We both had the same idea but didn't say it aloud. We just *knew*.

A little zip of excitement ran through me.

"Think that could be the answer?" I asked, hoping.

"Definitely," he assured me. "Has to be. Right?"

We both smiled. This was why we had earned our Junior Coastal Rangers troop badges faster than everyone else. We were just always on the same page, thought-wise. He could finish my sentences, and I knew that his school locker combination always used a variation of the numbers one, nine, five, and eight, because 1958 was the year Bigfoot was first mentioned in a newspaper.

It was good to know that when things were rough, we could still rely on each other.

"Okay," I said, turning around. "We've got the answer to the riddle."

"Are you sure?" Grumbones said, brow furrowed. "This is a one-time deal. I told you before, the Lake of Sighs is not meant for swimming. Plus, you'd break every bone in your body when you hit the surface. That can't be a good way to die."

I finally understood what my mom meant when she said the best piece of advice that she could give me was to always get references before hiring a roofer. Because I really was beginning to suspect that Grumbones wouldn't have any real references. Ten stars, my foot.

But I ignored him and spoke to the Bridge Guardian:

"The maker doesn't want you, the buyer doesn't use you, and the user never sees you. You are—a coffin."

"Probably for burying me, when I die of stress," Ben added in a whisper.

The gargoyle bowed its head. "Correct you are, we will not spar. Go freely now, the way unbarred."

The bridge shook as the creature pushed off the stone and its great wings flapped. Dust swirled, forcing me to shield my face again, and moments later, it had departed the bridge, along with the ward.

Unfortunately, it left behind a parting present.

Its great wings had created great winds. And those winds shifted a nearby lamppost, which groaned and creaked as it leaned . . .

Then toppled.

The lamppost crashed into the bridge with a terrible boom. Stone cracked. Not just a little either. An enormous fissure erupted in the middle of the bridge.

For a second, I thought the entire bridge had been cleaved in two.

"No!" Grumbones shouted, hands on his head. "What have you done?"

"The gargoyle did that!" I argued.

Our guide raced toward the fissure, and we ran after him, both of us confused and panicking afresh.

Legs pumping, we reached the giant crack, and came to a quick stop. Grumbones stepped over broken stone and peered down into darkness. "Not good."

I didn't care about the crack. I was just happy that the bridge wasn't broken. Not completely, at least.

"See?" I said, catching my breath. "There's plenty of room for us to walk around it and cross the bridge over there."

As soon as the words were out of my mouth, Grumbones screeched and reared back. He nearly fell into Ben, who bumped into me. In all the chaos, it took me a moment to spy what was going on.

At first I thought the crack was moving.

It was so much worse.

Sewer meeks. Hundreds of them, pouring out of the bridge's crevice.

All I could see were lizard tails and open mouths that were bright orange and filled with pointy teeth. And they were coming for us.

"Across the bridge!" Grumbones said.

At least, I think he said that. Ben and I didn't wait for instructions. We took off like there were hundreds of sewer meeks after us.

BECAUSE THERE WERE.

Around the crevice we raced, screaming bloody murder, dashing away from swiping claws. Darting out of reach of tiny bodies. One jumped onto my back. I dropped my shoulder instinctively and shook it off, flinging it over the bridge's railing.

Then Ben grabbed my hand, and we kept running.

And *running*.

Sewer meeks are fast, but not as fast as humans. Once we'd raced past several lampposts, we'd definitely lost them. Even Grumbones felt comfortable enough to slow down to a jog. He eventually bent over and gasped for shallow breaths.

"Holy mother," he said raggedly. "That there? That . . . was too close."

"Will they follow us?" Ben asked, squinting back across the bridge.

"They're territorial, tend to stick to their nests. Most likely those were below the crack." He huffed out a hard breath and nodded. "I think we're good now."

Relief flooded my limbs.

"Woo-hoo! We did it! We beat the gargoyle *and* the sewer meeks!" I said, fist-bumping Ben, who was somewhat happy until I knocked his sore finger. "Sorry. Still hurts?"

His finger was swelling. Grumbones took a look at it and sighed heavily.

"Why are you here, anyway?" he complained to Ben. "Morana's not even your old hag. What's your angle, kid? If you say the two of you really are too young to be dating—"

"WE ARE," we both shouted. Gross. Now my ears were heating up again. Great.

He held up his hands. "Sue me for living," he mumbled, then spoke to Ben. "I just can't figure you out, son. Why tag along?"

Ben gave Grumbones a furious look. "Helena's my best friend, and I'm sick of everyone assuming that it's more than that. I have to take crap from everyone at school, but I don't have to listen to it from you, too."

Wait. What? Everyone at school said that about us? How come he never told me? Now I was double embarrassed. I pretended like I wasn't. La-la-la. If I don't think about it, it doesn't exist. All I know are onions. I'm going to Detroit, and I have a basket of onions!

But Ben was still angry and wasn't done with Grumbones. "Babi Morana was like family to me," he said. "So if you call her a hag again, I'm docking you a star on your star card."

"Is that so?" Grumbones said, narrowing his eyes.

"And stop calling us babies, and nitwits, and sassafras," I added. "You're supposed to protect us, you know. That's your job. It's my fault Ben's here, but it's *your* fault he's injured."

"Yes, I can see he's injured, sassafr—"

I stared at him. Hard.

He inhaled deeply through his nostrils and spoke again, this time in a calmer voice. "Your little mistake is going to throw us off my schedule. Because now I'm going to need to stop and find some salve for your friend, or that finger is going to fester. Hope you're happy . . . milady."

"I'm not. But if we need to get salve, then let's get it."

"Fine."

"*Fine*," I answered sourly.

Grumbones surveyed the bridge behind us, looking for any stray sewer meeks that might have followed us out of the fissure. "Guess we've lost them."

"Can't believe we outran them and beat a real monster," Ben said, shaking his hand out.

"Goody for you," Grumbones said, buckling his saddlebag. "Defeated a dumb stone bird who's terrible at rhyming and eats bats for dinner. That was no *monster*." He gave us a smug smile. "Next time, you'll need steel weapons."

Ben and I gave each other a worried look while Grumbones set off to finish crossing the bridge.

Weapons of any kind . . . Neither of us had one.

CHAPTER 12
Town Square

Most bridges are straight and flat. This one wasn't. After we cleared the sewer meek danger zone, the bridge curved up and around like a ramp. Whoever built it must have haphazardly slapped it together and spent all their time designing the statuary and railings.

But the bridge *was* long; in fact, it took us more than an hour to walk across it, and still the moon stayed where it was, and the purple of the sky didn't lighten. It was as if everything were frozen in time.

I could tell by the way that Ben was looking up that he was wondering why that was too. But neither of us felt like asking. Grumbones had said time moved differently here than Above. Maybe night lasted longer in the underworld because of that.

Anyway, it didn't matter, because while we hiked behind Grumbones, I mostly wasn't thinking about time or the moon. I was thinking about what a terrible guide he was. Not only was Ben hurt but Grumbones hadn't really explained the whole don't-talk-to-strangers rule very well. *And* he didn't try to help us solve the gargoyle's riddle.

On top of all that, I was thinking about how he'd kicked Sir Krak's husked-out knee back in the flooded house and kept that letter, even though he'd said it was evidence.

Grumbones was selfish and pretty terrible.

Yet, at the same time, he was going to fetch some medicine for Ben. That was decent. And when we got to the end of the bridge, he told me that he'd ask his contacts if anyone knew anything about my Babi's stolen grave mementos. Also decent.

Outside of whether he was decent or selfish, there was the problem of getting around Hereafter without Grumbones's passport tattoos.

As in, we couldn't.

So as much as I disliked his company, we needed him. And that was just the way it was.

Besides, now that we'd escaped the sewer meeks and finally—*finally*—crossed the bridge, things were looking up. Light and noise was up ahead. Normal town noise: laughter, talking, and music—some kind of haunting violin music that was upbeat and sad at the same time.

It sounded like . . . a nighttime street festival.

"Listen up, children," Grumbones said as his tattoos glowed purple again when he approached a neighborhood ward. "We're entering a restricted area of the city called Old Town. And I'm going to leave you alone here for a few minutes while I fetch that salve."

"Alone?" Ben and I said, both of us thinking of the sewer meeks.

"What about all the constant impending danger?" I asked.

Grumbones held up a calming hand. "This is a safe place. Ish."

"Ish?"

"Safe-ish." Grumbones shifted his eyes to the side as if that weren't exactly true. "Look, there aren't any sewer meeks."

"What about the Nightmare? Or gargoyles with riddles? Or that grand admiral guy from the letter we found near Sir Krak's husk?" I asked. "In the letter, he talked about chopping people's heads off."

"Never mind him. That guy stays . . . in another part of the city."

"Where?"

"Forget him. You'll be fine. The souls in this district have been here awhile. Peasants, mostly. They're celebrating some dumb ancient holiday tonight, so just stay out of their way and don't ask them questions about why they're celebrating."

Ben sighed heavily.

"Do you want the salve or don't you?" Grumbones said.

"He does!" I said. "And we won't talk to anyone. Not even if it's an animal or a royal guard."

"Unlikely to see many royal guards on this side of the bridge," Grumbones muttered.

"Why?" Ben asked.

Our guide gave him an impatient look. "Okay, fine. You *can* talk to the townsfolk here. Just small talk, though, and only in the square. Do not leave the town square—that is the new rule. Repeat it."

"Do not leave the town square," we repeated robotically.

"Very good," he said. "No running away."

"Couldn't go far since we can't cross the district ward without your tattoo passport," Ben pointed out. "*You'd* better come back."

The corners of Grumbones's mouth turned upward. "I'll be back. It's my job, after all. You youngins just try to mind your own business and stay out of people's way. If they ask who you are, do not mention that you're Morana's granddaughter. She's a controversial figure in these parts. Her, uh, cantankerous reputation precedes her."

This upset me . . . for a second. Then it gave me hope. "People here know her?"

He shrugged, half-apologetic, as if I should expect as much. "She's hotheaded. Some folks don't like that. But it's not your job to worry what people do or don't like. You're just passin' through. Got it? Don't do what you do and ask a lot of your pesky questions."

I wasn't pesky; I was curious. Babi always said that was a good thing. Always be curious, always be reading and learning. That's what she told me. Which is why if she'd been alive, she would have told my principal where to stick my lunchtime detention.

"Don't ask a lot of questions, got it," I repeated to Grumbones.

"And keep it super casual," Ben said.

"Catchin' on real fast, son," Grumbones said, pointing an approving finger at Ben. "I'll be back soon with your salve. Don't leave the square. No talking about Morana."

"Got it," I said.

"Oh, and whatever you do," Grumbones warned, "don't drink the water here, for the love of St. Vitus. It makes folks as dumb as rocks."

After showing us where to enter the town square, he pulled down the brim of his fishing cap, turned in the opposite direction, and disappeared into a dark alley. I wasn't sure if I was happy to see him leave or nervous to be alone in a place filled with dead people.

If people at my school could only see me now. I really *was* Haunted Helena.

Funny thing was, for once, I really didn't mind.

The town square was lined with three-story row houses that all faced the center, their sharply slanting roofs gleaming. Hundreds of people gathered around small bonfires under strings of waxed-paper lanterns lit with candles. An open-air pub was serving fat steins of frothy drinks. Patrons looked relaxed and content.

"This isn't too bad," Ben said.

"Right? It's almost pleasant. Am I wrong?"

"You are not," Ben said, rubbing his injured hand.

There were even kids, hanging around a large well in the center of the square. The well was stone, but it had a big wooden platform built around it with a primitive roof, like an outdoor gazebo to protect it from the elements—one that was decorated with dried flowers and lanterns.

At this well, we strolled past a couple of girls who were a few years younger than us and dressed in ragged smocks. They were throwing dolls made of twisted roots and flowers into the well. They both clapped and cheered, and then turned around when they noticed us.

"Hello," a girl with a brown, smiling face called out. "You look strange. Are you a traveler?"

I weighed my answer carefully. Definitely didn't want to answer another riddle from a giant gargoyle. "Yes," I finally said. "That was a pretty doll you threw down the well."

"It's not a doll, it's a princess."

"Tonight's the Princess Festival," said her companion, a serious ginger-haired girl. "Our city will rise and bloom again when the princess is drowned, and the grand admiral wears the crown."

Um, hold up, now. What's this about drowning a girl?

Ben and I shared a sidelong glance that told me he was as creeped out as I was. And there was the fact that this girl mentioned the grand admiral person, from that letter in the flooded house.

Grumbones said not to mention my grandmother. He never said not to mention this guy.

Keep it casual, I said to myself.

"Um, so, the grand admiral is . . . ?" I prompted, squinting at the girls.

"The one true savior of Hereafter," the first girl replied.

Right. Okay. That wasn't helpful. The "friend on the inside" person who hired Sir Krak and threatened to cut off Sir Krak's head? *That* guy was their hero?

"And who is the princess?" Ben asked carefully.

"The princess of Hereafter," the ginger-haired girl said in a low, excited voice. Then she and her friend whispered to each other as if they shared a happy secret that they were bursting to tell.

I was very confused.

The serious girl explained, "The Rime Queen once ruled our kingdom. Then she abandoned us, and the Nightmare came to punish us for her misdeeds. When the well is filled with princess dolls, the House of Rime will fall. Our brave new leader, the grand admiral, will finally wear the crown and our people will be saved."

"Drown all the princesses!" her friend cried joyfully.

Double yikes. What was wrong with these people? Maybe the answer had to do with the water, because the smell rising up from the open well was . . . not pleasant.

Ben glanced into the well and signaled, so I looked. I wished I hadn't. Hundreds of wet dolls lay mounded in a watery grave, and something was swimming around them. Flies buzzed.

Don't drink the water, huh? Yeah, *no way*. That was not gonna be a temptation.

"I'm Tammy, and this is Mo," the smiling girl said. "Who are you?"

Ben gave me a nervous glance. Right. Keep it casual.

"Uh, Tammy, huh?" Ben said. "That name sounds pretty modern. When did you, uh . . . arrive in Hereafter?"

Wow, good question, Ben. I hadn't even caught that.

"Couple years back?" she said, not sounding sure.

Okay, so Tammy was dressed like a seventeenth-century peasant. The rules of the underworld were confusing. "Bet you miss things like phones and the internet. Pizza," I said, smiling.

She wrinkled up her nose. "Pee-sa? What's that?"

Whoa. Ben and I shared a look. Maybe Grumbones was right about the well water: it possibly made you lose a few brain cells.

"Isn't there some kind of lore about an underworld river that makes you lose your memories if you drink it?" Ben said to me in a low voice as the girls stared at us. "What if it's made all these people forget their lives aboveground?"

"Does all the water in Hereafter make you forget Above?" I murmured back. "It can't, right? If it did, then Babi might not remember who I am."

The thought of that made my stomach tense.

But it would explain why she hadn't answered our special summons for the last year. Had I been calling her, and she'd been like, *Who the heck is this brat?*

"Crap. I just had a thought," Ben said. "Maybe that's why the canal rats in the Boondocks live outside the city wall. Maybe the water isn't the forgetful kind of water there. You know? That area is closer to the surface, like Grumbones said. So the canal dwellers can remember their old lives. Maybe that's why they have electricity and jeans and noodle soup."

"What's noodle soup?" Tammy asked.

Oh, Tammy, you poor addled kid. *Please, oh, please don't let Babi be like this.* This entire journey would be for nothing if she didn't recognize me.

As if he knew exactly what I was thinking, Ben gently knocked his shoulder against mine. "It'll be okay," he whispered.

I hadn't known how badly I needed to hear that.

I nodded quickly, grateful for the support.

"We have the best soup. Come with us, and you can taste it," Mo said, beckoning for us to follow her.

Tammy nodded vigorously, as if this were the soup of the gods. "Follow us," she said, trying to lead us away from the well.

I waved my hands and didn't budge. "No thanks."

"Not hungry," Ben said.

Especially if it was made with well water. Gross.

The girls acted disappointed.

We definitely needed to ask Grumbones about this water thing when he came back with Ben's salve. For now, I wanted to continue to question—*casually*—Tammy and Mo about the story of the grand admiral and this Rime Queen leaving Hereafter.

But before I could do that, a huge blast of fire shot up from a beacon tower at the edge of the town square.

Fire?

Was that a signal fire? Were the townspeople calling for help?

People shouted and ran. Tables and chairs scattered as patrons fled the pub patio. Utter chaos. Panic. And I couldn't see what was causing it. Sewer meeks? A storm?

Then I heard it, from a dark lane leading away from the square.

A lone howl that froze the blood in my veins.

It sounded more monster than animal.

A battle cry. The town square was under attack.

"Howlers!" one of the peasants cried. "Take cover!"

Howlers? I whipped around, trying to get a look at these "revolutionists," as Grumbones had called them, but everything was chaotic. Who or what were the Howlers, even—human or animal? We didn't have a clue.

"This was supposed to be safe!" Ben said, alarm lining his face. "Where is our guide? We have no weapons!"

No weapons. No protection. I suddenly wished I could dive into the stinky well and bury myself under the pile of wet dolls.

The girls at the well called to us. "Come with us, please," Tammy begged, her face a jangle of fear and excitement, her feet dancing like a boxer's—as if she were used to their town square being under attack. "We know a place to hide! Quick, before it's too late!"

It might already have been just that.

The cobblestones rumbled beneath our feet as the Howlers came—how many? It sounded like hundreds. Enough to shake the ground and cause a string of lanterns to fall and set fire to a bale of hay. I couldn't see if the invaders were on horseback, but they sounded swift.

So I blindly followed the girls from the well.

I ran as fast as my legs would take me, Ben right alongside me. And when the girls held open an iron door to one of the row houses, we raced inside, utterly grateful. They barred the door and locked it behind us with a key as big as my hand.

"There we go," Mo said, sounding quite satisfied. "You're safe with us now. They can't get through that."

Thank goodness! My heart was beating so fast, I was worried it might burst. And Ben was gasping for breath, his face covered in sweat. But we were safe now. *Safe* . . .

Where exactly were we, anyway?

I looked around.

We were inside a pub.

It stank of ale and strong wine. Plastered timber walls were lined with casks and banners. A colorful stained-glass window covered the back wall, reminding me a little bit of our Victorian door back home in Forlorn. Next to it hung a painting that looked like it belonged in an Eastern European castle—a portrait of a grim-looking child princess in an elaborate black gown with a high collar and a royal pup at her side.

Boy, they really had an obsessive relationship with princesses around here.

Before I could get a better look at the princess in the painting, Ben made a low noise that directed my attention to the mob of townsfolk who were huddled together, gathered along one shadowy side of the pub. They all stared at us as if we were fish bait. A bucket of chum.

Or a sacrifice for their nasty old well . . .

I was probably imagining that, though. We weren't princesses, so we should be fine. And these folks were all scared, sheltering from their enemies outside. Likely they were just leery of us tourists.

So why did I have such a funny feeling in the pit of my stomach?

"Fine job, Tammy and Mo," the oldest man in the crowd said, stepping forward in formal robes that made him look important. He had a long, pale face that made me wonder if he had serious anemia issues. "And you managed it while the Howlers are afoot. Quick work."

Tammy smiled. "I had to think on my feet, Elder Bubba."

The medieval town elder was named *Bubba?*

"You did well, my child," the elder said before lifting a hand in our direction. He looked into my eyes and spoke directly to me. "We knew you'd come. Fate brought you to us."

"On festival night," a woman said behind him. "It was prophesied."

"Blood would be spilled and guide you to us." Elder Bubba's smile was big and wide. But he *sounded* like an axe-wielding psychopath, and that filled me with dread.

Were they talking about Ben's sewer meek bite? What the heck was happening? These people acted as if they were part of a cult. Fear was trickling over my skin, leaving goose bumps in its wake.

"I don't like this," Ben whispered.

Me neither. I had the worst feeling that we'd been duped and lured into the pub.

Elder Bubba exhaled a deep sigh of contentment. "After all these years, finally we shall have a proper sacrifice while the moon is shining."

Sacrifice? *Sacrifice?*

All my muscles tightened at once.

Ben went completely still.

"Do not be afraid," the town elder told me with his big, creepy smile. "This is your destiny."

Afraid? Heck yes, I was afraid. I didn't want to be sacrificed by a bunch of weird medieval cultists who had been drinking the well water. Maybe I could argue my way out of this? Or at least buy some time? There had to be a way to escape this.

"W-what about the Howlers outside?" I asked, backing up, but they didn't seem to hear me.

"All hail the princess!"

"Drown the princess!"

"Save our people!"

"DROWN THE PRINCESS, DROWN THE PRINCESS. . . ."

They were really chanting with gusto now, stepping forward as Ben and I backed up. The door to the pub was locked. Nothing on the other side of the room except the stained-glass window, but it was too high for an escape. Once again, I was painfully aware that we had no weapons. These people weren't demonic, exactly, so I doubted steel would do much good.

I didn't know what to do. So I tried to waste time by talking.

"You can't sacrifice me. I'm not even a princess!" I pointed toward Ben. "His family is way richer than mine."

"What the heck?" Ben said, flashing me an offended look.

"Neither of us is royalty," I clarified, not meaning to throw him under the bus.

"Doesn't matter. They aren't listening," he said quickly.

And they weren't. The crowd moved forward as a unit, taking slow steps and chanting in a singsong voice that sounded ecstatic and reverent. "Drown the princess, drown the princess. . . ."

Tammy and Mo held out their arms as they approached, as if they would sweep me up in a big bear hug. Or scoop me up and toss me into the well with their stinky dolls.

My panic was rising by the second.

"These people are psychotic!" Ben said as he accidently backed into a wooden bench.

"We have to get out of here!" I agreed.

How, I didn't know. The mob was getting closer, and we were running out of room. I looked around for a weapon. Then the weapon came to us.

Fur crashed through the stained-glass window. Glass flew across the tables, and the mob separated as a big gray wolf skidded into the room.

Wolf!

I had to look twice and make sure it wasn't a grizzly bear.

Nope. Wolf. Standing upright on two legs, like a human.

WEREWOLF.

Monster.

Screams erupted. The cultists scattered. Tammy and Mo hid under a table. The adults ran—but not fast enough. The werewolf lurched and caught Elder Bubba around the shoulders. His pale face disappeared inside the werewolf's enormous jaws. And with a horrendous crunch, his body fell to the floor without its head.

A sickening wave of terror washed over me.

My feet were rooted to the floor. I was going to pass out.

Ben grabbed my arm with shocking strength and yanked me out of my stupor.

"Door!" he shouted, pointing toward a dark corner.

A very small door. No idea where it led, but any place had to be better than this nightmare.

Forcing my feet to move, I raced alongside Ben, rounding tables and overturned benches, while screams echoed and werewolf teeth gnashed behind us. We headed straight for the small door and were relieved to find it unlocked.

Both of us were through in seconds, shutting it behind us before either of us could say a word.

We quickly discovered that there wasn't a lock on the door. This was some kind of food pantry, with shelves that held cheese wheels and clay jars. Working together, we pushed two heavy crates in front of the door to block it as best we could. Then we sank to the floor and caught our breath.

"Did you see?" Ben asked, chest heaving as he gestured loosely toward the door.

I nodded furiously. "The head."

"So much blood," Ben whispered. "Why do dead people even have blood?"

"No idea." I looked around the pantry for some kind of weapon. Really wished I had Ben's fabled anti-mugger necklace of steel beads right about then. "Why do dead people like stinky cheese?" It smelled like old gym shoes and dirty armpits back there. Maybe it was all the garlic bulbs that were strung up to dry.

"Hey, I just remembered," he whispered. "That painting out

in the pub of that Goth princess? Not sure if you noticed, but it looked a little like you. More than a little."

"What? No it didn't."

"Did so."

"Please stop." My chest felt as if a truck were parked on top of it. "Can't you see that I'm already completely freaked out? They weren't trying to drown *you*."

"They'd drown me by association! The guy in the back had a pitchfork, Helena. Oh, and way to make me into a scapegoat, with that whole 'his family has more money' line."

"Sorry, I panicked!" I said, genuinely meaning it.

"Next time, panic in the other direction," he mumbled.

Ugh. I already felt bad enough. I didn't need him mad at me too.

Exhausted, I gave up looking for a weapon—hurl a wheel of cheese at a werewolf?—and we huddled together for a moment while we listened to the muffled screams on the other side of the door. "You think Tammy and Mo are safe?" I whispered.

"I hope not. They lured us into this pub with the intention of doing us harm. If it's a couple of jerks versus some supernatural beasts, well, count me on Team Werewolf," he said bleakly. "Wish some werewolves would take out a few numskulls at our school."

He didn't mean it. But my mind conjured up an image of the three kids at the Beacon Corner Shop teasing me about being Haunted Helena. It was the absolute wrong thing to be thinking about at a time like this, but anything was better than listening to beastly chompings.

"Do people at school," I whispered to Ben, "really tease you about us . . . uh, you know? Being more than friends?"

He closed his eyes. "All the time."

"Why didn't you tell me?"

"Because. I don't know. It's embarrassing. And they're dumb. It's not important." He sucked in a hard breath. "Jeez, my finger hurts."

I hated that. I also hated the fact that I was now starting to wonder about some things. Like what if Ben had been spending more time with his Bigfooter friends lately because I was always busy being a loner? Or because he was embarrassed about what kids at school had been saying about us? That made my stomach queasy.

"Hey—" I started to ask him, but something made me stop to listen. It was difficult to pick out, especially over all the chaos still happening in the pub, but I swore I could hear something moving beyond the back wall of the pantry. What was it? It sounded—

"AHHH!"

We screamed as plaster exploded inward. Timber cracked. Half the wall came down, and fresh air whooshed into the small pantry. A shape moved in front of the great hole in the wall that now revealed moonlight and the dark alley outside. And when the dust cleared, I saw two shining eyes staring back at me.

They sat inside the head of a midnight-black werewolf.

One paw lifted.

All my nerves turned to glass and shattered.

Ben gasped.

But instead of killing me with a single swipe or biting my head off, the werewolf only held his arm in the air between us.

"Do not fear me, my lady," he said in a voice that sounded about our age. "I am here to rescue you. My name is Ike."

I peered at the wolf's face, wondering if this was a coincidence. Ike . . . like my grandmother's dogs? Ike the First, Second, and Third? They certainly weren't werewolves. They were all black like him, though. "But the townsfolk said you were the Howlers."

"That's what they call us. We are Grim Hounds."

Ben whispered from my side in astonishment, "Grim Hounds?"

"Not werewolves?"

"No, we are not transformed men. We are guardians of the underworld. Our home is at the chapel in the woods. Our mother sent us to protect you."

Ben and I gave each other a look. Who was his mother, and why did she care about us?

"There's no time to explain," Ike said. "The townsfolk lit the beacon, so reinforcements will come, armed. I need to give you this." He took a long chain from around his neck.

It was a small golden whistle. He carefully let it drop from his claw into my open palm. "We cannot help you escape the city wards here. Try to convince your guide to take you north of the city wall. There are no wards there, so you may travel freely. Sneak away from your guide and blow this whistle in the cover of the forest, and we will find you and take you to our mother. She will help you find the Rime Queen, whom we serve."

The queen? Okay, that was interesting, but I didn't know what to think. On one hand, the hound's name was Ike, which made me *want* to like him. But why was he telling us to sneak away from Grumbones? Sure, I didn't like him, but at this point, he was our one-way ticket to Babi.

And that's all I cared about. Not this wolf's Rime Queen.

"I appreciate your offer of help," I said as politely as I could, putting the chain around my neck and tucking the whistle underneath my shirt. It didn't seem wise to be rude to a beast with sharp claws and fangs. "But we are on our own mission."

"And no offense," Ben said, "but why should we trust you? That Grim buddy of yours? He's on the other side of this door on a killing spree in the pub."

"They are our enemies, and all the denizens of this land are already technically *dead*, my lord," the hound said.

"But they still feel pain," Ben pointed out. "I mean, it sure seemed like it."

"If you are concerning yourself with details of morality, they cannot be killed by us," the beast said. "We have fought this battle many times. Their souls just move to another part of the underworld. They'll have a chance to make their way back to Hereafter. Only the overseer of the underworld can bring true death."

There was someone in charge of all the kingdoms?

Ben said, "Wait. I thought this Nightmare was causing true death by harrowing souls."

"That is a different matter," Ike said. "No one knows where the harrowed souls go."

Huh. Maybe those hawk guards we spoke to in the Flooded District had just been guessing. I remembered that they had briefly mentioned the queen, but Grumbones had stopped them from talking about her. "I'm confused about this queen who you said that you served. The townsfolk were sort of talking like she caused the Nightmare to come to Hereafter because she abandoned the kingdom. Is that what you got from what they were saying?" I asked Ben.

He nodded. "Pretty much, yeah."

"Is your queen responsible," I asked the hound, "for all this harrowing?"

"No, my lady. I don't think you understand," Ike said in a soft voice, bowing his head. "Our leader is Queen Morana."

I blinked at him, dumbfounded. "My Babi?"

Ike stared at me, waiting.

This . . . couldn't be true. I looked at Ben. His eyes were as big as moons, but there was also skepticism behind them. And it was the same skepticism I was feeling. I mean, this was ridiculous. My grandmother couldn't be queen of Hereafter. She had arranged flowers and watched every season of *The Real Housewives of Atlanta*. She'd had an annual Eurovision party with her friends overseas. Cap'n Crunch had been her favorite breakfast cereal. . . .

Our favorite.

I laughed out loud, bubbling over with a little hysteria. "My Babi isn't queen of anything. Our mean neighbor Mrs. Whitehouse said she was queen of the harpies when our dog got into the trash and Babi wouldn't do anything about it, but that's about it."

Ike blinked at me with patient canine eyes shaped like almonds. "What was her dog's name?"

I looked at the hound.

The hound looked at me.

A rush of heat flooded my chest, and I began to feel lightheaded. "Are you . . . ?"

Ike the First. Was that who I was talking to right now? The original? I had only known Ike the Second, and Babi's last dog—currently on the tugboat with my parents—Ike the Third. I had never met Ike the First because he'd existed before I was born and was buried in Whispering Pines.

Or had I never met him because he actually only existed *here*?

"The grandmother that you knew Above is our queen Below," he said. "She raised me from a small pup. I was her constant companion until she left the underworld. When she left to pursue a mortal life, Hereafter fell apart. You must believe me, Princess."

In that moment, I began to. Just a little.

Shock rolled through me, and as Ben whispered words of disbelief, everything that the hound had been telling me began to sink in—really sink in.

How could this be? I would know if my grandmother was queen of the underworld. Right?

My grandmother, who'd told me endless myths and stories about the underworld.

Who'd spent her days arranging flowers for funerals.

Who'd spent her nights talking to a photo of her dead husband.

Who'd told me I would be able to talk to her once she was dead.

My mind snapped back to something I'd seen earlier, along with a comment Ben had made. I pointed toward the door. "That painting of the princess inside the pub . . . ?"

"Princess Morana, when she was a child," Ike confirmed. "And the young puppy is me."

My head felt dizzy. This was . . . a lot to take in. Dozens of questions surfaced at the same time, like why did all the townsfolk want to drown the princess if they had a painting of my grandmother up on their pub wall? And how did they think drowning the princess would help them? And shouldn't I have been asking the hound something more important? I was breathing too fast, feeling faint. My jaw was sore too. I stretched it out and felt the pop when it loosened.

Ben looked at me with anxious eyes and quickly asked Ike the one question I couldn't get out: "Where is Morana now?"

Yes! Exactly. Very important!

"She's imprisoned at the castle," Ike said. "Hostage. You are in grave danger, and—"

A gunshot tore through the night.

Another shower of plaster made me cough as Ike leapt back outside through the hole in the wall. In an instant, he bounded up the building across the alley. And as more buckshot blasted through the brick, the Grim Hound disappeared into the darkness.

Gone!

In his place was someone I really didn't want to see at the moment.

Our guide.

Grumbones pointed his shotgun at the roof, wavering, but didn't fire off another shot. He swiveled around and stuck the barrel inside the hole in the wall, and Ben and I raised our hands.

Ike had warned us that we were in danger.

I just hadn't realized he meant right this second.

CHAPTER 13

Dark Alley

As I stared down the barrels of Grumbones's raised shotgun, all I could think about were the times I'd doubted him. Like when we first saw him at the noodle house, and he looked like an evil Santa. And how he made the underworld sound like a theme park, but it was really just an *actual* death trap with freaky dead peasants who wanted to drown you. And how he didn't help us solve the gargoyle's riddle. And how he hid evidence we found in the abandoned house and kicked the husk of poor, harrowed Sir Krak.

For all I knew, Grumbones was the one who had stolen the mementos from Babi's grave.

But what I did know—what I knew at that moment—was that I trusted Ike.

And I did not trust the man pointing a shotgun at me.

The old man's white eyebrows knitted together. He dropped his gun to his side and said, "Put your hands down, you scaredies, for the love of . . . Wasn't aimin' at *you*. Was aimin' at the door behind ya."

Was that . . . true? I didn't know anymore. But I put my hands down.

"You shot at an innocent hound," I accused, furious.

"I shot at a dang underworld monster," he corrected. "If I'd wanted to hit it, I would have. I merely skeered it off." He pointed at the ground. "This here is called a rescue. Or maybe you haven't noticed the Saturday-night massacre going on right now in the pub?"

"We just escaped it, no thanks to you!" Ben snapped, his voice quivering with anger.

"Is there something you want to tell me about my Babi?" I demanded.

Our guide squinted at me. "Like what?"

"Who she is?"

I gave him a chance to come clean and confirm what Ike had just said, that Babi was this Rime Queen. Or maybe even that all the Grim Hounds had drunk the well water and were hallucinating that my grandmother was queen. Anything at all to explain the avalanche of information that had fallen onto me.

"I have no idea what you're talking about."

"Is that so?" I challenged. "There's nothing you haven't told us?"

His white beard was a little wild and flyaway, and he appeared startled, as if he'd miscalculated about me. For a moment, just a moment, the look on his face was unguarded and . . . weak. Maybe he wasn't used to being challenged. Either way, his moment of weakness didn't last long.

"Nope," he said.

I found myself staring into the deep-set, hard eyes of a man I no longer trusted.

"Come on," he instructed. "We need to hustle out of here before the Nightmare comes."

I didn't want to follow him. At all. But he tossed me a small brown jar with a corked top. "That's for what's-his-face. Ben. He don't look so good, and this district is no longer safe. We need to get him through the ward to somewhere quiet where he can rest and get that bite cleaned and bandaged up properly."

I glanced at Ben, and as much as I hated to admit it, Grumbones was right. Ben looked all sorts of horrible. Sweaty, eyes glazed over. Finger swollen. Maybe a moment before, his voice hadn't been so much quivering with anger as it had been just plain *quivering*. Looking at him now made me feel selfish for not realizing how bad off he was.

Ben was ill. Facts.

And we couldn't just stay here. The Grim Hounds had retreated, which only left us with potential stragglers from the angry mob on the other side of the pub door—and I didn't exactly relish the thought of facing them again.

If we wanted to set out on our own, Ben and I couldn't get through the wards without passport tattoos.

We were stuck with the guide, no bones about it.

So I swallowed my pride, kept my mouth shut, and followed the man I did not trust.

Miserable but resigned, we stepped out of the hole that had once been the cheese closet's wall. Grumbones watched the street and quickly led us down a dark alley, away from the chaos. We walked as fast as we could, hurrying down twisting streets and slinking through shadows, until the lights of the town square were far behind us.

All I could do was worry about Ben and think of everything Ike had told us. That the Grim Hounds believed my grandmother was queen of the underworld. Imprisoned. Hostage. In trouble. That Grumbones was not our friend.

If he wasn't our friend, he was our enemy.

"Where are you taking us?" I finally asked, voice cracking.

"I'm taking you to see your grandma. Didn't drink the well water, did you? Told you that stuff would rot your brain."

"That's not exactly what you said, but whatever," I mumbled. "And no, we didn't."

"But you told 'em *who* you were. The peasants."

"Nope, they already knew."

"Funny thing, but we saw a strange painting of young Babi inside the pub," Ben said boldly.

All right, Ben! Guess it was *on* now. How was Mr. Cranky-pants going to explain *that?*

"Thundering tarnation," Grumbones swore. "Forgot about that."

"You knew about it?" I accused.

He scratched his head. "Fanciful painting, wasn't it? That's what happens when you drink the well water. Should've thought to warn you, but I honestly didn't expect you to be visiting a pub. For one, you're not old enough to drink—I know that much, so don't tell me I'm wrong this time. And we wouldn't have even been there, but we weren't supposed to cut through the square. *Someone* had to get bit."

"Hey!" Ben complained.

Grumbones held up a hand. "What's done is done. Now we'll need to see if Merry Dead Plaza is empty."

"Merry Dead Plaza . . . ?" I repeated, thinking. Grumbones had me all riled up and twisted around, but the name of the plaza sparked something inside my head. "Oh! The Nightmare is supposed to have been there recently. We saw it on a poster, back at the Boondocks."

"This is the only way through unless we want to spend hours walking. Need to get to the clock tower."

I tried to remember Ike's instructions. Convince Grumbones to take us north of the wall. How was I supposed to do that when I didn't know where north was? "The clock tower," I repeated. "Where is that, exactly?"

"Nearby," he said, suspicious. "You plannin' on takin' my job now? Don't trust me anymore because you're softhearted about dogs—is that it?"

How did he know I was softhearted about dogs? Images from home of Ike the Third and the Shag Pack filled my head, but I guess he was only referring to me being mad about him shooting at the Grim Hound. Paranoia was beginning to set in. But he was right about one thing: I didn't trust him one bit.

"I—I just remembered seeing the clock tower on your map in the noodle house," I lied. "Just wanted to know how long we'd have to walk. Ben is hurt." That last part was true.

Grumbones's shoulders relaxed. "All right, fine. Nightmare or not, we need to cross the plaza because it's the most direct entrance to the clock tower from here. The way I was gonna guide ya is out of the question, now that we're detouring with a sick kid. This is our only choice. So stick next to me."

Oh, I would, all right. Keep your enemies close.

And keep your friends even closer. Ben was sweating buckets and looking weak. "I don't feel so good," he said. "My hand has a pulse."

Ben lifted it up in the pale twilight, and his bitten finger was swollen to twice the size it should have been. He couldn't bend it without grimacing. And I couldn't look at it without my stomach tightening in worry. I had the salve in my storm jacket pocket, but I didn't know if I should use it. What if it was dangerous? What if it made Ben worse? How could I trust Grumbones about anything?

I didn't know what to do.

Think, think, think!

"Did you have a chance to ask someone about my Babi's grave mementos when you were getting the salve?" I asked our guide.

He groaned. "Why do you care so much about a bunch of junk left on a grave?"

"Because they were mine!" I said impatiently. "They were how I was communicating with my grandmother."

"You communicated with her?" Grumbones said, surprised.

I kicked a pebble in the alley. "I tried. She told me how to do it, but . . ." I shook my head. "It doesn't matter. I'm here now, aren't I? And Babi and I were a team. You wouldn't understand because clearly you are a lonely old coot who never had anyone to love you when you were alive."

"You know so much about me, do you?" he said, a little huffy too. "Just because I'm lonely now doesn't mean I was lonely Above."

I pitied any person who was forced to spend quality time with the likes of him. But I was also peeved that he admitted he was lonely, because I knew what that felt like, and I didn't like relating to him.

"Now stop yappin' about things that don't matter," he complained. "If you care about your sick friend, you'll focus on him—not a bunch of cemetery trash. Got it?"

"Got it," I mumbled, resentful and resigned.

He strode ahead of us, done with our conversation, and slipped inside a creaking iron gate. "Through here."

We walked down a stone path overgrown with tall weeds toward a hanging lamp with scrolling metalwork that arched between two spired buildings. The metalwork spelled out MERRY DEAD.

Grumbones slowed and whispered for us to stay on guard. "No merry locals here that I can see. Not anymore. Just got to make it to the clock tower," he explained. "Don't be fooled by the time. It ain't worked right since the Siege. But if it *does* go off and the Nightmare's around, we're sitting ducks."

"What?" I said, alarmed.

"The Nightmare is attracted by bells. A few of its favorite haunts around the city have bells. A chapel on the south side, a lighthouse, and this place. But last time I came through, there was another problem. Just a small one. So stay behind me. Don't turn on your headlamp, and don't make a sound."

He entered the plaza before I could ask why.

If the town square was a modest local football field, the plaza was a World Cup arena. It was long and rectangular, and tiled with fancy stone to create a design—one that looked like hundreds of coffins lying side by side on the ground. The spires of the buildings here were capped by skulls, and the length of the plaza was filled with marble sculptures of giant dancing skeletons. Smiling, joyful skeletons.

Merry dead.

And it almost was merry. Pleasant, at least. The plaza was softly lit by gas lamplight. If Ben and I hadn't been touring the underworld with an untrustworthy man with a shotgun, I might have wanted to spend time here and explore. But my best friend was sick, and I was mad, and as soon as we started following Grumbones across the flickering shadows of the plaza, I was pretty sure I'd spotted that other problem our guide had mentioned.

We weren't alone. Not exactly.

Merry locals might not have been there, but something else was. Their husks. *So many.*

Seeing one glassy husk of a harrowed body in an abandoned house was creepy. Seeing a hundred husks spread out beneath dancing skeleton statues was gruesome. Enough to make Ben moan.

And if *that* weren't enough, after we'd sneaked past the first dancing skeleton, Grumbones swore under his breath, breaking his Underworld Guide Vows to us once again as he stuck out a hand and waved for us to stop and be quiet.

Something dark swooped down from the twilit sky. It began to land in the middle of the plaza up ahead—too far away to notice us—but when it perched on one of the husks, I got a faint look at it.

A giant bird with enormous black wings . . . and a human woman's head.

Harpy.

Like what Mrs. Whitehouse had called my grandmother, only an *actual* harpy.

The monster wrapped its talons around the husk, flapped its great wings, and flew off with it, disappearing into the sky.

Before I could open my mouth to speak, another birdwoman flew down and repeated the same task a few feet away from where the first had landed.

I was beginning to see why Babi hated birds so much.

Ben wobbled on his feet next to me. Not good! I put a hand on his shoulder to steady him until the second monster flew away.

But Grumbones didn't give Ben any time to rest. He gestured for us to move forward. "Come on, now. There'll be more. Don't let 'em spot us, or they'll carry you off instead."

"What's happening?" I whispered. "Did all these people get mass harrowed by the Nightmare here?"

"I think it's made this place its lair," Grumbones admitted reluctantly. "Like a spiderweb."

"You're . . . guiding us through a monster's lair?" Ben said, voice weak and mildly angry.

"Buck up, kid," Grumbones whispered in a huff. "Keep moving. Too late to bail now."

I knew he was right. We'd passed through a purple ward to get here, so we couldn't even go back to the freaky town square without Grumbones's help. All we could do was move forward, sneaking through the shadows, stopping when the harpies swooped to snatch up another husk.

"Where are they taking them? And why?" I whispered during a lull when we were moving forward.

In the gray light, even Grumbones looked concerned. "The harpies move the husks here from around the city. Might be some kind of temporary storage facility. Sometimes they come and retrieve them, move 'em somewhere else. Don't know where or why."

I counted the giant dancing skeleton statues as we went. Ten behind us. Three ahead. And now I could see the clock tower, plain and clear. It had three big purple dials on the front with elaborate moon designs. Once upon a time, it was probably pretty, but part of the tower was falling apart. Maybe it had gotten struck with some kind of big weapon during the Siege, and that's why it didn't work right anymore.

The Siege . . . Now I was wondering if that really had to do with my grandmother. Grumbones hadn't told us enough details about the Siege or why it had happened. "Local politics," he'd called it. What if the local politics involved my family?

That made me angry at Grumbones all over again.

As I was studying the clock, fuming to myself, a harpy flew down. At least we were past them now: they were gathering husks behind us. We paused to allow the pair to collect their silent cargo, but as they flew away, I listened to their wings and spotted something strange on the clock tower.

Two shuttered doors next to the largest dial opened slowly. Clockwork figures began emerging from within: robed Death with a scythe, and another figure, a woman, with a large key.

My pulse increased rapidly.

"Grumbones!" I whispered, tugging the sleeve of his coat.

But it was too late.

The clock tower came to life. Chiming, chiming, *chiming*. The bells rang out and echoed across the plaza, so loud that Ben and I had to cover our ears.

Hundreds of bats flew from the eaves of the plaza buildings into the purple fog above. I thought the bells had driven them out. Wrong. The stones below our feet began to shake rhythmically.

The skeleton statues had come to life.

They were dancing.

"RUN FOR COVER!" Grumbones shouted.

Where? We'd been hiding behind the skeleton statues the entire way through the plaza. The only sanctuary left was the husk people, and no way was I getting near those—not with the harpies coming back.

But as we raced behind him, Grumbones found shelter under the arched promenade of a nearby building. It was lined with massive square columns that were lit by candle sconces, casting deep shadows. The three of us skidded to a stop in the darkness as the bells continued to ring.

It was hard to get my bearings when I couldn't hear anything other than the ringing. The bells were deafening, causing me to twist around constantly, glancing over my shoulder for danger. The hiding spot Grumbones had found looked like it could have once been the outer area of something fancy, like an opera house or a bank. I wondered if people had been lined up where we were standing when they'd been attacked by the Nightmare.

Best not to think things like that.

As we sneaked around the columns, the clock tower bells and the dancing skeletons stopped. Finally! Only now I was afraid of what else besides us might have heard the bells. Grumbones definitely acted as if he were thinking the same. I jiggled my ear to rid myself of the internal ringing that persisted, and as I did, just up ahead through the columns I spotted two men in tricorn hats and capes climbing out of a window.

"Look!" Ben said, having spotted them too. We tried to hide

behind one of the columns, but it didn't matter. The men weren't interested in us: they had crossbows, and they were aiming at the harpies.

"What the . . . ?"

Grumbones watched them. "Those dummies are trying to defend the husks," he told us. "Probably people they know, fellow comrades. Defending them is a touching but pointless act of heroism."

"Doesn't seem to me like you know all that much about being a hero," I grumbled.

He snorted. "You aren't wrong about that, sassafras. Heroes are suckers. Heroes give everything they have and still end up losing it all and getting stuck down here with the cowards."

Unsurprising that he felt that way, honestly. But I didn't have time to argue with him because something had caught my eye near the two men shooting crossbows.

A light blue mist, shimmering and shifting.

The mist was roughly the shape of an octopus. And as it passed under an arch and one of the lights from the columns shone down onto it, I could see it better.

They weren't tentacles. Those were tendrils of hair. Long hair, all wild and slowly blowing around. And beneath the hair was the ghastly face of a woman, pale and glowing.

Dread welded my feet to the ground.

I watched in terror as a windstorm whirled in her wake, tossing up dirt and causing her ragged dress to ripple and snap.

The woman's mouth was wide open, fixed into a permanent scream. And she was silently floating up behind one of the men with the crossbows.

I had the awful, sickening feeling that the clock tower bells had woken up the lair's occupant. The spider in the web. The one creature in Hereafter we'd been warned to avoid.

We'd finally found the Nightmare.

CHAPTER 14

The Clock Tower

Waves of fear crashed over me as I cowered in my hiding spot behind the stone column. The glowing monster looked too surreal to exist, and yet there she was.

I watched as the Nightmare floated farther off the ground and opened her arms behind the first man with the crossbow. Tendrils of white electricity crackled around her arms. Her entire body glowed with a pale blue mist that created strange shadows.

Mist and shadow, that's what she was made of.

And I was almost sure she was going to take that man's soul.

Fear engulfed me, but I knew I had to be right. We all knew it. Ben whimpered beside me as he clutched my jacket. It was too much even for tough old Grumbones, who laid his forehead against the stone column and closed his eyes, hiding behind his long white hair.

I was the only one who watched.

The Nightmare's mouth opened, jaws extending impossibly

wide to reveal a swirling black pit. Her victim swung around, dropped his crossbow, and stumbled backward a half step. His friend ran like the wind toward the skeleton statues in the middle of the plaza, taking his chances with the harpies.

This guy didn't have that luxury.

The Nightmare's electrical tendrils reached out and gripped him in a shocking embrace, like a police officer with a Taser. The man shook uncontrollably while blue mist swirled around, cocooning him. Then she hovered over the misty cocoon and began screaming.

And screaming.

I covered my ears in horror. I wanted to crawl up inside myself and hide. I wished I could turn around and go back to Ludo's boat, walk all the way back up those steps to the cemetery, and race home to my bedroom.

The Nightmare's scream was a million times worse than the bells.

It was high-pitched and wrong, somehow backward. Screams are forced out from your mouth, but this scream? It was an inward scream.

The Nightmare was draining the very life from that poor man's body.

His soul.

It flew into her swirling mouth, along with everything else inside him. Blood. Bones. In a whoosh, everything he was . . . was gone. The blue mist faded.

Then he was still. Empty. Nothing left but the outer shape of what he'd once been, a moment preserved in time.

A husk.

That poor, poor man. For all I knew, he had lived hundreds of years ago and could have been a jerk. But in that moment, I felt nothing but sympathy for him. No one should have to go out like that. It felt so wrong. So monstrous and cold that I couldn't stop a tear from falling down my cheek.

Babi told me that one of the kindest things you can do for a stranger is to remember them when it would be easier to forget. I would try to remember him.

As I steadied myself, blinking back tears, I couldn't stop staring at the husk. Or the monster. Something glinted in the courtyard's light: a shiny, occult-looking object dangling from the Nightmare's neck. I couldn't make it out from where I was. We were too far away. And I definitely didn't want to get any closer.

Ben's grip on my jacket released. He swayed at my side and, before I could catch him, collapsed into a heap on the ground. As he did, his miner's hat fell and bounced against the stone, and the metal surrounding the glass light made a terrible. Loud. Ringing. Noise.

I winced and braced myself. But it was no use.

The Nightmare's head jerked in our direction.

We'd been spotted. The Nightmare began floating between the columns toward us, electricity crackling ominously and wind swirling.

Grumbones swore a single obscene oath. He pushed his lantern staff into my hands and bent down to scoop Ben's limp body into his arms. But that was harder than it looked because Ben was seriously passed out, and Grumbones tripped over my foot. I nearly dropped his staff.

More swearing.

I got my footing back. And as Grumbones tried to pick up Ben, I checked to see where the Nightmare was. Her misty form vanished right in front of my eyes. Poof! Gone.

My heart raced madly. I rotated my head around wildly, searching for her.

Then she reappeared in front of another column.

So much closer.

How did she do that? She could move across great distances in a flash?

I could see her terrifying face so much better now, along with that strange pendant around her neck. Some kind of talisman that looked more solid than she did. But just because she was made of mist and shadows didn't mean she wasn't a substantial threat. Anything that devours souls with ease is dangerous. Though we still didn't know what happened to the souls of the dead that she harrowed. Like Sir Krak.

Maybe I really should have been wondering where harrowed souls of the *living* go.

The Nightmare shimmered, then disappeared again.

"Sh-she's almost here!" I stammered, gripping Grumbones's wooden lantern staff with trembling hands. "Hurry!"

Grumbones grunted as he struggled to hoist Ben into his arms.

Come on, come on . . .

A tremor shook me from the inside out as my fear worsened.

My gaze darted between Grumbones and the space where I had last seen the creature. Then I smelled something funny. I'd smelled it once before, out on the harbor, when a building had gotten struck by lightning up the beach, a few yards away from where Babi and I had been picking up shells for our collection. It had smelled like burning plastic mixed with chlorine. The scent of a lightning strike. Ozone, my Babi had said.

That's what I smelled now.

Right when the Nightmare reappeared in front of us.

Grumbones shifted Ben in his arms and yelled at me, "Run, girl!"

He didn't have to tell me twice.

I gripped the gnarled walking staff and ran next to Grumbones, out of the columns, into the open air of the plaza—hearing the harpies swooping above but not caring, because anything was better than the electrical ghoul behind us.

I didn't look back to see if the Nightmare was gaining on us, because I knew she was. I could feel it. And I kept picturing her vanishing and reappearing closer. *Please no!* But I could also see Grumbones's destination: a wooden door at the base of the clock tower.

As we raced up to the door, I saw that it had no handle, and I panicked that it might not even be a real door at all—what if it was just one of the doors that those clockwork figures paraded out of when the bells rang? And what was Grumbones mumbling to himself as he was running? I distinctly thought I heard him say, "Yemoja is going to kill me."

That was Granny Booker's first name.

How the heck did Grumbones know Granny Booker?

WHAT WAS GOING ON?

Then a familiar figure stepped out of the shadowy stonework.

Fizzle the vulture! Good old birdbrain, showing up when we most needed help! Was that weird? A little, sure. But this was the underworld. To think that he had once scared me. Not anymore. I knew my onions pretty well, buddy. And right now, the onions behind me were the scary thing, not the monkish vulture in front of me.

"Need a hand, Mr. Grumbones?" Fizzle called out.

Normal voice, not the otherworldly *leave a penny* voice. And now he had regular bird eyes too. I was running too fast toward the clock tower to stop and ask why.

"That would be helpful," Grumbones replied curtly as the tattoos beneath his clothes glowed their magical purple light. "Open a local portal, please."

"Where to?" Fizzle asked.

"Somewhere safe and quiet," Grumbones said. "This kid is sick."

"Flooded District is the safest place," Fizzle said.

"Not there!" Grumbones shouted, looking back at the approaching glowing mist. "We can't go back. Where's an exit to Above? Think!"

"Rime Castle, of course. But I can't get you there. The castle's special wards block my entry," the vulture said. "You could always try to petition the lady in the Perilous Woods and see if she might help the child."

"She tries to capture me every time I go near there! I can't risk losing my magical passport." He hesitated, unsure. "I guess we could steer clear of her. Take us to the Vineyard Château," Grumbones barked. "Now!"

The doorkeeper drew a handle on the door and swung it open just in time.

"Behind me, sassafras!" Grumbones called out.

I zoomed into the tower. "Hey, Fizzle. No time to chat!"

"Milady," Fizzle acknowledged, looking sad. The last thing I heard him say before he shut the door behind us was, "I am *so* sorry."

Sorry? What in the world for? He'd just helped to save Ben and me from the Nightmare.

If Ben could just hang on a little longer, I'd find a way to finish saving him myself.

CHAPTER 15

Vineyard Château

The first time I ever saw Ben pass out was when we were ten and hiking in the woods south of town, trying to get our Junior Coastal Rangers badge for "Insect Expert." We poked under the wrong rock and Ben got bitten by a snake. It wasn't venomous, but we didn't know that. I guess we both sort of panicked and thought he was going to die. Maybe I was the one who said it. Anyway, that was when his eyes went all weird and he zonked.

Passed out cold.

I shook him. Shouted. He didn't wake up right away.

We were alone in the woods, and for a few terrifying seconds I didn't know what to do.

Now Ben was passing into and out of consciousness, mumbling under his breath. We weren't alone in the woods, but we *were* alone with a dangerous old man—and I still didn't know what to do. That memory of younger Ben with the snakebite flashed in my head as I entered through Fizzle's door in the clock tower. Even after it shut behind me, I could still hear the crackling from the Nightmare's windswept electric tendrils—just for a moment.

And then I was hung up in time.

In limbo.

Nowhere.

The stone floor whooshed out from under my feet, and a swift breeze blew my hair around. I blinked, and I was no longer inside the clock tower.

I was standing on a hill above the city, outside a country château.

Vineyards stretched out on the rolling hills leading down to the edge of the city streets. The clock tower was visible from here—half a mile away or more.

Fizzle's portal had moved us this far? I guess we were safe. It was hard to tell.

Grumbones stood by my side, holding Ben. "Made it through the portal," the guide said, sounding tired. "Close, though. Your friend and his bite nearly got you killed."

"He's hurt!" I shouted. "I don't want you touching him. How do I know you won't make it worse?" I mean, yes, somewhere inside my head I was rationally aware that Grumbones had helped to save Ben—maybe? But for the life of me, I couldn't tell if he was on our side anymore. Was he putting us in harm's way on purpose, or genuinely helping to get us to Babi? How could one old man be such a hot mess?

"How come you didn't tell us we could move around the city using portals?" I demanded. "And how do you know Granny Booker?"

Grumbones scowled at me. "What the ding dang are you talking about, girl? I realize you're upset right now, but cut me a huss, here, all right?"

"What does that even mean? Why can't you talk normal, old man?"

"Keep your voice down. The Nightmare isn't the only thing out here."

Oh. Crap. I glanced over my shoulder, wary. "Where are we?"

"North of the city wall."

Oh. My heart pounded faster. There were woods in the distance. Were they the right woods? Grim Hound Ike's woods? I wasn't sure, but I had hope. Just a little.

Mostly I was scared for Ben. He was starting to come to, mouthing indistinctly in a breathy, weak voice. But he wasn't exactly conscious.

"Let's just get Ben inside the château and put some salve on him," Grumbones said. "You can yell at me some more there. Apparently every dang thing is my fault now."

"Let's just assume that," I said darkly.

"Fine."

"Fine!" I snapped. While Grumbones wasn't looking, I checked to make sure the golden whistle was still safely inside my shirt.

Ike the Grim Hound. I trusted Ike. And maybe, just maybe, he wasn't far.

While Grumbones carried an incoherent Ben, I trudged at his side across a wild lawn to the back of the sprawling, dark château. Barrels of wine were stacked near wagons, sitting abandoned along a driveway that wound through a yard overgrown with vines and dried wildflowers. The driveway ended at an imposing iron gate guarded by two female stone lions, one with her nose destroyed. Grumbones pushed open the creaking gate with one shoulder.

"What is this place?" I asked in a low voice, a little nervous that he might be leading us into a trap.

"Belonged to a baron. After the Siege, the creatures in the woods drove him out. It's been abandoned for a while. We shouldn't stay for long, but we can get the kid patched up."

I closed the gate behind us, peering into the mist at the edge of the property. Creatures in the woods, eh? I wondered which creatures. Good ones or bad? Regardless, Ike had told us about these woods, and they were *right there*. Just had to get Ben fully conscious.

And find a good time to escape.

Grumbones's staff felt good in my hand, though the lantern was hard to get used to. Its swinging flame lit up an unkempt courtyard with some petite trees growing around a dried-up reflecting pool—nothing but dust and a couple of shallow puddles of rancid-looking water. Behind the pool was a vine-tangled pergola with three stone benches.

"Here," Grumbones said. "I'll put the kid down to rest. Stick the staff in the dirt there, sassafras, to give us a little light."

As soon as Grumbones set him down, Ben grunted on the cracked stone patio and tried to sit up. Then he blinked, groggy, and looked at me clearly for the first time since we'd left Merry Dead Plaza.

"High," I said.

"Low," he replied in a weak voice. "Helena? Where . . . are we?"

"The Bad Place," I half joked. I was just so relieved to hear his voice.

"Got your grandmother's sense of humor," Grumbones mumbled as he dug out a metal box from his pack.

I wanted to ask how he would even know Babi well enough to be aware of that, but I was too concerned about Ben. "Don't try to move, okay? We're going to fix up your hand a little. You fainted, remember?"

"Ugh," he grunted. "Embarrassing. I feel woozy."

"Shh," I told him. "It's just the sewer poison coursing through your veins. Poop and urine, and people's vomit."

"Not funny," he said with a groan.

"A little funny?" I asked.

"A little," he amended.

"You know what would be a *lot* funny?" Grumbones said, pulling out from his little metal lockbox a roll of old fabric wound up into a ball. "Having to amputate your best buddy's hand because you didn't follow instructions. Where's the salve?"

"Amputation?" Ben said, sitting up too fast and then groaning.

Grumbones pushed him back down. "Don't get excited, Booker. We aren't there yet."

"How'd you know my last name was Booker?"

Good question. We'd given him Babi's name, but . . .

"I'm magical," Grumbones said dryly. "You told me? In the noodle house? Has the poison hit your brain, or were you already this barbecued?"

"I'd like to barbecue something, all right," I mumbled, giving him the evil eye along with the jar of salve as I fantasized about what I could do to him with that lantern staff.

"Big talker," Grumbones said. "Not so soft anymore, are ya? Underworld toughens ya up fast."

"Hello? I'm dying here," Ben reminded us.

Grumbones sighed. "I suppose. Now, son, listen up. This salve is made from some cave mushrooms that will slow the toxins from multiplying in your bloodstream. I ain't gonna lie to you. This is gonna hurt real bad."

"What?" Ben tried to snatch his hand back, but he was too slow. Grumbones was fast, and he spread some of the salve over Ben's swollen finger with a stick from the patio. Ben screamed. Grumbones tossed the stick aside and clamped a hand over Ben's mouth. "Help me hold him down, girl!"

I felt awful doing that, but Ben was kicking now. He must've been in so much pain, and that made me sick in my heart. As he calmed down, wilting against me, I glanced at the stick Grumbones had tossed aside; it had begun disintegrating. But Grumbones was already wrapping up Ben's finger in a rag and tying it off.

"Ben? *Ben?*" I said. "If you've hurt him . . . ," I warned our guide.

"Immokaay," Ben slurred. "Whew. Oh my Sasquatch."

"Hurt like the devil, didn't it?" Grumbones said, his gold tooth glinting as he smiled. "Told ya. But it should feel a little better soon. Won't cure ya, though. You're still gonna need to get that poison out."

Ben and I stared at him.

"Excuse me?" I said. "What do you mean?"

"He's got plenty of time," Grumbones assured me, then added under his breath, "hopefully."

Panic fired through me. "Please explain *now*. My best friend's life is on the line, and it's my fault he's here in the first place."

Ben gave me a soft smile and slurred, "Naah. I wouldn't've missssed all this fun. Ride or die, baby!"

Oh my word. The last time Ben had been this sick, he'd vomited up a dozen frozen pizza rolls and half his body weight in Sprite after coming down with the flu two years ago.

Grumbones sighed. "I know a healer in another kingdom, if we can get back to Ludo so he can ferry us."

"All the way back to where we started?" I said, anxiety rising. We'd barely made it here in one piece. What were the chances we could make it back?

"Or," Grumbones suggested, "you could just take him to a doctor once you get Above. The salve will stave off the poison. As long as the whites in his eyes don't turn green and spotty, he's good. Many hours before you have to worry about the poison going off. Many."

"Hours Below, or hours Above?" I asked.

Grumbones squinted. "Is that a trick question? He's got plenty of time. Maybe even a day or two once the salve is working at peak. Probably."

Probably? How would we know when it was working "at peak"? What the heck kind of loosey-goosey treatment was this?

I leaned close to Ben and looked into his eyes.

"Are they green and spotty?" Ben asked.

"Nope. All clear," I assured him, hoping he couldn't tell how worried I was.

He relaxed. "Okay. Well, I do feel better." He hiccupped. Twice. "Just super thirsty . . ." His gaze flicked to the dried-up reflecting pool.

"Nuh-uh," Grumbones said, shaking a finger. "Never drink underworld water. Haven't I taught you nothin'? That's rule number one. Just going to have to tough it out. Now, you need to rest and let that salve kick in real good. I myself could use some shut-eye."

"We're setting up camp here?" I asked.

"Just until he's rested," our guide said. Then he looked down at Ben. "When you can walk without me carrying you, kid, we'll get going again. Don't need you slowing us down when we're facing enemies. Get your strength back."

I was worried the sewer meek poison would "go off" before that happened, but I had to admit that Ben was in no shape to stomp around the city. What if we bumped into the Nightmare again?

Grumbones coughed, took a swig from his flask, and then lay down on a stone bench close to the iron entrance gates—to guard them, he said, "in case we have company." I tried to convince him that I could take guard duty, but he just snorted. "You wouldn't even know what to be on the lookout for, kid. Tend to your buddy and wake me in a couple hours. I'm takin' a quickie cowboy nap."

Now I was his personal assistant? Ugh. I detested him with a white-hot burning fire.

When he said he was taking a nap, though, he meant it. He shifted his cap over his face and was snoring in no time. Loudly. Guess we really were staying here for a while.

I took off my headlamp and set it next to Ben. It felt good to have it off.

"Are you sure you're really feeling better?" I asked Ben in a low voice as he pulled himself into a full sitting position, cross-legged.

"Promise," he said. "Still a bit grogs, though."

I chuckled. "Grogs?"

"Groggy. Whatever. How did we get here?" he asked, glancing around the courtyard.

"You don't remember the Nightmare? Seeing Fizzle? The door in the clock tower that portaled us here outside the city wall?" I explained the rest quickly.

Ben looked stunned. "No bull?"

"No bull."

"Wow," Ben said, eyelashes fanning slowly. "I must have been *o-u-t*. Did you . . . did you ask Grumbones about all that stuff that the Grim Hound was telling us? About Babi Morana being queen?"

I shook my head and glanced over at our sleeping guide to make sure he wasn't listening.

"I've barely had a chance to think about it," I admitted to Ben. "It's still hard to believe. How could she be queen of the underworld *and* my grandmother?"

Ben nodded as if he understood, and studied his bandaged hand. "I've been thinking about that. I mean, we know from what Ike said that Babi left the underworld to pursue a mortal life. I think that's how he put it."

"Why would you choose to do that if you were queen down here?"

He shook his head. "No idea, but Grumbones definitely knows her, right? He's described her fiery personality, and he knows her name—"

"He knows *way* too many people's names," I griped. "It's weird."

"Grumbones said there was the Siege in Hereafter a few decades ago, and that's when everything got destroyed here."

"The kingdom supposedly fell apart when Babi left. But why?"

"War," he said.

"To be at war, you need an enemy."

"The Nightmare?" Ben suggested.

"She eats souls; she doesn't destroy buildings. Who would my grandmother's enemy be? Who would start a war?"

Ben cradled his injured hand. "Only know of one other player down here with military ties. That grand admiral dude."

Right. The letter we'd found near Sir Krak's husk was from the grand admiral. And in it, he talked about ground troops and cutting off Sir Krak's head.

"Wonder where he is?" I mused.

"Don't know, but the Grim Hound said your grandmother is being held hostage in the castle. And that's where Grumbones is taking us."

Yeah. Were we being taken there to have our heads chopped off by the grand admiral? I kept thinking about the letter we'd found by Sir Krak, and something felt off about it. About the way that Grumbones had told the hawk guards that he definitely didn't work for the grand admiral—and they'd seemed relieved. But had he been telling the truth?

We needed someone with more information who could shed some light on all this.

"The woods around this place . . . ," I whispered to Ben, feeling a small rush of excitement. "This is where Ike told us to go. To call for a rescue."

He blinked lazily, then shook himself. "These are *the* woods? Okay, okay . . . We should leave while Grumbones is asleep."

Exactly! However, Ben still didn't look so hot. He probably really did need to rest. Much more so than our jerk of a guide, but I didn't know how long he'd be napping.

"We have time," I told Ben.

His shoulders relaxed. "You think?"

Even though I wasn't sure, I still nodded. I didn't want him worrying too. "Let's try to get you rested up, okay?"

Time passed slowly in the courtyard. Neither one of us could sleep, though Ben lay down and tried to nap. I could always tell when he was asleep because he had this little dripping-faucet sound that he made when he breathed. We'd spent the night at each other's houses way too many times over the years, so I knew it well.

Restless, I explored the courtyard, tiptoeing around Grumbones, but there wasn't much to see. When I was done, I plopped down by Ben.

He gave up trying to sleep and sat up next to me, yawning. "*Really* wish I could drink that water," he mumbled. "That's how they get you. Drag you into the underworld and then don't let you have any food or drink. Classic."

"That's Persephone. She was forced to spend part of the year in the underworld because she ate a pomegranate seed."

"Mmm, I could chow down on a pomegranate seed right about now," Ben lamented. "Or some of that noodle soup from Pokie's that Grumbones says is so good. I wonder if the soup there is safe, you know . . . since the Boondocks are kind of in the Liminal Lands?"

If Ben was craving underworld soup, he was definitely hungry. Hmm . . . I dug around inside my storm jacket pocket and pulled out the remainder of my stash of bubble gum. "It's not soup, but will this do?"

"Score! Pedro bubble gum, my hero," Ben said, smiling a little as he accepted a couple of pieces. "The sugar will sustain us."

"If it doesn't give me lockjaw first," I joked.

"No dentists in the underworld. Better be careful. You could end up like me, with some weird homemade remedy to cure your injury."

I grimaced. He was only teasing, but I felt awful that he was poisoned. And as we sat together in the dark courtyard, listening to Grumbones snore, my brain wouldn't stop thinking about the fact that it was my fault, technically, that Ben was here. He hadn't wanted to enter the Doorless Tomb. I'd convinced him because I hadn't wanted to do this alone.

Because I was a coward.

"I'm sorry," I told him in a low voice.

"For what?" he asked.

I scratched my neck. "Everything. Bringing you here. And for what we were arguing about earlier today. You are . . . important to me."

He didn't reply right away. Just sat with his arms loosely cradling his knees.

Then he said, "Sometimes I don't feel like it. It's like you'd rather spend time alone than with me."

"That's not true."

"I've invited you to hang out with Miguel and Gabby, like, so many times? But you always blow me off."

"The Bigfooters?"

He snorted. "See? There you go, looking down on it. It's a paranormal club, Helena. People who are interested in the same stuff that we are. Look at us! We're in the underworld."

Obviously I knew that. "Your club is for you."

"And what activities are for you?" he said, narrowing his eyes. "Detention at school?"

"I'm not happy about the detention!" I said a little too loudly, then looked back to make sure Grumbones wasn't waking up.

"But you choose to take long walks on rainy beaches by yourself instead of spending time with me and my club. It's like you prefer being an outcast. You've changed, and I don't understand why."

"My grandmother died!" I whispered hotly.

"And I'm *so sorry*," he said. "I've been sorry this entire year. But I don't understand what that has to do with us. I'm your best friend. You should be leaning on me—and not just for trips to the underworld."

"I do lean on you."

"Only when you want something from me. But when I want you to do things with me, you always have something 'better' to do. And it's usually on your own. How do you think that makes me feel? When you only call me to help you with graveyard rituals, but you won't answer my texts about, I don't know, dumb stuff like homework?"

A spiraling panic wound through me. "I need to tell you something."

"Okay . . . ?"

I felt as if I might be sick. The secret I'd been carrying around all these months suddenly expanded several sizes and was too big to stay inside me any longer. "Babi and I got into a fight before she died."

"You did?" he said softly, squinting. He glanced away for a moment and cleared his throat, as if he didn't know what to say. "You never fought."

No, we did not. And I really didn't want to tell Ben why Babi and I had been arguing. That was the thing about secrets. When it came time for revealing them, they could find darker hiding places.

But this one had hidden too long.

I shyly looked at Ben and admitted, "We fought about you."

A moment of silence stretched between us. Ben blinked at me. "About me?"

My chest felt as if it were going to cave in. "Babi thought that . . . that—" I couldn't get it all out. "She thought I was spending too much time with you," I said, feeling tears well. "That I needed to make more friends."

Ben looked dumbstruck. "Why?"

"I don't know! That's why we argued. And, you know, we *never* fought. But I yelled at her, and we said terrible things to each other, and . . . that was the last time I saw her alive."

I didn't tell anyone for months. I was too ashamed. Then I finally told my dad because I was worried that my argument with Babi had caused her heart attack. He assured me that it hadn't.

But it took me a long time to believe him. I still wasn't entirely sure I did.

"I've felt so guilty. I didn't want to avoid you. But I wanted to honor her wishes . . . and at the same time, I was confused why she'd ask me to . . . uh, I don't know, cool it with you, or whatever."

Ben gave me a look with hooded eyes. "I think I understand. It's the same reason that kids at school tease me."

I nodded. I understood that now too. But we were just friends! And that's what I'd tried to tell Babi. It was just that she was strong-willed, and I guess maybe I was too. So it hadn't gone well.

"I'm sorry," I whispered. "I'm so sorry."

I was embarrassed to cry in front of Ben. But after an awkward moment, he reached out and pulled me into a hug. His long arms felt familiar and good around me, but mostly they felt like the one thing I needed from him.

Acceptance.

"You should have told me," he whispered.

"I know," I said. "I'm sorry."

"I'm sorry too. I *was* spending more time with my club because all this time I thought you were avoiding me."

"Mostly I've just been missing you," I admitted.

"I've missed you too." He squeezed me tighter. "You're still my best friend, you know."

"Always," I vowed, feeling as if a pile of bricks had just been lifted from my chest.

We released each other and chuckled awkwardly. I brushed away tears and glanced over my shoulder. I was a little worried I'd wake up Grumbones. The last thing I needed was him seeing me crying and calling me a baby.

"How can he sleep so hard in this place?" Ben asked as we both tried to pretend as if we hadn't just gotten emo together.

"I wish you could," I told Ben. "So you could get up the strength to walk."

"I can walk."

Could he? Enough to escape the château with me?

I wasn't sure. When I shifted around on my haunches to check Ben's eyes for poison—all clear!—the scent of lilies of the valley wafted up from my storm jacket. That reminded me that Grumbones had blown me off when I'd asked if he'd inquired around about my stolen mementos during his jaunt to get the salve. But why should I trust anything he said?

I *could* check his stuff, secretly.

Just to be sure he didn't have my mementos.

After all, I might never have this chance again.

"Helena . . . ," Ben warned when I told him my plan. But he was curious too. "Be very careful. Do not wake him."

I held up a finger to my lips to signal to Ben to remain quiet, and then I sneaked over to the saddlebag. Slowly, gingerly I unbuckled the bag. Grumbones's hat moved up and down on his face with every snore, and each time it did, my heart felt as if it would burst out of my chest. Finally the closure came loose, and I was able to lift the flap.

Grumbones stopped snoring and shifted. I stilled. Waiting . . .

He began snoring again.

I carefully peeked inside the dark of his pack, looking through his things. A rat's nest is what it looked like—a big jumble of this and that. Papers, cards, twine, keys, his flask (which stunk of cherry cough medicine and strong alcohol), three more bottles with cork stoppers (all shapes and sizes, but no labels), a pocketknife, a tin of sardines, something that looked like a bomb, shotgun shells, a coupon for a free bowl of Pokie's noodle soup (frequent customer reward), a booklet of magic spells—

Magic spells? Like the booklet Ben had found in the cemetery about talking to the dead, written by Fizzle. Only this one was titled *Changing Your Identity in the Underworld: A Complete Guide to Being Anonymous in All Four Kingdoms*.

What the . . . ? And look, stuck inside: here was the damp letter to Sir Krak that we'd found near his husked-out body back in the abandoned house.

I held it up for Ben to see, but he was smiling to himself and looked like *he'd* been taking swigs out of Grumbones's cough-drop-scented flask. The booklet was too big to fit into my pocket, so I took Sir Krak's letter and left the booklet while I continued to dig through the saddlebag.

He had more stuff in there. What the heck was this? Some kind of small handbell, the kind people ring in choirs, with a trigger that released the clapper; symbols were carved on the handle.

The bell *definitely* seemed important, and it was small enough to fit into my jacket pocket, so I took that. And once I'd stashed it, I spotted the thing I wanted, at the very bottom of the bag, right below where the bell had been.

My drawings of Big, Little, and Tiny. And the photograph of me and Babi.

Grumbones was the grave robber? All this time, it had been him? *Him?*

Either that or he had managed to find the mementos and hadn't told me. Both scenarios stank. He was withholding information from me. Why?

My heart squeezed painfully as I stared at the crumpled papers in my fingers. The photograph of me and Babi and Ike was creased permanently. Seeing her face now made fresh tears fill my eyes.

Bony fingers clamped around my arm.

"What do you think you're doing in my stuff, sassafras?" Grumbones said, one mean eye fixed on me from the edge of the black fishing cap.

Terrified, I jerked my arm back, clinging to the photo. He was shockingly strong, holding on to my arm; the other hand grabbed one free edge of the photo. I wasn't going to win in a tug-of-war with him, and I feared the photo would rip.

Stalemate.

"Thief!" I accused, gripping the photo's corner. "Liar! This isn't yours, it's mine. I asked you to help me find it, and you lied."

"You finished?"

"I've got plenty more, and I'll bet you deserve all of it. Want to tell us why you failed to mention that the Grim Hounds think my grandmother is queen of the underworld?"

He stilled.

"*Yeah*," I said, giving him my best dirty look, inherited from Babi herself. "We found out that and more. We know you're a cheap liar. Ike the Grim Hound said we're in danger with you, and now that I've found my mementos in your stuff, I know I was right to believe him."

"Okay, first, sassafras—"

"Stop calling me that!" I shouted.

The ground shook behind me, and he looked over my head—just for a second. Long enough for me to snatch the photo of me and Babi away. I stumbled backward and stuffed it inside my storm jacket, delighted that I'd won. I even cackled a little.

Until I heard Ben scream.

I swung around to see him arching away from the reflecting pool, where two gooey shapes were emerging.

Twin monsters. They crawled out of the stagnant puddles, up from the ground itself, bursting through the tile, and they looked like men who'd been dipped in shiny black engine oil—goopy and oozing, and a little iridescent in places where the light hit.

They looked exactly the same. When one moved, the other moved in the same way. Doubled. As if they were mirroring each other.

"Reflection spirits!" Grumbones shouted. "Don't attack them! They'll mirror what you do back at you. Move away from them, or they'll catch you!"

The creatures were fully out of the ground now, crouching in the reflecting pool and swaying, heads turning in tandem, as if they were searching for a target. They found one in Ben. He sloppily scrambled to his feet. They did the same. Ben shoved a lock of curly hair away from his eye. They both mimicked the gesture on their lustrous faces.

Ben tried to take a step backward and tripped on his own feet, almost falling. Then he lurched forward.

The reflecting men lurched forward.

Their heads turned to meet Ben's, only a few feet away, and a ghoulish smile lifted on their oil-slick faces.

"Back away, son!" Grumbones shouted.

Ben was scared, though, and instead moved sideways, toward us. The reflecting men followed him, which only made Ben confused and more panicky.

"Grab my flame staff," Grumbones told him. "You can set 'em on fire with the lantern!"

Ben hesitated. It was out of reach. He'd have to move closer to the oil men to get it. And now that I was looking at it . . . Why was Grumbones asking Ben to fetch it, when the staff was just as close to us?

Was he *trying* to put Ben in danger?

Anger flared inside my chest. Why would I trust this man? At worst he was a grave robber and at best a liar. He'd shot at Ike, who'd warned us that Grumbones was trouble. So why on earth would I think he was actually going to help us in good faith?

Whatever Grumbones's game was, I knew one thing.

I wasn't going to let him hurt Ben.

"Fetch your own staff!" I shouted, shoving Grumbones as hard as I could toward the reflecting men.

I wasn't strong, but I had the power of surprise on my side. Grumbones stumbled forward onto the reflecting pool tile and landed on his hands and knees. The spirits turned away from Ben and trained their oily gaze on our guide.

"Come on!" I shouted at Ben, holding out my hand. "Now!"

Eyes wide, he rocketed toward me. I grabbed his clammy fingers as the reflecting spirits closed in on Grumbones.

"You nitwits!" the old man shouted behind us.

I didn't look back. I just held on to Ben for dear life, raced out of the courtyard, and pushed open the creaking iron gate. And we escaped the château, running for our lives, across the vineyards, into the mist . . . into the edge of the Perilous Woods.

CHAPTER 16

Perilous Woods

Mist circled us. We zigzagged around bushes until I couldn't see the château anymore. Until we had to slow from a run to a walk because we were making too much noise, crashing through the underbrush.

Ben's breath sounded ragged. I was so worried for him.

Worried for both of us, that we would run into some unseen ward—that we would need Grumbones after all.

But we didn't. Ike had been right. It seemed that we could travel freely here.

The forest was quiet and dark. Moss-covered trees stretched into the fog, their roots blanketed by ferns. I pressed on as best I could, getting tangled up in vines, tripping over stones, and dragging Ben along with me. His grip faded and his weight felt heavier and heavier to tug.

I didn't know if Grumbones would escape from the reflecting-pool spirits and come after us, or if there were other dangers here.

"We need to keep moving," I encouraged, wishing I hadn't left my miner's hat behind.

"I . . . can't," he complained, sounding disturbingly out of breath. "Please . . . Helena. B-blow . . . Ike's whistle."

Maybe he was right. It was time.

I stopped in front of a big oak and dug out the golden necklace that was hidden inside my shirt. Then I put the whistle to my lips and blew. No sound came out. I blew again.

"Dog whistles make no noise to human ears," I told him. "Is it the same for Grim Hound whistles, you think?"

Maybe.

There could have been other reasons why we didn't hear it. I was worried we were in the wrong woods, after all. We could've walked too far. Or not far enough?

"He didn't say how long the rescue would take," Ben pointed out.

"What if the whistle broke when we were running from the Nightmare, or when I was trying to pull away from Grumbones?"

"It's probably magic, or something?" Ben said, his voice a mix of hope and doubt, overlaid with a thin sheen of sickness that was making his eyelids heavier and heavier. A twinge of worry went through my stomach.

I blew the whistle again.

Still no sound.

Ben and I huddled together against the tree and waited. Seconds ticked as we listened.

In the distance, something rustled in the underbrush.

Yes! A noise!

My heart sped up. Was it our rescue, or danger? Something was definitely approaching. . . .

Two shapes emerged in the fog. One big and gray, one smaller and black.

I held my breath and clung to Ben.

"My lady," Ike's voice said.

Thank goodness!

"You came," I said, relieved.

"I told you we would," he said. "This is my brother, Shuck."

When Shuck stepped into the moonlight, I recognized him as the Grim who had ripped off Elder Bubba's head inside the pub. I didn't know whether to be thankful or frightened until he canted his head politely and bowed.

I guess even wild wolfy hounds have manners.

"Hello, Mr. Shuck," I said. "I guess you've saved us twice now. That town elder was going to drown me."

"You would not have been the first." Shuck spoke in a deeper voice than Ike, one that rumbled through the ground. "He's drowned two tourists since I last relieved him of his head. At least it will take him a while to find his way back to the town square."

"A few years," Ike confirmed.

Oh wow. Things really did work differently in the underworld. But I didn't care so much about Elder Bubba, serial drowner and cult leader. I had more urgent matters. . . .

"Sorry, but my friend Ben here has been bitten by a sewer meek," I told the Grim Hounds. "Grumbones put salve on it, but he said the poison needed to be removed. I don't know whether he was lying. Can you help us?"

Ike and Shuck looked at Ben's bandaged hand.

Then Shuck said in his booming voice, "We will take you to our den mother. It's safe there."

"Can you walk?" I asked Ben, concerned.

"If it's not far."

"Come, children," Ike said. "Just through the trees."

A sense of calm washed over me as we followed the Grims through the dark woods on a narrow, hidden path lit by pale moonlight. The earth smelled damp and clean, and there were no signs of anything following us. Nothing menacing in the shadows. No evil lurking. And it felt good to have bodyguards like Shuck and Ike scouting the way. Reminded me of my Shag Pack back home.

I hoped Big, Little, and Tiny were okay. Maybe they were still in the gift shop, if Grumbones hadn't been lying to us about the passage of time being different. Who even knew? He was a fink, so it was hard to tell.

When Ben made a small noise of appreciation, I looked up to see what he was observing. Between a pair of massive oak trees, the Grims had led us to a clearing in the forest with an old stone chapel surrounded by a graveyard. Stained-glass windows with designs of trees and flowers were on each of its four walls. Otherwise, it looked nearly identical to—

"Whispering Pines Cemetery gift shop," we said together.

Ben chuckled nervously. "How is that possible? It looks almost the same."

I half expected the chapel door to open and the Shag Pack to stroll out.

When the door *did* open, my breath caught.

A woman in a hooded gray cloak stepped out of the chapel. Both Grims padded up to her and sat majestically by her side.

"Welcome to Chapel Perilous," the woman said. "I am the Grimmother."

This woman's voice sounded familiar, yet shadows hid her face inside the hood of her cloak. I didn't like that. What was she trying to hide? It made me anxious.

But Ike the First trusted her.

And through him, she'd helped to get us away from Grumbones.

Ben and I hesitated. I supposed it felt odd to meet someone who didn't want to attack us or drown us in a well or challenge us to a riddle that might end in us falling to our death.

"Who is this person? And why is there a graveyard in the underworld?" Ben asked in a whisper near my ear.

Good question.

"Because the underworld changes with the memories of its souls," the Grimmother said. "Memories and dreams. Fears, too. The queen saw them all, and I think it made her curious to know what mortal life was like Above. Which is how this whole fiasco started in the first place."

My ears perked up at the mention of the queen. "Which fiasco would that be?"

"Between your grandmother and the grand admiral," the Grimmother said. "The Siege. War. Battle for the crown, among other things."

My pulse rocketed as a rush of excitement went through me. Finally someone was telling us *something*. Information was like candy around here. I wanted to shove it into my mouth until my cheeks were rounder than a squirrel's.

"So, let's say that I believe you that my grandmother is the queen," I said. "You're saying that the grand admiral *is* my grandmother's enemy? Who is he, exactly?"

The woman sighed. "Come, children. I think we'd better talk

quickly. Things are more dire than I realized, and if you don't even believe . . ." She shook her hooded head.

"It's okay," Ike told me. "The Grimmother wants to help you. It is safe here. You can ask for the help you need."

I glanced at Ben. He was still standing and conscious, but very tired. I offered him my arm for support, and when he nodded, we walked together.

My stomach fluttered as I cautiously stepped onto the chapel's graveled path, passing through a low iron fence surrounding the graveyard. When I stopped in front of the Grimmother, she pulled down the hood of her cloak.

Ben gasped. Or maybe that was both of us.

Because we stared into the face of someone we both knew.

Gray, messy hair. Tooth of a wolf around her neck on a gold chain.

The cemetery tour guide who knew all her onions.

"Miss Neja?" I whispered, surprise making my jaw hang open.

She gave us a soft smile. "Nice to see you. Wish it was Above and not here."

"But how?" I asked. "You're not dead. Are you?"

"Not last time I checked," she said, smiling. "You met Ludo? I'm a bit like him."

"You don't eat bugs, do you?" Ben asked.

"Bugs are very nutritious. High in protein, low in fat," she pointed out. "But I'm vegetarian."

I shook my head several times, blinking. "But, but . . . How are you here and there? You move between worlds? You're immortal, aren't you?" I asked all at once, unable to stop myself from blabbering in a hyper voice.

"Don't have to say it *that* way, Helena. It's not a dirty word, you know," she teased. "I suppose I am, sort of? I can be killed, but it's complicated. My official job Above is Grave Guardian. You already knew that, really. It's just that I do a little more than give cemetery tours and sell key chains."

"Because you're *immortal*," Ben harped. "Which you failed to mention to us."

"I don't go around announcing it up there, Ben. It's a need-to-know situation. And it's not like I lied to you. I'm a cemetery custodian, and I'm a friend to all hounds—"

Uh, these Grims weren't like the stray dogs in Whispering Pines, but okay.

"—and because of my work, I have a free pass to travel between the realms."

"Above and Below?" I asked.

"Yep. Oh, and I used to do a little soothsaying on the side."

"Soothsaying?"

"Foretelling the future," she explained. "To be honest, that hasn't worked out so well, and how I got my job is a story for another time. All that matters is that when I'm Above, in Forlorn, I protect Whispering Pines Cemetery. Down here, I try to protect your grandmother, even when she's too stubborn to want my help. And right now, she's in a bit of trouble."

The barricade of doubt inside my head that had been stopping me from truly believing that Babi could be queen suddenly broke, and I hesitantly experimented with a newfound acceptance.

My grandmother was queen of the underworld.

My grandmother was queen of the underworld.

HOLY CRAP, MY GRANDMOTHER REALLY WAS THE QUEEN OF THE UNDERWORLD!

Miss Neja gave me a satisfied look. "We on the same page now?"

"My Babi? Mine?" I said, reeling. "All those chats you had with her at the cemetery gift shop . . ."

She nodded. "Yup. I'd known your grandmother forever. Sort of literally." She chuckled.

"My granny was part of that chat group too," Ben said, a little wild alarm behind his eyes. "Did she know? She didn't know. Right? If I went home right now and asked her?"

"It's never wise to ask folks Above about folks Below," she replied, shaking her head.

That seemed like good advice.

"And I obviously couldn't say anything myself," Miss Neja said. "It wasn't my place. And it's not important now. Because Morana's in trouble."

Everyone was in trouble. Babi. Ben. The stress was making my chest feel heavy. The shock of everything was going to give me a heart attack before I made it to thirteen. "What kind of trouble? Ike said she was being held hostage?"

"Sadly, I cannot save her. But you still might be able to. Are you willing to try?"

"I would do anything," I told her. And now more than ever, I meant that with all my heart.

"Excellent. Then let's not waste time."

She took out a brass hunting horn that was hidden in the folds of her cloak and blew it. I knew that sound.

"That's the same horn Ben and I heard in Whispering Pines when we first met Fizzle," I said.

"Yes," she said. "When you told me about the vulture, I knew something was wrong. Fizzle rarely gets summoned to Whispering Pines without me knowing about it. But before I could survey the grounds, you'd already gone. I told you to stay in the shop."

Ben moaned. "I wish we'd stayed, trust me."

"I think I've figured out some of what happened," she said. "You used Fizzle's summoning book to enter the underworld?"

We nodded. I felt a little sheepish for having kept that from her. But how was I supposed to have known she was an underworld being? "I just wanted to talk to Babi. I guess I should've asked for your help? Would've been so much better than talking to an eyeless monk and walking down all those stairs. Or do you take the stairs down too?"

She held up her hand. "I do not. And back up to that one thing you said."

"Better than talking to an eyeless monk?"

She pointed. "That's the part that concerns me. I'll tell you why in just a moment."

I didn't like the sound of that, but before I could question her, the gravel shook under my feet. Something was coming.

"Horses?" Ben whispered.

From out of the mist, a fancy carriage emerged that was led by two enormous black stallions. A carriage driver in a Victorian coat sat high above them, his skeletal face hidden behind a scarf. Two socket eyes glowed in the shadow of a towering black top hat.

"Don't be frightened," Miss Neja said. "This is the Phantom Carriage. It will take us through the Perilous Woods to the Crown District. I'll ride inside with you. Ike and Shuck will keep guard outside, right, boys?"

"Yes, Mother," they said.

"It's okay," Ike said. "We'll watch the road for you."

"Thank you," I told him.

Up two steps, we climbed into the waiting carriage. The small door closed behind us with an eerie creak.

Inside were two purple velvet seats facing each other. Ben and I sat together on one while Miss Neja sat across from us. She tapped the top of the carriage, and the driver cracked a whip.

Then we were moving.

Through the carriage's window, I watched the small chapel shift out of sight before Ike appeared. He was running alongside the carriage; Shuck ran on the opposite side.

"So," Miss Neja said, crossing her hands on her lap. "I'm sure you have questions. . . ."

So many. I hardly knew where to start.

"Before anything else, my most urgent question is about Ben," I said as the carriage bumped along the wooded path. "He got bit by a sewer meek."

"Our guide put some weird mushroom salve on me," Ben said.

"Nasty things, sewer meeks. Let me take a look." By the light of the lanterns that hung near each seat, Miss Neja examined his bandaged finger. Sniffed it. "Duskcap salve. This is good, strong stuff. It slows the meek poison. Your guide knew what he was doing. He saved your life."

Huh. So Grumbones actually did one good thing. Didn't make up for all the bad stuff.

She peered into Ben's eyes.

"Am I okay?" he asked.

"You'll need to see a doctor when you get home." She looked at me. "Be sure you do."

"Do what?" I asked.

"Get Ben home," she said gravely.

My stomach twisted as Ben made a small, worried noise. The way she said it made me think there was a chance that it wouldn't happen. But she assured him that he'd be okay and patted him on the knee. I think this made him feel better. I tried to feel the same way.

And now that we knew he was okay—at least for the moment—we moved on to other questions.

"Miss Neja," I said. "Ike said Babi is being held hostage in a castle. We need to know why, and how she got to be queen of Hereafter. And also, who is this grand admiral person? Our guide, Grumbones, was useless and told us nothing."

"He was the worst," Ben agreed.

"Apart from saving your life," Miss Neja murmured, brows furrowed, as the carriage sped and the trees flew by the windows. "We don't have a lot of time, but I think I need to fill you in on how the Siege happened, because it has everything to do with why you're here right now. Remember when I showed you the drawing on the wall of the gift shop and told you the quick fable about our friend Billy, who knows everything about onions?"

"How could we forget Detroit Billy?" Ben said.

She smiled. "Well, now I have a *very* short story for you about how your grandmother and I met, Helena, a very long time ago. Let me see now. . . . It was around the time when Leonardo da Vinci lived, and after book printing had been invented."

Ben and I stared at her, both of our mouths hanging open.

"Now, I know what you're thinking," Miss Neja said. "Morana Novak looked very good for a woman who'd been walking the earth since the 1400s. But see, when she first came Above, she was the same as me. Immortal. And she stayed that way until she moved to Forlorn."

"Forlorn?" I said.

"It's a special town. But we'll get to that. Because my story starts at the Boondocks."

"Where we entered Hereafter?" Ben said.

She nodded. "Back then, in the time of da Vinci, Morana was still queen of Hereafter and living down here in Rime Castle. Oh, hold on. This should help explain things."

Miss Neja lifted the cushioned seat next to hers, rustled around in a storage space beneath it, and pulled out a worn book. The gilded spine read *1,001 Goofs, Gags, and Giggles.*

"Wait, wrong one." She pulled out a second book. This one read *The Histories of Hereafter*, and the author listed was Fizzle.

"Wow, ol' birdbrain really *is* an author, huh?" Ben said, impressed.

"Quite a good artist, too," Miss Neja said, thumbing through vellum pages. "Ah, here we are. Read this passage. It's short. I believe you'll find it enlightening."

How the Queen Lost Her Kingdom

A young underworld queen named Morana loved to travel with her trusty dog. She delighted in all the beautiful things as she toured her kingdom, for its denizens would bring their memories from Above and change the landscape of the underworld. The more she saw of Above, the more she desired to see it.

One day, she traveled outside the wall of her

realm to discover even more new things. And while she was there, a scheming court advisor who was trying to get her dethroned suggested she go fishing with the locals, to get to know the people of the Liminal Lands. When she asked the advisor where to catch the best fish, he lied and told her to fish in a forbidden canal.

There she caught a white eel. It was too small to eat, and it had no eyes, but the no-good advisor told her it would be an insult to the locals if she didn't keep it.

So she put the eel into a fishing basket. And when she got back inside the city walls, the eel began wriggling and thrashing awfully. She threw it down a well, returned to the castle, and forgot about it.

But the well water became foul, and no one could catch the white eel to remove it. The eel grew and grew, until it had two feet and could escape the well at night and walk upright like a man. It moved to a cave near the Lake of Sighs and sneaked around in the fog while people slept in their beds.

And while it sneaked, it ate birds.

And dogs.

And when it was strong enough, the white eel began slipping into the townsfolk and using their bodies to do very bad things.

It stole.

It set things on fire.

It caused chaos around the city.

But the worst thing it did was hide inside the body of the no-good court advisor and sneak into the castle. Because that's where it found the young queen, and it played a terrible trick.

The white eel told the queen that she could leave Hereafter by a special door and travel Above freely among the mortals. And whenever she was ready to come back to Hereafter, all she had to do was fall in love.

The young queen fell for his trick. She and her trusty dog left her kingdom and went Above.

"Where?" I asked Miss Neja, interrupting my reading. "Where did she go when she left the underworld and went Above?"

"The Kingdom of Bohemia. Now known as the Czech Republic—to the capital, Prague. She was smitten with the bridge there," Miss Neja said. "The one over the Lake of Sighs down here had recently been built at that time. I think the memories of plague victims from Prague built it."

"Wait, as in the Black Plague?" Ben said.

"It wasn't a great time for the world," she admitted. "Keep reading. . . ."

At first, the queen was happy Above. Then she became worried about her kingdom. She wanted to return Below. But falling in love was harder than she'd expected. So when she was traveling around Europe, she asked a chapel soothsayer in a churchyard to reveal when she would fall in love.

But when the soothsayer used her magic, she

saw that the queen hadn't just been tricked by the white eel. She'd been cursed with an ancient affliction known as the Curse of the Lonely.

"Curse of the Lonely?" I said. "That sounds awful."

"It is," Miss Neja said, looking solemn. "You don't make friends easily. No one wants to have anything to do with you. Think of a hermit living in a cave. That's what that curse ends up doing to people. It made Morana miserable."

My heart hurt just thinking about it. Maybe because it sounded a little bit like my own life.

"Read on," Miss Neja encouraged.

The curse wasn't a normal curse, because the white eel was not a normal eel.

He was a trickster demon from the deepest, muddiest mire of the demon world.

His name was Wyrm. And Wyrm was trying to take over the young queen's kingdom.

"Wyrm?" Ben said aloud. "We saw that word, remember? The graffiti poem?"

I nodded energetically. "In the Flooded District. Something about House of Rime falling and Wyrm rising."

"Like any villain, he has his fair share of fans," Miss Neja said, shrugging. "One person's trash is another's treasure."

"Yeah, but a demon?" I said.

"He's quite charming," Miss Neja admitted. "And back when Morana was under his curse, walking the earth, she knew that the only way she could get back to the underworld to save her kingdom was to fall in love. But that wouldn't happen for five hundred more years, in the 1970s, when she met a young American soldier who was just about to be sent off to war in Vietnam. They fell in love. And voila! The Curse of the Lonely was broken. Queen Morana became just a mortal woman."

My head felt light and airy with all this new information. "My Babi wasn't human until the 1970s?"

"Yep," Miss Neja said, then read the top of the book upside down, skimming the lines with one finger. "Let's see, you already know that. . . . Okay, skip to this part. Read this."

> But curses are funny things. Because once the queen was in love, she didn't want to return to the underworld. She wanted to stay Above and marry the soldier. Which she did. They had a child together. And theirs might have been a happy story, but the curse's effects lingered. The soldier died in a shipwreck.
>
> And Morana grew old. Powerless. Mortal. In love but separated from her husband.
>
> Lonely.
>
> All she could do was care for her new mortal family and wait for death so she could return Below.

"What the heck?" I said. "This is a terrible story!"

"Worst story ever," Ben agreed.

Miss Neja nodded. "I'm afraid it doesn't get happier. Because when your grandmother finally died and returned to the underworld, she found it in shambles—as you see it today. Wyrm had appointed himself as grand admiral and raised a fleet of demons from beneath the Lake of Sighs."

Armies come by land. Navies come by water. Grumbones had told us some of this. We just hadn't realized he was talking about a demon war that was meant to ruin my grandmother's kingdom.

"The Siege," Ben whispered.

"Yes," Miss Neja said. "Wyrm's troops set fires and toppled buildings. They flooded an entire neighborhood. On top of that, Wyrm put up magical barriers around the city to make it easier to contain everyone. Then he poisoned the water to brainwash them."

The well water!

"He took up residence in the castle," Miss Neja explained, "where he captured Morana the minute she entered Hereafter. He was waiting for her. Because the one thing he wanted was to be king of Hereafter. He had the crown, but he could not wear it and wield its power."

"Why?" Ben asked.

"He couldn't figure that out," Miss Neja said. "And when Morana would not share the crown's secret, he created a terrible magical creature to terrorize the city."

Ben and I stared across the carriage at her, waiting. But of course I knew exactly which creature she was talking about. "The Nightmare."

"That's right," Miss Neja said. "She's something called a servitor, made for one purpose. She steals the souls from the city's inhabitants. I suppose Wyrm thought that if the former queen of Hereafter would not help him become king, he would get his loyal subjects one way or another. So he began taking the queen's subjects by force, hoping it would make her give in and reveal the crown's secrets."

"It didn't, though?" I guessed.

"Nope," Miss Neja said with a quick shake of her head. "So Wyrm did the last thing he could think of to convince the queen. He lured Morana's only granddaughter into the underworld as leverage."

"Lured? I wasn't lured," I said, offended.

Miss Neja crossed her arms. "Where did you get Fizzle's summoning book?"

"Found it in Whispering Pines on a bench," Ben said.

"That was a trap," Miss Neja said. "Likely one of Wyrm's soldiers set it there. He's got people Above and Below who do favors for him."

A low noise escaped my mouth. My head was spinning. I didn't know what to think about any of this.

"My hounds have picked up rumors down here," she said, "that Wyrm has been planning something for a while now. He wanted to get you down here, Helena. I'm sorry I don't have better news to report. Or a better story to tell."

"I don't like this story very much," Ben said in a small voice. "I liked the one about Detroit Billy and his onions better."

Miss Neja nodded in sympathy. "I'm sorry you got dragged into this, Ben."

"It's pretty epic," he admitted.

"I know Morana blames herself for everything that's happened over the last few hundred years, and indeed, she made mistakes," she said. "But the white demon is crafty. He's made Morana miserable. He even tracked her Above. He was watching her in Forlorn and creating havoc there. Worms will be worms."

"No," Ben said, eyes wide.

"The Forlorn Worm is *Wyrm*?" I whispered.

"I'm afraid so," Miss Neja said. "He can travel back and forth like me, but he can't stay Above for long. He's most powerful in his natural form—a water serpent, his Forlorn Worm form. But he can utilize another body for a couple of minutes and hitch a ride, so to speak. In fact, I believe you've already met him. When he slithers into his victims, he magically removes their eyes."

Chills ran down my arms. Ben sank into the carriage seat, hiding in the collar of his peacoat.

"The eyeless vulture wasn't Fizzle," I mumbled.

Miss Neja shook her head.

But the Fizzle I'd seen at the clock tower had had eyes. That's why he'd apologized. Because the demon had used his body to lure us down here.

"Oh, children," Miss Neja moaned. "I told you to stay inside the gift shop. But it's too late now. You're here, and maybe that's what your grandmother wanted all along. I have to believe she has a plan of her own to beat him."

"You don't know?" I asked.

Miss Neja twisted her mouth to one side. "I haven't been able to contact her since she died and Wyrm captured her."

Crap.

"What if she isn't even here?" I asked as my old fear resurfaced. "No one has seen her. What if the Nightmare harrowed her?"

"No. She's in the castle," Miss Neja assured me. "As for the rest, why don't I tell you what I know, and then maybe we can figure out precisely who this Grumbones person is."

"Wait, you don't know that, either?" Ben said, brow furrowed. "What kind of soothsayer are you, anyway?"

For the first time since I'd met her, Miss Neja's perky attitude sagged. She glanced outside the carriage window and murmured, "I lost my soothsaying powers many years ago when I bet them in a fiddling contest with a trickster. . . . It's a long story for another time." A brief blush of embarrassment stained her cheeks; then she shook it away. "Regardless, I can see nothing of the future now. It's like walking in the Grum. So I just concentrate on my other work, like keeping an eye on this place. I did while your grandmother was away, and since her imprisonment upon returning, I continue to try my best to repel Wyrm's forces."

"If that was your job, to watch the kingdom while Babi was Above, then how did it get this bad? I mean—" I was going to point out all the devastation we'd run into around the city.

Miss Neja held up a hand. "For one, my powers as guardian are limited. In the old days, I took care of a single churchyard. Not an entire kingdom."

I supposed that was legit.

"Then came the city wards. Wyrm found out about me and wouldn't let me inside. I'm stuck out here, beyond the wall. Only a few can travel through the wards. Wyrm. Fizzle, who can open portals when he's not possessed by the white worm. And apparently your guide. Which makes him a curiosity to me."

I definitely agreed.

Just who was Grumbones, anyway?

CHAPTER 17
Phantom Carriage

The Phantom Carriage took a turn through the Perilous Woods and sped through another patch of fog. I quickly checked to make sure Ike was still keeping up alongside it, which made me feel better. Not much. Some.

Miss Neja folded her hands in her lap. "Do you have any questions, children?"

"Where exactly is Wyrm from?" Ben said.

"A place called the Abyssal Plain," Miss Neja said. "It's a very deep part of the demon world where the Old Ones dwell. If he were where he *should* be, he'd be able to reach neither mortals Above nor the dead in Hereafter. I don't know how he got into the underworld canal, except that it's a place between worlds, so that probably made it easier. But I know that as long as he's able to roam Above and Below, he's dangerous."

I guess it was a little like layers of an onion, as Grumbones had told us. Maybe Wyrm had wriggled his way between the layers. "Why does he want to rule Hereafter?"

She hesitated. "I think, but I'm not certain, that he actually wants to be human. He's able to possess humans—dead or alive. But he doesn't own a human body. And I don't know why, but he believes that being ruler down here will get him some kind of power over life and death."

"Seems like he already has that with the Nightmare," I said. "What's he planning on doing with all the souls he's sucked out of the harrowed husks?" I thought of the harpies.

Miss Neja shook her head. "I'm not sure. I know that he made the Nightmare with magic."

"What did you call it?" I asked. "A serve . . ."

"Servitor," Miss Neja explained. "Have you ever heard of a golem? That's a creature built from clay and brought to life with a magic spell. A servitor is similar. But I don't know how to destroy her. Arrows bounce right off. I think her skin is made of the same substance as the husks, strangely enough. So you'd think she'd be brittle and could be broken. But no."

I remembered the shiny necklace that I'd spotted around her neck when we'd seen her harrow that poor man in the plaza, and I told Miss Neja about it. "You think that could be the source of her magic?"

"Could be what makes her tick, sure. But how do you get close enough to grab it? A couple of folks in a district on the other side of the lake tried to crush her with a boulder that they pushed off a building, but they missed. The Nightmare transported up to the roof and harrowed one before she could run away." Her eyes flicked to Ben. "My dear . . . are you feeling all right?"

He was staring out the window. "Thought I saw something in the trees. . . ."

She nodded. "Lost souls. They can't hurt us. Don't look, though. Keep your eyes in the carriage. On me."

Ben blinked at her. He was worried. I watched him for a moment, checking the whites of his eyes—*still okay, whew!*—then tried to refocus on what Miss Neja had been saying.

"We're running out of time, so let me get to the heart of the problem," Miss Neja said. "Wyrm is holding Morana in the castle, and he has the Rime Crown. But he can't wear it."

"Why?" I asked.

"Because he's a demon," she said, eyes bright with excitement. "He's in the wrong level of the underworld. Doesn't belong here. So the crown is just a trinket to him. Basically, think of it like . . . he has your grandmother's laptop, but doesn't have her password, so he can't use it."

"Oh, okay," Ben and I said.

"But the crown has immense power, and on Morana, it would allow her to get control of the kingdom again. She could repair the damage Wyrm has done and kick all his minions out. Someone needs to rescue her and get the crown back onto her head."

She meant me. And Ben, who was looking worse and worse. "I don't understand."

"The castle is back inside the city proper, and I can't breach the city walls," she said. "Ike and Shuck can enter the town square—but that is as far as they can go into the city. But if you can sneak into the castle, maybe you can help your grandmother recover the crown. Then she'll do the rest."

I stared at her as the carriage rolled along the path. "But Ben and I have been lured here. We'll be expected. This is a trap."

"It could be," she said. "But there's no one else who can get inside the castle wards. Because Wyrm's not going to let just anyone inside Rime Castle. Only you."

"I'm bait?" I said, alarmed.

Miss Neja squinted one eye shut. "More like you've got a golden ticket to the event of the century. You've just got to outsmart the evil monster inside and rescue the queen in order to enjoy yourself."

Ben groaned. "This is all a load of bunk. The booklet that was left in the cemetery, that was Fizzle's book—*How to Talk to the Dead*. If we hadn't had that dumb book, we wouldn't be here. That birdbrain helped Wyrm! He's the same as that scheming court advisor from the story in your book, Miss Neja."

"Please don't blame Fizzle," she said. "He may have been possessed by Wyrm, but he's not the white demon's servant. He's an underworld creature, loyal to the Reaper."

"As in, the Grim Reaper?" I asked.

"Yup. The top dog of the entire underworld," she confirmed. "The big boss. Head honcho. Death itself with a capital *D*."

"If the Reaper is the big boss, why can't we just ask him for help? I mean, if he rules the underworld, it seems like he wouldn't want Wyrm up in his kingdoms, causing mass destruction with the Nightmare."

"Good point," Ben said groggily. "Seems like he should've already booted him out. Doesn't he care about a demon invading his people?"

"The Reaper doesn't show up when you snap your fingers," Miss Neja scoffed. "Over the centuries, I've seen my fair share of powerful underworld gods—good, bad, and ordinary, and none have so much as *spoken* to the Reaper. You have to be high up on the food chain."

"Higher than queen of the underworld?"

"A queen. Not *the* queen. Your grandmother only rules over the humans from Above that pass on to this kingdom. The underworld is a big place. There are all kinds of things down here. Humans aren't the only things that die, you know."

My mind turned. It was all so overwhelming. Babi was in trouble. We couldn't ask this Reaper entity for help. Fizzle wasn't to blame. Miss Neja didn't have any more answers. But she also wasn't bringing up the elephant in the carriage. "Seems to me that the real villain here today is Grumbones. He's the one who lured us here, pretending to be a friendly guide. He's the liar!"

Miss Neja squinted. "For the death of me, I just can't figure out who he is."

"We thought you could tell us," Ben said, sounding hopeless.

"I've only heard whispers from some of the souls around the city who've sent word to me today through Ike and Shuck. But the whispers are about two underworld guides."

"Two?"

She made rabbit ears with her fingers and wiggled them. "Apparently Wyrm sent a mercenary posing as an underworld guide to lure you down here, kidnap you, and take you to the castle. But there was a second man claiming to be a guide, and that's where things get strange. Because I'm not sure who sent the second man. Was it Morana, who'd somehow managed to send someone to fetch you? Or perhaps a third party? Whoever they are, rumor is that before you showed up, these two clashed and the Nightmare harrowed one of them." She drew a line along her neck with her finger.

Ben and I shared a wide-eyed look. I was positive we were thinking the same thing.

"The husk in the Flooded District," I said. "We found a letter nearby that was from the castle. It said it was paying someone to deliver an asset."

"You're the asset?" Ben whispered in horror. "But that would mean Sir Krak is . . . ? Who is the real guide?"

Real guide. Fake guide. Sir Krak had had brochures in Ludo's boat. Those had *seemed* real. Grumbones's "official" guide license had looked pretty fake. Plus, there was all the lying and stealing. And he was super irritating.

Then again, he had saved Ben's life.

Ben's eyes narrowed. "Don't you see? Grumbones *is* the mercenary! Sir Krak was the real guide, on his way to warn you. But someone sneaked into the abandoned house in the Flooded District, sicced the Nightmare on the guide to kill him, and then took his place. Grumbones is Wyrm's mercenary. Grumbones is a fake guide."

Miss Neja listened to his theory and frowned. "Look, I don't know exactly who Mr. Grumbones is. All I know is that he's not from Hereafter, and Fizzle says he's been traveling around here asking a lot of questions about Morana. Fizzle suspects he goes by another name, but he isn't sure."

If Fizzle thought Grumbones was a highly suspicious type, then why did Fizzle help him at the clock tower, opening up a portal for us to the château? It seemed to me like there was a certain amount of respect between them, but maybe I had been imagining that. . . .

"I found a book among Grumbones's things," I said, suddenly

remembering. "It was something about changing your identity in the underworld. A guide to being anonymous."

"See? Fake!" Ben said.

Miss Neja looked concerned. "Another of Fizzle's titles. But," she pointed out, "only the Nightmare can make a husk. How would Grumbones have summoned the Nightmare to harrow Sir Krak? The Nightmare doesn't just hang around the Flooded District. It tends to be attracted to certain loud noises."

Like bells.

I retrieved the handbell that I'd nabbed from Grumbones's saddlebag. "Would this make a noise loud enough to attract the Nightmare?"

"A Deathbell," she murmured. "Well, well . . . where did you get this, Mr. Grumbones, you naughty boy, you? This is a magical weapon, children. It calls all sorts of nasty creatures. And yes, it would get the Nightmare's attention. She would hear this from the other side of the city. This is a magic bell. *Very* dangerous." Miss Neja looked at both of us. "Where is Grumbones now?"

We explained what had happened, and how we'd gotten away at the château. She took it all in stride and seemed to know exactly what we were talking about with regard to the reflecting spirits. Miss Neja was always calm and collected, but that coolness was on a whole different level down here. Grimmother. So strange to think that she could be in both worlds.

She rested both hands on her knees. "Well, there's no way of knowing whether these mirror spirits from the château have taken Grumbones out of Hereafter permanently. He could be buried underground for years and rise again later, or he could be shifted to another part of the underworld. We just don't know. I do worry that he is a little like me and can move between Above and Below. He might not even be human. . . ."

Her face fell suddenly as she stared at Ben.

I turned to see what she was looking at, and my stomach knotted.

Green, in the whites of his eyes. Tiny pinpricks of dots—like a toxic rash.

My entire world felt as if it had just been tackled and brought to the ground.

"Oh, Ben—no, no, no!" I said, throat squeezing painfully as fear filled up my head.

"Don't . . . feel good," he mumbled, blinking rapidly.

Miss Neja checked his temperature with the backs of her fingers against his forehead. "He can't stay here, Helena," she said very seriously. "If he does, he will die and be stuck here for eternity."

"No!" I cried.

"I don't want to die," he whispered.

He couldn't die! That was impossible. I wasn't going to lose my best friend. I had already shut him out for the last year. I needed time to make that up to him—in some place other than a decrepit underworld kingdom. I needed . . . Ben.

"How do I get him back home?"

She clasped his hand. "If you accompany him and go back through Fizzle, you will not be able to return."

"Ever?"

She shook her head. "That is the rule."

No! It wasn't fair! My thoughts scattered like birds. "But . . . Ben. And I can't come back? What about my Babi? She needs my help too."

Miss Neja peered through the window with a worried look in her eyes. Now I was seeing something too. Something in the trees, running alongside the carriage past Shuck. Something almost invisible and moving very fast. I had a terrible feeling that whatever it was, we didn't want it to catch up. That it was worse than the Nightmare. What if it was Death himself?

What if Death was coming for Ben?

"There's one other way," Miss Neja said, snapping her fingers to get my attention. "I can take him in the carriage, up through the cemetery. Just me and Ben."

"You mean, I stay here? Alone?"

"No," Ben huffed out in a sickly voice. "I won't . . . leave her."

"I won't leave him, either," I said, reaching for his hand.

A terrible howl in the woods made me jump. Another howl answered from the other side of the carriage. Ike and Shuck. Warnings.

The carriage shook violently and veered to the side. Hinges creaked as the black fabric above us sank in four places.

Something was on top.

Terror washed over me. I grabbed Ben's arm, but he was too sick to panic. He was more in danger of tipping out of the window than dying of fear. His eyes were fluttering shut, and he was talking to himself.

"Can't leave Helena. Can't leave . . ."

The driver cracked his whip. The carriage sped.

The thing above us sank lower and moved toward Ben's window.

We were going too fast. The wheels sounded as if they could fly off.

"Don't worry about all this," Miss Neja said, gesturing toward the carriage roof. "I knew this would happen. It's why I took you this way. Remember when I said there were only a few people who could pass through the city wards? I didn't mention one other option. A one-way option. There's a way of getting through the ward if you're small enough and fast enough, and if you go through at just the right speed."

"Speed?" I said, rattled.

"If you want to save your grandmother, you'll have to jump out of the carriage," Miss Neja told me. "It's okay. I'll tell you when. Listen to everything I'm about to tell you."

"I need to go with Helena," Ben mumbled.

"No, you must go home, my darling," Miss Neja told Ben. "Do not be scared. When we get back, you will be alive but death-kissed. You will see things you didn't see before you journeyed through the underworld. Don't be afraid."

But he was. And I knew that because *I* was terrified. What if he didn't make it? The poison could kill him. What did our doctors Above know about sewer meeks?

What if I never saw him again?

Tears filled my eyes. "Ben, no. I can't leave you. I'll go home with you."

"Don't be a nitwit," he said, and attempted a smile.

"Don't quote Grumbones to me!"

"Go save your grandmother," he said in a faint voice. "Be Haunted Helena."

I locked eyes with him and nodded. I could do this alone. Me. For *him*. My best friend, the only person weird enough to follow me into the underworld.

"You can do it," he said.

Here comes Haunted Helena, I thought with a gust of pride.

The carriage shook as though it were going to explode.

But Miss Neja just smiled at me. "I'll get him home to Forlorn. And you'll be all right, I do believe. You have a basket full of onions, and you are on your way to Rime Castle. You know your onions, and that is all that matters."

I didn't know if that was really true anymore. I didn't know jack about onions. But I did know two things: Ben needed her help, and my grandmother needed mine.

CHAPTER 18

Icy Moat

I lay in the road at the edge of the Perilous Woods, gasping for breath as I watched the Phantom Carriage speed away. It wasn't long before the fog covered its tracks. But when I could no longer hear horses' hooves pounding the ground, I felt all the hurt in my bones.

Jumping out of a moving carriage in the underworld had not been on my bucket list. And when that hurt went away, it was replaced by an aching fear that settled deep inside my chest.

Ben was gone. I didn't know if he was going to be okay.

My Babi was being held hostage by an evil demon.

And I was now very much alone in the underworld.

No guide. No map. Only a general idea of where to go, out of the forest and then toward the castle. And no idea what to do when I got there.

Miss Neja had promised that the castle was close and that I couldn't miss it. She was right about both. As soon as I emerged from the trees, the city lay in front of me under a night sky that was spotted with white. It had started snowing.

That was okay. Because the Phantom Carriage had taken me all the way around to the northwest side of the lake. And there, just a short hike up a hill, was the castle I'd been promised.

A grand one, by the looks of it.

I set out in its direction as snow dusted the ground, thankful that I was wearing my trusty red rubber rain boots. I was even more thankful that I didn't see anything moving in the landscape, because the closer I got to the castle, the harder the wind blew and the colder it got. All the trees and bushes were covered in ice and hoarfrost. My storm jacket was not warm enough.

I really wished my Shag Pack were here to keep me company, but maybe it was okay to be alone sometimes. It gave me a chance to focus on the castle and how I was going to get inside.

Rime Castle was impressively ominous: inky black, with a dozen needlelike towers puncturing the clouds. I was approaching it from the back, which could be a good thing. Grumbones had said no one was allowed to just waltz into the castle, and as much as I hated to admit it, he was probably right. Likely there would be guards out front. Probably not friendly ones either.

Whether I tried to get into the castle from the front or the back, the problem was its defenses. First, a massive wall topped with icicles circled the entire castle. Below that wall was a moat. Water. Lots of it. Some of it was iced over. Some wasn't. If ever there was a piece of ice that shouted, *Don't walk on me, I WILL crack*, it was this. And who knew what kind of underworld monsters dwelled beneath its dark surface?

But it wasn't all bad. I reached the back gate by crossing a short wooden drawbridge that lay over the icy moat. The drawbridge was lowered, attached by two fat chains to the castle's wall. The iron gate, however, was shut tight.

Was it warded?

An icicle fell when I jiggled the gate. If there was a ward, it didn't zap me. Or stop my hand. Strange that the place where Wyrm was keeping my Babi prisoner wasn't warded, when the rest of the city was. That made me suspicious.

"Is there a latch or a key?" I mumbled to myself, shivering as the snow fell around me. There were no guards out here, and when I peered through the iron bars, the yard around the castle looked dark and barren.

"It's a tricky one," a scratchy, low voice said behind me.

I spun around to find the last person I wanted to see standing in the middle of the drawbridge.

Grumbones. Guess he escaped the mirror spirits after all.

I wanted to scream. Run. Clobber him with an icicle. My heart sped frantically when it dawned on me that he might feel the same way about me right now.

"No key," he said. "Locked with soul magic. In other words, you gotta spill blood to get it to open. The castle's current occupier has a flair for the dark and dastardly."

I didn't respond. I just stood where I was, back to the gate, as panic crested over me in long, rolling waves. A long silence passed between us while snow fell all around.

"Where's your pal?" he finally asked.

"Why do you care? It's your fault he got sick."

"So that's how it's going to be, huh? I'm getting iced out now? We're enemies?"

"You sound mad."

"What? Me?" He opened his arms and shrugged. "Why would I be mad? For you shovin' me into a couple of wretched oil-slick spirits? Or on account of the two of ya stealin' my stuff and runnin' away like deserters?"

"You're calling *me* a thief?" I said, furious as I fumbled inside my jacket pocket and flashed him the photo of me and Babi. "I found this in your saddlebag. You're the one who stole precious, private things from a grave. That's low-down."

He tilted his fisherman's cap up to wipe his forehead, then settled it back down. "I didn't steal those things off your grandmother's grave. I can't go Above. You ever think I might have a good reason to have them in my possession? Or you just make assumptions left and right?"

There was no use arguing with him about this because I could see what he was doing. Trying to waste time and get me to let my guard down. He was going to try to trap me.

I shoved the photo back into my pocket and glanced around, peering out of the corners of my eyes. Well. Scratch that. He *had* trapped me. I was stuck at the gate, and there was no way inside. I could try to make a run for it, see if I could get past him on the drawbridge.

Otherwise, I was cornered. Like a stinking rat. On top of a moat. Made of ice.

"Why are you even here?" I asked. "I'm really curious how you found me."

He pointed at the snow. "You ain't exactly inconspicuous. No one else out here with boot tracks like that."

He had tracking skills. This place was nowhere near the

château, where we had left him. And that made me more afraid than I already had been. After all, I was standing in front of a fake guide. Who knew what he was capable of doing to me?

"I meant, why are you even doing this?" I said. "Who are you? I know you aren't a real guide. What's your deal? You said you don't get paid in cash, but that was just one of your many lies, huh? This Wyrm demon must be giving you some kind of big reward for me."

"Whoa-ho-ho," he said. "Sounds like someone's been digging up dirt since I last saw you. Hold on—I know now. Ben's gone. You were near the woods. You been to see the Grimmother, ain't ya?"

"Grimmother?" I mumbled, eyeing the moat's banks below. Maybe I could jump into the water? Could I make it across before something ate me? "Don't know what you're talking about."

"Yes, you do," he said in a singsong voice. "She took the kid back Above. On account of his bite. Only other standard way out of here is Fizzle—or asking the Big Cheese to take you, and I'm betting that lily liver didn't have the guts to petition the Reaper."

"Those are the only ways out, huh? What happened to all the doors you told me about? The ones you insisted only you knew— that you'd marked on your map? Those were a lie?"

"No, little sassafras, we used one, if you recall. It was in the clock tower. They're called portals, and Fizzle guards them. You can use the portals to get around the city or go back Above—but they're one-way access. So if you use one to go Above, you ain't comin' back down unless you know how to find Fizzle in the land of the living. And that's a whole other thing."

I blinked away snowflakes. "Whatever, liar. I just know I haven't seen a single mailbox. I can't believe we bought your lie about that dumb star card."

"Okay, yes. *That* was a lie," he admitted.

"Knew it!"

"But I am a guide. Official one. In my own kingdom."

"Shut it. You're a fink. Grumfink, that's *you.*"

"What did the ol' Grimmother tell you about me?"

"Why would you care?"

"Because you're slandering my good name!"

This time I laughed. "You're not a real guide! You're a murderer." I took out the Deathbell from my pocket. "She told me about this—that it's a magical weapon. That it summons the Nightmare."

He held up both hands. "Whoa, whoa, girl. Be careful with that."

"Because it's a weapon? And you used it to call the Nightmare to harrow that poor knight in the Flooded District?"

He stared at me, eyes squinting. "You don't know what you're talking about."

"Oh, really? Because I'm pretty sure you murdered the soul of a real guide—and then you swapped places with him so that you could take me to that Wyrm guy instead! Am I right?"

He laughed. "Sassafras, you're a walking example of how a little bit of knowledge is dangerous. No. You're not right. You're *some* right, but overall you're very wrong."

"What does that even mean? I hate all your riddles. You never tell the truth."

"Oh, really?"

"I know you're a liar who's using a fake identity—yeah, I saw your book about being anonymous in the underworld."

"Got reasons for that."

"Don't care, because worst of all, you're a murderer."

Grumbones tugged the twirl of his mustache, chuckled darkly

to himself, and then turned to look at the moat. He didn't respond right away. Maybe because I'd figured out his devious plan. Maybe because he was trying to figure out a way to murder me, too. . . .

"You're right. I did call the Nightmare to harrow that man you saw in the abandoned house," he finally admitted. "I used the Deathbell you have in your hand. It's a wicked weapon. It calls the Nightmare, and she came and took Sir Krak's soul."

His honesty took me by surprise. I didn't know what to make of it, so I just kept pressing him. "And when we found the letter that was the evidence against you, of course you hid it."

"That letter wasn't written to me. It was Sir Krak's letter," Grumbones said. "I had him harrowed because he was a dirty mercenary who betrayed the queen. Wyrm hired him to steal your grave mementos, lure you down here, and bring you to the castle."

"Exactly! Wait . . . what?"

He turned to face me. "Don't believe me? Wyrm has got your gram-grams locked up inside that castle, and Sir Krak was only too happy to kidnap you because he's a coward who won't stand up to Wyrm."

"You're telling me Sir Krak can travel between Above and Below, and that's how Fizzle's book ended up in Whispering Pines? That's how he stole my grave mementos?"

Grumbones shook his head. "He sent a sewer meek. You wouldn't recognize them in your world. They look like those clown seabirds on the coast with big orange feet."

Puffins? Of course! The one I saw trailing me on my walk from the Beacon to Granny Booker's! I *knew* I was being followed. And that's why the sewer meek that bit Ben looked so familiar: its orange teeth.

"Birds," he mumbled. "Never trust a bird when you're Above. Nine times out of ten, they are other beings in disguise from another plane of existence, and half of those beings are demons—if they aren't pooping on your head, they're stealing your soul."

That's what Babi always said.

Grumbones shook his head. "Anyway, Sir Krak planned to lure you down here and take you to the castle. But I got to him before he could kidnap you. You came down here anyway, because you're as stubborn as a mule, apparently."

I felt conflicted. If I bought into this story, that would mean that Grumbones was telling the truth. Did I believe him . . . ?

Part of me wanted to, but then I remembered something.

"There's a crack in your story," I said. "Why did you pretend to be our guide? Why were you escorting us to the castle if that's where Sir Krak was supposed to take us? Sounds like you killed him and took over his contract so you could get his payout from Wyrm."

"Oh, you got it all figured out, have ya?" he scoffed. "Wrong. I wouldn't work for Wyrm if it meant true death, harrowing—you name the punishment. Nothing would make me work for him. Now, yes, it's true, he needs you at the castle because you're the queen's weakness, and he wants to wear her crown. But it's like Cinderella's slipper—it don't fit him, see? Wyrm has tried everything in his power to get the queen to tell him how he can wear the crown, but the queen is holding out on him. Whoever wears the crown rules Hereafter. It's got power. He wants it. And he thinks you're the key to breaking Morana."

Grumbones knew about all this? Well . . . so what? That only proved that he'd been withholding information from me this whole time. "Okay, so you were taking us to the castle . . . why?"

"To help the queen."

Right. Didn't believe that. "Not for sightseeing, then. Guess the Dream Tower was a big scam, huh?"

"Pretty much," he admitted. "But Sir Krak wouldn't have taken you there either. That wasn't a lie. He was dirty, sassafras."

"And you aren't? You lied to me. Withheld information. I know you aren't who you say you are," I accused. "Who are you?"

"I'm Grumbones. I'm a guide."

"Bull. I saw that book in your saddlebag. You've changed your identity somehow."

Grumbones took a step closer. "That's true. I did. But it was out of necessity. When I died, Wyrm wanted my head on a spike. So I changed my identity with magic and stayed hidden. I was good at that—learned all about stayin' alive in the jungle Above. So I found out how to camouflage myself down here, too."

I didn't trust him.

And he'd lied to me and Ben. He'd shot at Ike the First.

"I couldn't tell you two who I really was. If I did, Wyrm's demons would come after us. They've been chasing me through the kingdoms for years. I had to stay one step ahead of them. You aren't Morana's only weakness, you know."

What was he talking about?

"Don't come any closer!" I warned him, heart racing. The gate was right behind me. I felt so trapped. Scared. Confused.

"Steady now, girl. You don't know what that bell can do," he said, raising his hands slowly, as if he might snatch it from me. "Hand it over before someone gets hurt. There's a better way to do this."

He was a fink. He'd killed Sir Krak, so Ben's theory had been correct. Therefore, Grumbones had to be the fake guide . . . didn't he? It was so hard to sort out everything I'd seen from everything he was telling me. But the facts were that Grumbones had kept Wyrm's letter instead of handing it over to the hawk guards, and if he were innocent, he wouldn't hide evidence.

If he were secretly working with my Babi to help her—like Miss Neja suspected one of the two guides was—he would have told me and Ben right from the start. He would have warned me about Wyrm. There had to be some way he could have shared that with us without putting us all in danger, as he claimed.

Right?

Why did adults never trust kids with the truth? Even Miss Neja didn't, and I knew she was good and decent. My mom admitted holding back the truth from me to protect me sometimes. Mostly, though, it seemed to be sneaky adults who were trying to hide bad things.

Grumbones definitely fit that description in my head.

And I was sick and tired of being on the wrong side of need-to-know situations.

"Tell me who you are!" I demanded.

"Why couldn't you have just followed directions?" he snapped, anger tightening the line of his brow and hiding his eyes. "Why did you bring Ben down here, anyway? It was supposed to be a simple trip through the city. That kid ruined everything."

Now he sounded like Babi a year ago, when we'd had our one and only fight. *Spending too much time with Ben. Friends will be your ruin.*

"Shut up! You rotten old scumbag!"

"Watch your mouth!"

"You watch yours! Ben is a million times the person you will ever be. And I'd rather be bitten by ten sewer meeks than go anywhere with you again."

A look of fury transformed his face. "We'll see about that!"

His hand lurched toward the bell.

I jerked back. My elbow hit the gate and caused my finger to slip on the handbell's trigger. I felt it give way as pain shot up my arm.

The inner clapper of the bell released. It was heavy in my hand. And before I had time to stop it—

The handbell rang out. Only once. But loudly.

No! I didn't mean to!

Shock rooted my feet to the ground as I held my breath, unsure what would happen next. Maybe I hadn't done it right. Maybe it needed to be rung multiple times, or there was a special magical phrase that had to be uttered.

But even as I told myself this, I knew it wasn't true.

The snow around us stopped fluttering in midair. Nothing moved. No wind. The water in the moat below stopped trickling.

Dead silence.

Grumbones's face fell. He shut his eyes and bowed his head. He looked . . . defeated.

But also . . .

Relieved? That couldn't be right.

"It was an accident!" I said in a panic.

"It was duty," he said in a peaceful voice.

Duty? What was he talking about?

At the far end of the drawbridge, a light appeared. Blue mist, crackling with tendrils of electricity. The Nightmare had answered the bell and was heading straight for Grumbones.

I flattened myself against the iron gate as the Nightmare hovered over Grumbones. Maybe she remembered him from the abandoned house. Maybe she just attacked the first person she saw. I didn't know. But she wasn't going after me. As she stalked him, I gawked at her, like you'd watch a car crash. Unable to tear my eyes away. My heart filling up with terror.

And a painful regret that sapped my own spirit.

It was one thing to push Grumbones toward the mirror spirits. He'd had a fighting chance. I knew he didn't with this creature. And I wished more than anything else that I could take it all back. But I guess my Babi had been right once again when she'd told me that you can't unring a bell.

Now that I was closer to the Nightmare than I had been in the plaza, I could see that Miss Neja was right: the creature's skin was made out of the same brittle, shell-like material as the harrowed husks that she created. She was like a floating insect, crackling with energy. And as she descended over him, he seemed resigned to his fate.

I couldn't watch another harrowing. Not again. Not one I caused myself!

Not Grumbones.

Despite all the lies, and all the horrible, irritating things he'd said to us, he had done a few good things. He'd gotten that salve for Ben, and Miss Neja had said it was the right medicine. And he'd carried Ben through Merry Dead Plaza when we'd been running for our lives.

Oh God. What have I done?

Wallowing in anguish and guilt, I cried out to try to stop her, but she didn't hear me.

It was too late.

My throat was like a vise. My knees felt weak enough to give out.

I wished I'd never come to the underworld.

I wished I'd never seen this man's face.

But as the Nightmare opened her swirling mouth, and he stared up into her face with the same dull expression worn by the other man I'd seen harrowed, something changed. Something in the way he held himself. He was straining. Turning his head away from hers, as if he could break her harrowing spell if he looked away long enough.

For a moment, anyway, it seemed to help. Grumbones's shoulders relaxed, just slightly, and his face softened as he gazed in my direction. An odd look came over him, one that was tender and sentimental, and it made me feel even guiltier than I had thought possible.

He smiled at me gently as he spoke.

"Goodbye, Helenka."

But that couldn't be right. No one called me Helenka but Babi. *No one.* It was a Czech nickname, and he'd even gotten the pronunciation right.

How would he know my private nickname unless he'd talked to Babi?

He'd claimed to know her. *Number-One Dragon*, he'd called her. But if he knew her well enough for her to tell him my special name, then—

Were they friends? Or . . . what?

Was Grumbones not the bad guy I'd thought he was?

No! No, no, no!

While he smiled at me, his tattoos glowed around his wrists.

Then, on his chest, a bright light began blazing from a circular symbol tattooed there. It shone through his clothes like an exploding sun. And right before my eyes, his appearance briefly changed.

Santa's evil twin melted away, and just for a moment, like a glint in a mirror, underneath was a huskier man with a gentler, younger face.

One I recognized from old photographs in my Babi's room.

The photographs that she had used to talk to her dead husband in the underworld.

The grandfather I'd never met.

The man in front of me now, held within the Nightmare's unstoppable thrall, looked just like him. He had a kind, funny face with sharp eyes and a sillier version of the mustache he'd sported while in disguise. His hair was military-short, and he was wearing green army fatigues and black boots.

Yes, he looked like my Babi's old photos. But he also looked so much like my dad that I could have mistaken him, had we been Above.

I felt as if someone had kicked me in the stomach.

"Don't lose your gumption now, kid. You're everything I wanted in a granddaughter," he said in a younger voice, but one that still sounded like him. "I might have failed you, but Morana raised you up right."

I cried out in confusion. My head emptied. My brain wouldn't work, no matter how hard I tried to force it. I needed to think of reasons why this was another one of Grumbones's lies.

But I couldn't.

He knew too much about my family . . .

Because he was family.

Shock unwound inside me in rapid spirals and made it feel as if the ground were falling away from my feet.

But my crisis of faith didn't matter to the Nightmare. Her harrowing black hole could not be stopped.

As his soul drained from his body, he tossed something at me. "For protection. Save your grandmother. Save all of us."

I caught something silver. A necklace? No.

Old U.S. Army dog tags. They read:

NOVAK

ADAM B

RA16461822

O POS

NO PREFERENCE

"NO! WAIT!" I tried to run toward him, but he held up a hand.

"No, kid. Soul magic. The gate. Ge—"

He didn't finish.

I covered my face with one hand and sobbed. The mystery of Grumbones was solved. He wasn't fake. He'd been on my side the entire time. And I'd just killed him.

My own grandfather.

CHAPTER 19

Rime Castle

Back home, in Babi's old room, she'd kept all her favorite photos in pretty frames on top of her dresser. Dozens of them. Her friends in Europe. My parents. Me. Ike the First. But of all the pictures she'd kept, the majority of them had been of Adam Novak. Pictures of them together. Of him holding up a big fish he'd caught in the Forlorn harbor. Of him in fancy military dress. With his army pals, in Vietnam.

Every time I'd asked her about him over the years, she'd said that he was funny and irreverent. And that he'd lost his parents in an accident, so she'd been the only real family he'd had.

Now he had no family because I'd stolen that away from him too.

All this time I'd been calling him Santa's evil twin, but I was the actual bad person.

I'd harrowed my own grandfather.

Tears streamed down my face. I hadn't felt this empty and alone since Babi had died.

Yet the underworld would not allow me time to even think, much less grieve, because I was startled as the iron gate behind me slowly opened.

Soul magic. Grumbones's harrowing had opened the castle ward.

Somewhere in the back of my head, under all the shock and pain, I knew I had to move. But that creature still floated above the empty husk on the drawbridge. And I couldn't make myself leave.

The Nightmare was done with Adam "Grumbones" Novak, the U.S. captain who'd been an army medic in the Vietnam War. The man who'd drowned when his ship had crashed off the coast of Forlorn after his tour of duty had ended. He'd never made it home to see his newborn son, my father, who was named after him.

His grave sat empty next to my Babi's in Whispering Pines Cemetery, because they never found his body—though my parents search the Pacific for it, year after year.

The man Babi said she started dating because he was the only other Czech American in Forlorn, which was a terrible reason to date someone. He didn't even speak Czech, so she had to teach him everything about the Old Country. And he had to teach her everything about the woods and hiking. And they were friends with the Bookers.

And then he drowned.

And that was all I really knew about him.

All the onions I knew about my own grandfather.

But what I *did* know, in that awful, terrible moment, was that it was too late to do anything about what I'd done. And that if I wanted to save Babi, I'd need to leave him before the Nightmare moved on to me.

I just didn't think I could do it.

"Psst," a tiny voice said.

I looked around, snapping out of my tear-filled daze long enough to find the source of the voice. It came from the snowy ground, near a bush.

A skeleton rat with black, glossy eyes.

It sat on its skeletal hind legs, and it was motioning to me.

"You," it said in its meensy rat voice. "You are the queen's girl. The princess. I can help you. I know secrets."

"I'm no princess," I said, miserably wiping my nose. "My grandfather is dead, and it's all my fault because I didn't trust him. I . . . *killed him*. Not on purpose, but that doesn't matter, because I thought he was a bad person, so I might have done it anyway?" And that was a hard truth to admit, even to a rat. I sobbed. "I didn't even know his real name when I was with him!"

"Sure you did. That was his army medic nickname in Vietnam."

"It was?"

He nodded. "Grumbones is my friend. And just because he's harrowed doesn't mean he's gone. But if you don't want to end up like him, you need to move before *she* spots us."

I glanced back at the Nightmare. It was hard to look at Grumbones's harrowed body. A little sob rose up in me and choked its way out of my mouth. I didn't even know that "Grumbones" was his army nickname. How much had Babi kept from me?

But it wasn't her fault I was in this situation. Worst decision ever to use Fizzle's dumb summoning book. Look what it had gotten me! A grandfather dead—*deader?*—by my own hand. A poisoned best friend who might or might not be alive. I didn't even know if he'd made it out of the underworld.

Now there was an empty space where my heart had once been, and it ached so badly.

I couldn't stop crying. The Nightmare was definitely going to hear me.

"There, there, Princess," the skeleton rat said. "It'll be all right. My name's Donk, by the way. Follow me. I can get you into the castle."

It was probably a terrible idea to follow a talking rat skeleton, especially one named Donk, but I was already making awful decisions that day.

I had nothing to lose.

So when he scampered through the snow toward the back of the castle, I strung my grandfather's dog tags around my neck alongside the Grim Hound whistle and trudged across the lawn after my new companion.

Donk ran pretty fast. Maybe having no internal organs helped to not weigh you down. But I caught up to him when he waited beneath a gargoyle dragon with a long tongue.

I really didn't like gargoyles.

This one, however, hung off the edge of the castle and pointed toward a simple wooden door that was lit by one lantern.

"Oh no!" the rat said.

"What?" I turned around to see the Nightmare coming through the gate.

Not good.

"She's never gotten past the moat. Maybe she'll give up the chase once we're inside," Donk said, talking more to himself than me. "The gate's not usually open. No one's ever carried the Death-bell inside here either."

"I didn't mean to kill him." Here came the tears again. Don't judge me.

"Please don't cry," Donk said, the bones of his little rat skull turning downward into a frown-like shape. "Milady? I know you're upset, but we're in danger. I normally get inside through a hole because I can't reach the handle. . . . A little help? Pull yourself together until we're inside, away from her. Crying is for when you're safe, and we ain't that."

It was tough being shamed by a rat, so I wiped my nose on my storm jacket and looked around. "What is this, anyway? Where does it lead?"

"Cellar door," he said.

That sounded okay. Better than being out here in the cold with the Nightmare. So I opened it and stepped inside, Donk racing between my boots, then closed it behind us to shut out the snow.

It was a cellar, all right. Dark and dank, full of wine barrels. Water puddled on the uneven dirt floor. A couple of lit torches were set into iron holders on the wall, so if I squinted, I could pick my way around wooden shelving to the dim stairwell.

A tremor shook the floor and rattled all the shelves. Just for a few seconds.

Earthquake? Did they have those in the underworld?

"What was that?" I whispered.

Donk shook his head. "No idea, milady. Has never happened before. I think we should keep moving."

"You know your way around the castle?" I asked the rat.

"Indeed I do."

"Can you help me get to my Babi? And maybe tell me where this demon named Wyrm is, so I can avoid him?"

Donk hopped up the stairwell. "That will prove difficult, milady. He is tricky."

"Guess we'll have to be trickier."

We climbed in silence, but he was slow on the steps, and I didn't know if the Nightmare could get into the castle, so I offered to carry him. His little bony feet felt strange in my hand, and his beady black eyes peered up at me.

"I didn't mean to do it," I told Donk. "I mean, I *sort* of did. But I thought he was bad."

"Who?"

"Grumbones. I thought he was trying to kidnap me. When he was, uh, alive, back in the land of the living? He died before I was born. I didn't know who he was."

The rat nodded. "Wouldn't worry too much. He won't hold it against you. I've known the ol' captain for years. I slept under his berth on the ship when he left Vietnam and was with him when it sank. Anger-wise, he gets hot fast but cools fast too. He doesn't hold a grudge. It's one of his best qualities."

I remembered something Grumbones had told us: *Rats are some of my best companions.*

"Besides," Donk said, "this is only a slight variation on his original plan. He knew a soul had to be sacrificed to open the gate to the castle and get you inside. I think he was hoping to draw out one of the demon guards and battle them, mano a mano. You know, fair fight? If he got killed, at least he could make his way back eventually."

That's right. . . . Ike had told us that when the townspeople got "killed" here, their souls just moved to another part of the underworld. But we didn't know what happened to the harrowed souls.

Torture? True death? Maybe some kind of horrible demon plane. Who knew where I had sent my grandfather's soul when I'd called the Nightmare to come take him.

"Why couldn't my grandfather have just told me who he was?" I said, anguished.

Donk's tiny face turned to look up at mine. "You don't understand how crafty Wyrm is. He's been chasing the captain since we got down here. We've hopped from kingdom to kingdom, in hiding. The captain got killed once already, and it took me ten years to find him."

"Ten years?"

Donk nodded. "When we finally got back to Hereafter, he found a magic woman in the Boondocks who gave him a book that helped him change his appearance and conceal his identity. A cloak-and-dagger spell that hid him *real* good. But in order to keep hidden, he had to constantly drink a nasty potion."

The flask that smelled like cherry cough syrup!

"But couldn't he have told *me* who he was, at least?"

"Names have power down here. If he told anyone his secret, the spell would have broken, and Wyrm could have tracked him. I was the only one who remembered who he really was because I was there when the spell was cast. Well, me and your grandmother, back when she was still Above."

"You heard them talking?"

"All the time, until she ended up down here again. Then she got trapped in the castle."

Right.

"Trust me," Donk said. "I know he *wanted* to tell you who he was. He was so nervous to meet you. Nervous and excited.

Told me he ate his weight in noodle soup, he was so wound up."

I touched the jacket pocket where I'd stashed the Deathbell. It made my heart hurt.

"Through this door, quick," Donk told me. "I think I hear the Nightmare coming."

We entered an empty medieval kitchen—one that was warm and inviting, with a fire burning and some kind of stew bubbling in a black pot over it. I ducked under braids of garlic bulbs that hung from the low rafters.

Another tremor shook the walls and all the tin plates. I held on to a butcher block table for balance. Then it was over. "Really don't like that," Donk mumbled. "Turn left here."

We were in some part of the castle that was built for the servants, and the kitchen connected to other rooms. I followed the rat's guidance as we made our way through some dark stone passageways, listening for the Nightmare's telltale electrical crackling. Maybe she wasn't following.

I *really* hoped she didn't use her teleporting ability.

"Here!" Donk said. "Go through there. Quick!"

I opened a set of double doors.

We stepped into a long, strange room. It was a dining hall that stretched up two stories. In the center was a heavy table piled with candelabras and platters of food: pork and baked apples, fancy cakes that teetered ten tiers high. It smelled delicious. The table was so long, I couldn't see where it stopped.

Endless table. Endless dining room. Candles cast shimmering light onto the walls. There were no windows, and it felt like nighttime. No people here either. The entire castle felt deserted.

And extremely unsafe. At least the tremors had stopped.

"What is this?" I whispered to Donk as he asked to be set on the floor, where he scurried along behind chairs encased in dark red velvet. Were there a hundred chairs lining this table? More? How far did it go? How many people lived here besides my Babi?

"The dining hall. We must hurry. And do not eat the food," he warned. "I made that mistake my first day here. If you want to keep your skin, stay away from the cooked cabbage."

Didn't have to tell me twice. There was cake on this table. Who would go for the cooked cabbage? "My dad makes pizza," I told him as I jogged down the hall.

"The diver."

"You know about him?"

"Lots of time to shoot the breeze in the afterlife."

I glanced behind us. This didn't feel right. Hereafter was in ruins and suddenly there was a rich feast before us? Who had cooked this? Was it magical food?

"How long does this table go on?" I asked.

"Wyrm built this with magic. It's supposed to be a trap," the rat said. "It's the endless dining hall. You walk until you get hungry. Then you eat the food. Then the room ends, and you think, great! But you'd be wrong, because you ate the food and lost all your skin, and now you're stuck roaming the castle grounds for all eternity as a skeleton."

I grimaced. What a terrible trap. "Okay, no. There must be another way. Think, Donk."

"Hold on—I can eat the food to make the room end. Duh," he said. "I'm already stuck. The cabbage is just past those cakes. . . ."

Why he liked cabbage so much, I didn't know. But another tremor shook the castle and all the chandeliers clinked. Guess I spoke too soon.

But there was something even more concerning.

When I looked behind us, I spotted the crackling blue mist of the Nightmare. Her wind field was blowing chairs around and knocking plates off the table. And that wasn't all: a strange shadow slithered on the opposite wall across the table. For a moment, I thought it belonged to the Nightmare, but no. She was slow-moving tendrils. This shadow was like a fat snake.

And it stopped when I watched it, as if it saw me looking at it.

Shadows don't do that.

Shadows don't blink, either.

Panicking, I grabbed something off the table to protect myself. A butter knife. Great. Was there nothing sharper here? I threw it to the floor and whispered, "Eat the cabbage, Donk. Eat it *now!*"

Jumping onto a silver platter, the rat nibbled a pile of cooked vegetables, and what do you know? Donk was right. Just ahead, the end of the dining hall appeared in the darkness: a grand, curving staircase that led to a second story.

"Go!" I said, making a dash for the stairs.

He scampered across the platters of food, knocking down goblets of wine and scattering chocolate-dipped rose petals. At the end of the table, he leapt onto my shoulder, and we raced to get away from the Nightmare and the snakelike shadow.

CHAPTER 20

Throne Room

p the curving staircase we went. An iron chandelier fell past the railing, and I screamed as it nearly hit Donk and exploded on the floor below. But things only got worse on the second floor.

A tiny waterfall was trickling down the steps from above. It was as if someone had left the water running in a bathroom and the tub had overflowed. When I crested the top step, water splashed over the toes of my boots. The entire second floor was wet.

Maybe the tremors had caused a leak somewhere.

"What's going on up here?" Donk said in a frightened voice.

"It's not normally like this?" I whispered.

"Describe normal," he quipped. "Wyrm is always changing things. Every time I find a way up here, he moves the traps around. Once I got lost in a maze for a month. The captain was about to travel to the cat world to look for me."

We sloshed across an enormous open room with no roof, the night sky above us. Moonlight provided enough illumination for me to walk, but not enough for me to make out what was at the end of the room . . . which tightened my stomach.

"Keep going," Donk encouraged in a whisper. "We're close."

"What is this place?" The floor was tilting upward, and it reminded me of being in a stadium or a movie theater, where you had to climb to get to your assigned seat. We also had to weave around columns that held up nothing.

"Throne room," Donk said. "It used to have a ceiling. And furniture. Last time I was in here, there were steps about halfway up this ramp. Throne is at the top."

"Is my Babi here?"

"Should be, yes," Donk said, sounding worried. "But we need to be vigilant here. . . ."

I didn't let my guard down, nervously flicking my gaze around the vast chamber as my eyesight adjusted to the moonlight. We passed tattered banners hanging on the columns—banners with the heraldic wolf crest that we'd seen in the Flooded District. Snowflakes fell, and the farther we climbed, the less water there was on the floor. It still ran down past my boots, but now it was just a trickle on the bottom of my soles.

When we were about halfway across the room, I could make out some unlit torches on the columns. And stairs leading to a big stone platform. And on that platform, dark shapes.

I slowed my pace, wary.

If I squinted, I could see all the way to the back of the throne room. At first I thought there was a crowd of people standing on the platform in the dark, but after a few blinks, I realized they were just husks. Hundreds of them lined up in neat little rows like soldiers. Silent statues.

A silent army.

In front of that army sat an empty throne.

To the right of the throne was a single husk.

To the left of the throne was a small iron cage. And inside the cage, a female figure huddled in the corner. She stood up and pressed her face against the bars of the cage.

"Helena?" she called out.

"Babi!" I shouted, racing up the stairs and across the platform.

"Is that really you?" the woman in the cage asked, sounding unsure.

I stopped in front of the bars. I was unsure too.

A face that was both familiar and strange stared back at me. Same silver bobbed hair. Same cunning eyes. Even the same nightgown she'd been wearing the night she died, which was both comforting and upsetting, honestly.

Yet gone was the bright red lipstick and the sly smile. She was weak and tired. Frail.

Was it my grandmother? Not a trap or an illusion?

I'm ashamed to say I was filled with fear and uncertainty.

She was supposed to be a fiery dragon. Strong. Tough. It made me feel small and helpless to see her like this. After everything I had gone through to get here, I desperately wanted it to be her, but part of me wished it weren't.

"Babi?" I whispered, afraid to touch her.

She blinked at me a few times, then looked at my hand. "Donk," she said, cutting her eyes at him sharply, "if that white demon is making me see things that aren't here, you'd better tell me now. Because this is the last straw—you hear me? Wait until I get out of this cage! I will tear him new eyeholes."

Now, *that* was the Babi I knew. Stubborn and bossy, didn't take crap from anyone. She might have looked frail on the outside, but her mind was just fine.

I sucked in a ragged breath as tears flooded my eyes and spilled down my cheeks. It was more than I could have ever hoped for, her standing in front of me after the last year of absence. As if she'd been on the longest trip ever, not dead. How could she be dead when she was standing in front of me?

"Babi," I choked out between sobs, "it's really me!"

"She's not lying, your highness," Donk told her. "She and her friend Ben traveled all the way from Above to find you."

She squinted at me, suspicious. Looking me over as if I were fake. A copy.

"Together before, together again," I said, leaning against the cage bars as I tried to reach for her with my fingers.

Yet still she didn't believe me. "The demon is crafty. I've been fooled before. . . ."

Frustrated by her stubbornness, I wiped away tears and fumbled inside my jacket. "Here," I said, shoving the proof I had through the narrow space between the bars, the photograph of us. "I put this on your grave, but someone stole it. Fizzle opened a portal in Whispering Pines Cemetery, and Ben and I rode on Ludo's boat, but Miss Neja had to take Ben back up because he got bit by a sewer meek. I know you're probably not happy that I brought him here, due to what we argued about the last time we talked."

Her mouth made a little round shape as she gasped, and then her eyes softened. "My sweet Helenka," she whispered.

I clutched her fingertips through the cage. "I've missed you so much."

"I've missed you, my sweeting. We must be quick, though. Did you run into—" She hesitated. "Anyone you know? And were you captured?"

My fingers trembled around hers. The empty space where my heart had been ached and ached. I couldn't tell her about Grumbones. I just couldn't. My eyes welled with fresh tears. "I—I wasn't captured," I told her. "I came to get you out of here."

"FAMILY REUNIONS ARE SO TOUCHING," a voice said, otherworldly and strange. One that made my skin crawl and all the hope inside me sink to the bottom of my feet. I once thought it was Fizzle's voice, but now I knew better. Especially because of the way Donk ran up my sleeve and tried to hide in my collar.

Wyrm.

Where was he? I couldn't see a body. Only the reflected ripple in the chitinous husks where he slid around the silent statues on the floor. He was circling the outskirts of the platform, making his way toward the cage.

"Stay away from us, demon," I warned.

"NOW, NOW. LET US NOT RESORT TO NAME-CALLING. YOU MAY CALL ME WYRM OR GRAND ADMIRAL. I WOULD LIKE US TO BE PARTNERS, HELENA. DID I NOT TELL YOU BACK IN THE CEMETERY THAT YOU COULD COME TO THE UNDERWORLD AND SPEAK TO YOUR GRANDMOTHER? PROMISE MADE, PROMISE KEPT."

"She's in a cage!"

"*I SAID SPEAK TO HER, NOT HUG HER. DETAILS ARE IMPORTANT.*"

"If you touch my granddaughter, I'll make it so you never existed," Babi warned him.

"*BIG TALK, MORANA. IF YOU CAN DO THAT WITHOUT THE CROWN OF RIME, THEN BY ALL MEANS, PLEASE GO AHEAD. I AM WAITING.*"

The air near the throne shuddered, and a pale fog appeared. It swirled and became dense, until it formed a cloud-like shape: a skeleton man dressed in an old-fashioned military uniform from the eighteenth century, with a three-sided hat, tall boots, and a sash, looking a bit like one of the Three Musketeers.

He lounged on the throne, grinning beneath the brim of his tricorne. He wasn't real. He was made of white clouds. Smoke. An illusion with no actual body.

And yet, my skin grew clammy with fear. I didn't know what he could do to me. How much power he had.

But looking at him now, I did spot one detail in the room that I hadn't noticed before.

A silver crown hung from a pointy tip at the top of the throne.

The Crown of Rime. That was it? What this entire mess was all about? A dumb old headpiece that wasn't even that pretty. Not even gold. No jewels. Sort of tarnished, too.

"*I SEE YOU EYEING MY CROWN, HELENA.*"

"*My* crown," Babi said, pointing a finger at her chest. "I don't see you wearing it, tough guy. If you could, then you wouldn't have me locked in this rattrap. No offense, Donk."

"None taken, Your Highness," Donk said.

"*YOUR GRANDMOTHER HAS NO POWER WITHOUT IT. THIS*

IS WHAT HAPPENS WHEN YOU TAKE CHEAP ADVICE FROM THE CHAPEL SOOTHSAYER. YOU ARE CAVORTING WITH THE WRONG SIDE, LITTLE GIRL. SO HERE'S MY NEXT PROPOSAL. TALK TO YOUR GRANDMOTHER. CONVINCE HER TO TELL ME THE SECRET OF HOW I CAN WEAR THE CROWN, AND I PROMISE THAT I WILL LET THE SAD, OLD WOMAN OUT OF THE CAGE."

"She doesn't look sad," I told him. "She looks angry."

"'Angry' doesn't begin to describe what I'm feeling toward this piece of filth," she mumbled.

"*EH, POTATO, PO-TAH-TO,*" Wyrm said with a shrug of his misty skeleton form. "*YOU SEE BRIMFIRE, I SEE AN OPPORTUNITY FOR S'MORES. TALK TO YOUR GRANDMOTHER AND LET US MAKE A DEAL, YES?*"

Ugh. He was more irritating than Grumbones. I mean . . . my grandfather. Best not to think about that now. I needed to focus on getting Babi out of that cage, but how?

Obviously we couldn't let Wyrm possess the secret of the crown—whatever that was. The crown held some serious power, and clearly he was already maxed out. Nope.

I needed to get the crown to Babi. But even if I could run past the demon and snatch the crown from where it hung on the throne—unlikely—the crown itself was too big to slip through the bars of the cage. I could already see that from where I stood.

"Trust me, I've been trying that for months," Babi whispered. "Never going to happen. You've gotta get me *O-U-T*."

Right, okay. Cages have locks. All of them. Even demon cages. And, yep, there was a keyhole. Problem was, I didn't know where the key was.

"It's not in this room," Donk said from my shoulder. "He's hiding it somewhere."

"Where?" I whispered. "I can't traipse around the city looking for a key."

"Those stinkin' wards. Rats!" Babi complained. "Again, no offense, Donk."

"None taken, Your Highness," he said again. "Though might I suggest that you demean birds and not rats? Since when have I ever caused you trouble, ma'am?"

"Good point indeed, Donk," she said. "If we get out of this, I'm promoting you to senior court advisor."

If we got out of this.

Think, think! Glancing around in a panic, my eyes lit on the husk of the man that stood next to Wyrm's throne. I knew that husk. It was the first one I'd seen, back in the abandoned house. The demon saw me looking at the husk's feathered hat.

Wyrm's impish smile widened.

"THIS IS SIR KRAK, MY MOST TRUSTED MINION AFTER SIX HUNDRED YEARS. HE WAS QUEEN MORANA'S LAST COURT ADVISOR, A KNIGHT WHO TRICKED HER INTO FISHING FOR ME IN THE CANAL. HE WOULD ALSO THROW YOU OFF A CLIFF IN A HEARTBEAT, BECAUSE HE IS POWER HUNGRY. THAT MAKES FOR GOOD MINION MATERIAL. I WOULD INTRODUCE YOU, BUT YOUR GRANDFATHER HAD HIM HARROWED. MURDER RUNS IN THE FAMILY, THOUGH, DOES IT NOT?"

I knew what he meant. He was talking about me. He knew what I'd done to Grumbones. And even though it was coming from an evil demon, it still made me feel as if I'd been punched in the stomach. I also worried that he was going to tell Babi outright what I'd done. Shame and worry collided inside me.

Wyrm just chuckled darkly and slung a misty arm over Sir Krak's husked shoulder.

But he wasn't our only problem.

Down below the platform, the Nightmare glided across the throne room. She was still a distance away and floating slowly over the water, but it made me feel sick. I could run from a harrowing; in the cage, Babi could not.

"*SPEAK OF THE DEVIL . . . THERE SHE IS NOW. MY BELOVED NIGHTMARE. WHICH SOUL SHOULD SHE TAKE FOR MY ARMY, THE OLD OR THE YOUNG SOUL? PROBABLY THE YOUNG ONE. UNLESS THE QUEEN HAS SOMETHING THAT SHE WANTS TO TELL ME . . . ?*"

"Don't tell him, Babi," I said, struggling to find the Deathbell in my pocket. "I have a plan."

Miss Neja had said the Deathbell was a weapon, right? It could summon the Nightmare. Could I control the servitor with it? Maybe get it to take the demon's soul? If he even had one.

"*YOU HOLLOWED OUT YOUR GRANDFATHER. NO ONE ELSE NEEDS TO DIE, LITTLE ASSASSIN.*"

His words twisted painfully inside my chest like a rusty dagger. He wasn't wrong. I knew what I'd done. I just didn't want my grandmother to find out.

I squeezed my eyes shut briefly, as if I could hold it back.

But there was no stopping it now.

"What's that snake talking about, Helena?" Babi asked.

I looked up at her with shame, fresh tears welling in my eyes. "Not now. Please."

"Tell me," she demanded firmly, but I could see the fear in the lines of her face. And that made it so much worse.

"Oh, Babi," I cried. "I didn't know it was him. He was using magic to disguise his identity."

Her eyes slid to Wyrm, who coolly smiled at her. "I DIDN'T NEED TO FIND HIM AFTER ALL. YOUR LITTLE ANGEL DID THE DIRTY WORK FOR ME. SO THOUGHTFUL!"

"I thought he was trying to trick me," I argued. "But he was hiding from the demon to get me here to you."

"No," she whispered. "That can't be right. No! He's gone?"

"I'm so sorry. I didn't know who he was." With trembling fingers, I pulled out the dog tags that hung underneath my shirt and showed her.

She stared at the dog tags, recognition and then shock in her eyes. Then her forehead dropped against the bars. "Adam. My Adam. Hundreds of years, I searched for you. . . ."

"Oh, Babi, I'm so sorry," I cried.

"YOU ARE DEFEATED, MORANA. GIVE ME THE SECRET OF THE CROWN."

Babi clung to the bars of the cage and turned her tear-stained face toward the throne. She didn't look defiant anymore. She looked broken. As though she were considering giving in to Wyrm's wishes.

"No, Your Majesty!" Donk whispered, racing down my arm to leap through the bars. But she didn't pay any attention to his tiny rat pleas.

This was all my fault. I had to fix this. Had to!

I grabbed the trigger of the Deathbell as the Nightmare floated up the platform's steps. And even though it made my stomach sick,

I knew I had to use it again, this time to save us. I pointed the bell toward Wyrm, and I rang it.

The Nightmare wavered. Then she sped faster toward me.

Wyrm laughed. "LITTLE ASSASSIN, YOU AMUSE ME. BUT YOU JUST HASTENED YOUR DEATH. MORANA, TELL ME THE SECRET OF THE CROWN NOW, OR YOUR GRANDDAUGHTER WILL BE HARROWED."

"Don't you touch my granddaughter!" Babi said.

"LAST CHANCE TO STOP THIS OR YOU WILL BE ALONE FOR ALL ETERNITY. . . ."

Panic fired through me. Anger, too. I loathed this demon and his horrible creature. My Babi was locked up, and I couldn't think about Grumbones or Ben or I'd fall apart.

But as the Nightmare came toward me, they were *all* I could think about. How sick Ben had looked in the Phantom Carriage before I had jumped out. Grumbones's face before he'd been harrowed. My fingers reached for the dog tags and closed around the smooth, rectangular metal.

For protection, Grumbones had said about them.

But my brain was making connections, and as I held on to the dog tags, all I could think about was Ben's story about the mystery lady in Forlorn who had pulled off her beaded steel necklace and used it as a weapon against a mugger. . . .

And then there was what Grumbones had told us:

Silver don't kill nothin' here. What you want is steel to put down any demonic creatures.

What were old dog tags made from? Had to be stainless steel, right? I wasn't positive, and I had no idea if it would work against the Nightmare. But I had no other option.

That wasn't exactly true. I could have given up. It would have been easier. After all, I was basically just a kid trying to battle a monster on my own. Just like with the three kids in the Beacon Corner Shop back home, it wasn't a fair fight, and this time I couldn't run away.

But when I thought of Ben's poison-weary eyes staring back at me, I didn't want to run away. I wanted to fight so that I had a chance to see him again.

It wasn't a fair fight, but I wasn't alone. People needed me, and I needed them. I had to try!

Hands shaking, I wound the dog tags' chain around two fingers to make sure I had a good grip. *Is this right?* I didn't know. I was so scared and felt so unsure.

Energy crackled. Blue light filled my vision.

"IT IS TIME, MY ANNOYING QUEEN," Wyrm said to Babi, sounding irritated. "IF YOU DO NOT TELL ME THE CROWN'S SECRET, THEN YOUR GRANDDAUGHTER'S SOUL WILL BE SENT TO THE DEMON PLANE, ALONG WITH THE OTHERS. AND WHEN I FINALLY RULE HEREAFTER, SHE WILL RETURN AS MY LOYAL SERVANT, BOUND TO DO MY BIDDING."

Aha! Some truth from him. That's where all the harrowed souls were. Which meant my grandfather was still alive? In a demon plane, which totally sucked. But alive!

That tiny bit of news boosted my hope and gave me some fortitude.

"TELL ME NOW, QUEEN," Wyrm prodded.

"Don't tell him, Your Majesty!" Donk cried. "It's a trap!"

"Helena!" Babi called out.

The Nightmare floated in front of the cage and opened her

arms to me. The horrid black mouth gaped. Tendrils of hair moved as if they were alive. Blue mist enveloped me.

A painful tug wrenched inside my chest. She was devouring my soul. I'd seen it happen in Merry Dead Plaza . . . and to Grumbones. I just hadn't understood until now what it actually meant. Why it was so inescapable.

A couple of years ago, my father had decided he would install electricity in Babi's flower workshop that sits in our backyard—with my help. Only he isn't an electrician, and I wasn't a good helper. I touched the wrong wire at the wrong time, and the electrical current that went through my body was so painful, all my muscles tightened up. I couldn't move.

That's how I felt as the Nightmare took my soul.

Pain pierced every part of my body. I tried to jerk away, but it was too much torment. I couldn't understand how Grumbones had found the strength to even speak through this. Maybe I was weaker than he was, because I wanted to give in and let her take all of me. To make this pain stop. At least I'd get to see my grandfather again in the demon plane. . . .

Babi was shouting something behind me. A phrase I didn't understand. Another language? Magic?

Her words were like someone snapping their fingers to get a dog's attention . . . if the Nightmare were a dog. The creature turned her eyes away from me to glance at my grandmother.

When she did, the blue glow around me faded just a little. The pull in my chest still gripped me, but in that moment, it loosened slightly. Waves of relief and panic crashed over me in succession.

I could move again!

I didn't know for how long.

I had to act now.

I can do this, I can do this. . . .

Gripping the chain again, I pulled my arm back and lashed out, swinging the dog tags like a whip. The speed of it surprised me. Steel struck the Nightmare's chest. The blow wasn't strong enough to knock her backward. She stood, stalwart.

But the steel was a razor against her supernatural flesh, slicing her chest open.

Blinding blue light shone out.

The painful tug inside my own chest stuttered, faded, and then . . . stopped. My knees buckled a little with weakness, but *sweet, beautiful relief!* The pain was gone! But were we safe?!

The Nightmare's horrifying tendrils sagged. That was promising. But—

Her head lifted.

She was still alive.

I nearly cried out in agony. That had been my only shot! She was injured, sure, but I didn't know for how long, and, and . . . What else could I try? I had to run now, and running wasn't an option.

"STOP THAT!" Wyrm bellowed. His smoky form leapt from the throne and furiously smogged its way toward his wounded creature. And me.

Fear shot through me as I scrambled to back away from what I'd done. But as I did, the glint of the necklace around the Nightmare's neck caught my eye.

A talisman that kept the golem-like creature alive? No. It was a key.

A *key.*

Everything inside my head cleared like a chalkboard being

erased. New plan! Racing Wyrm, I doubled back to the Nightmare, two quick steps, and reached out to grab her necklace. As hard as I could, I snatched it.

But the chain didn't break.

In a shower of sparks, her entire head came away with the chain and tumbled to the floor.

Her body remained standing. Still. A silent husk.

Horrified, I stared at the head on the floor. There was no blood. She wasn't real. She was a construction. A doll, made of magic and light.

And from the back of the room, a terrible cracking sound reverberated.

All the husks began falling apart. Sir Krak. The others. They shattered and crumbled into piles of broken bits.

"*NO! WHAT HAVE YOU DONE?*" Wyrm floated to the servitor's head. Anguished. Furious.

I worried about the husks—did that mean Grumbones couldn't come back from the demon plane? Had I just done more harm than good?

Something tickled my leg, but before I could startle, I realized Donk was climbing me like a tree. When he leapt to my shoulder, he whispered into my ear, "You got the key to the cage!"

Oh! Yes! I'd almost forgotten. I hoped he was right. While Wyrm was distracted with grief, I swiveled around and quickly stuck the key into the lock. One turn was all it took. The lock opened.

All I wanted to do was hug her. But I knew we weren't out of danger yet. I raced to the throne, jumped up onto the seat, and grabbed the crown. It was kind of heavy. I met my grandmother halfway between the cage and the throne, and just as Wyrm rose from his broken Nightmare, Babi put the crown on her head.

A pearlescent light streaked down her body, causing her skin to glow softly on her cheeks and under her fingernails. One moment she was an old lady in a nightgown. The next, she was a magnificent dark queen in a swirling gown of silver mist and a mesh of flowing chain mail. Pinpoints of starlight glittered behind her eyes. Snowflakes frosted her lashes.

And the jagged silver crown? It looked as if it had always been there. A part of her.

"The crown's secret," she said with a smile, "was that I had to give it up willingly. Rules of the underworld are simple. You just can't break them."

Eesh. So true. I'd definitely learned that the hard way.

Wyrm must have too. He screamed as if his soul were being devoured.

But I wasn't listening. I was too busy gazing in awe at the magnificent woman standing in front of me.

Rime Queen. Underworld royalty.

Holy terror of Forlorn.

My grandma.

"Ahhh, finally. I have my powers again," she said in a rough voice, cracking her neck from side to side. She shook herself off. Her hair was wild. Her skin looked as if it were frosted over with ice crystals. But otherwise, she was the Babi I'd known when she was alive.

With a cool crown and a little extra glow-up.

"Babi?" I said. "Are you okay?"

She smiled at me. "Better than okay. I'm an immortal queen of the underworld. Let's kick this buffoon out of my kingdom."

"Watch out!" Donk said, scurrying near my feet. "He's trying to possess the Nightmare!"

Donk was right. A white mist was slithering into the headless Nightmare.

"Only one way to get rid of the demon. Fire," Babi whispered, looking around the water-filled room. She raised her hand toward a torch on the wall, and with a flick of her wrist, the torch caught fire magically. My Babi, Firestarter! If all the kids at school could only see her now, they wouldn't call her a mean old bat, would they?

But almost as soon as it ignited, the flame disappointingly went out.

"Has Wyrm cursed everything in my castle?" Babi complained, flicking her hand toward other torches. One by one, they lit up, then snuffed out.

Maybe they were just Wyrm's illusions, like the endless table downstairs.

"I WILL NEVER GIVE UP, MORANA." The demon had formed a smoky skeleton head on the Nightmare's body and was using it to talk. If he possessed the creature long enough, could he make it move again? I didn't want to find out. If fire was the way to get rid of him, we needed it—and STAT.

"Can you just conjure up a fireball?" I asked Babi.

She gave me a pointed dark look that confused me for a second, and then I remembered where I'd seen it before—when I'd asked her last year if she'd backed into our neighbor Mrs. Whitehouse's car but I hadn't realized Mrs. Whitehouse could overhear our conversation from the driveway.

Babi didn't want me to ask that question in front of Wyrm. Which meant . . . she didn't want him to know the answer. So she couldn't conjure a fireball. She needed something to ignite.

Hold on. I could help with that!

Quickly I dug around in my storm jacket pocket and took out the paper tube of fireplace matches. It was smooshed and the cardboard was a touch damp, but the lone, last match remained inside.

A slow grin lifted Babi's face. "Hold that steady, will ya?"

"*YOU CANNOT BURN ME. WHAT DO YOU HAVE THERE? NOW, LITTLE ASSASSIN, BEFORE YOU DO ANYTHING RASH—*"

If we didn't do anything rash, I was going to die of a panic attack. While Babi flicked her wrist, I stuck the long match against the wound in the middle of the Nightmare's open chest.

It caught fire. And I do mean *fast*.

Donk squealed and jumped up my arm to the safety of my shoulder.

The creature's husk was aflame. Its chitinous skin crackled and popped as it burned. Flames spread to the husk pile that had once been Sir Krak, and then farther back, to the other fallen husks. Soon the entire back of the throne room was one massive blaze.

"Yes!" Babi cried happily. "Purge the demon from my kingdom."

Was it working? I wasn't sure if it was smoke from the fire or Wyrm's head changing, but I could no longer see his face on the Nightmare's body.

I just wished I could see some proof that he was truly gone. I wanted to collapse, but I couldn't let down my guard until I knew for sure.

Plumes of smoke rose into the sky, blocking out the moonlight. I coughed, eyes burning. Donk was saying something in my ear, but I couldn't quite catch it. And another tremor shook the walls, which only made the situation worse.

Then, out of the corner of my eye, I spotted a white form slithering behind the flames.

Wyrm was still here.

"Babi! He's not dead. I see him over there!"

And the demon was escaping.

From somewhere behind me, Babi called out, "Wyrm, show yourself!"

The white creature rose from the flames, and Wyrm coalesced into his misty human form, mumbling some kind of quick-and-dirty magic spell. He raised a hand above his head, and a big black bird glided down from the sky.

A vulture.

That could only mean one thing: Fizzle. Doorway. Portal.

Escape.

"No, Fizzle!" Babi raised her hand, and an icy white light shot toward the bird.

It was too late. Extraordinarily fast, Wyrm slipped inside Fizzle and became the vulture-headed doorkeeper with no eyes, quickly sidestepping Babi's beam of light. He opened a door that didn't exist on the back wall of the platform, slipped through it, and disappeared.

He was gone, along with the door.

My grandmother shouted several profanities. Queen or not, I guess she hadn't changed much. That gave me some comfort, despite the dire situation.

But I felt some of her sharp disappointment. "After all this, we lost?"

Babi turned to look at me, and her face softened. "After all this, my kingdom is free."

And *she* was too. That was the most important thing.

Before I could ask what we should do next, the room shook again. And this time, it didn't stop shaking. This was no tremor.

It was an earthquake.

CHAPTER 21
Lake of Sighs

Snow turned to rain, and lightning lit up the sky.

"To me, Helenka!" Babi yelled, one hand on the wall. "It's flooding."

I didn't understand how that could be possible. Was the water rising from the lower part of the throne room? The stairs were now submerged, and water was spilling onto the platform. The water had just been an inch on the floor below, maybe less. The rain wouldn't flood the room like this. How was it rising so fast?

"Babi!" I shouted over a hard gust of wind that blew in from the sky above us. "How are we going to get out? Is there another exit up here? The dining hall is blocked."

Wine casks and cakes floated into the room from the lower levels of the castle.

"It's okay. Do not worry. It will all be okay now," Babi assured me.

How could she say that? We were trapped.

A wave of water flooded across the throne platform, and suddenly I lost my footing. Donk clung to my jacket and shouted as I waded, pushing off from the floor. The floodwater rose impossibly fast. It smelled sharply of wine.

"Steady now. I will make a bubble around us, and we will swim out," Babi told me.

"Can you do that?"

"I believe so. I'm weak but getting stronger by the minute." Instead of flicking her wrist, she swirled her arm, and a silver light formed a bubble in the water around her. She reached for my hand, and I splashed over to her. As soon as I entered the bubble, I felt more buoyant. It was so easy to float with her. Weightless.

And it felt so good to hold her again. Like she was alive.

"That's it, Helenka," she said as we floated in the water together. "Hold on to me. That's my girl."

"Are we really safe now?" I asked her, my arm around her shoulder.

"We will be," she assured me. "There's no need to be frightened right now. We aren't going to drown. My bubble will protect us as we tread water."

That made me relax a little. But not much. "Where did Wyrm go?"

"Don't know. Back to his plane, perhaps. He has many nests in the underworld, too. If he's here, I will find him, don't worry. I have my crown back, and my powers will eventually be fully restored. He hasn't won, Helenka. You saved us," she said, swimming with one arm as the waters rose.

"How can you say that? Your castle is flooding. This is a disaster!"

"This is just one of Wyrm's tricks. And a weak one. He can't flood me out. Foolish demon. We will rebuild!"

Donk scurried to the top of my head. "Try to paddle faster, will ya? I don't like my feet getting wet."

A massive purple light exploded in the night sky, and it sounded as if fireworks were going off in the city. "What's that?" I asked, frightened as I watched the sky, which was getting closer as we bobbed along in the rising waters.

"Don't worry, keep treading water. That's all the city wards going down," Babi said with a delighted smile. "Finally. Now all my royal guards can get back inside the castle. Miss Neja, too! By the way, did you see Ike? Is Neja taking care of my Grim puppy?"

It was strange to hear her talking about them so casually. I knew them, and I knew her, but it was hard to wrap my head around knowing them all together. Worlds were colliding. "He's fine—" I was a little frustrated. "Babi, ugh, you could have told me about all this before you died."

She made a pouty face. "I told you about the underworld all your life, my sweeting."

"Not that you were queen! Not this! You told me myths and legends. Stories."

"There is truth in every story," she said mischievously with a little wink.

"But you don't understand," I said, frustrated again that she wasn't taking this seriously. "I've been trying to talk to you for a year. Your summons didn't work."

"Sure it did. I've been dreaming of you while I was in that cage." She gave me a soft smile. "I heard every word."

My heart squeezed painfully. "You did?"

"I did," she said gently. "Wyrm's magic prevented me from answering. I'm sorry."

Visions of our last fight when she was still alive filled my head. And it was like a year hadn't even passed. I was still angry, confused . . . and teeming with regret.

"Babi," I said, feeling very small and vulnerable, "do you remember the last time you saw me Above?"

She nodded. "It wasn't great, was it? Arguing was a terrible way to end things."

It was the very worst way to end things. I wasn't sure I could explain how that fight had haunted me all these months. It had sat in my brain, darkening every thought I had. It had nearly ruined my relationship with Ben.

"Babi, I need to tell you something. I came all the way here to tell you something," I said, feeling the horrible weight of it pressing into my heart. "I didn't even know you needed help when I started all this. I just came here to tell you this."

She moved a hand through the water and waited. "I'm listening."

Now that I was finally here, it was harder to say than I'd thought. But it was important, so I made the effort.

"I needed to tell you . . ."

"Yes?"

"I'm sorry."

She reached one hand over the water to cradle my cheek. "Oh, my darling. I'm sorry too. I'm so very sorry."

I didn't *want* to cry, but it was like trying to stop the rain: pointless. "I thought I couldn't talk to your ghost because you were mad at me. Because I disobeyed you. Because I couldn't stop being friends with Ben. He was my weakness."

"Your . . . ? Oh, no, my love, not at all." She shook her head.

"Do you want to know a secret? Sometimes grandmas can be wrong. Even ones who are queens," she admitted. "And when I told you to stop spending so much time with Ben, I was looking at you and seeing myself."

"I don't understand," I said.

"When I lost your grandfather, it was the worst pain."

I hung my head. Guilt and despair washed over me.

She lifted my chin with her fingers. "I didn't want you to lose someone and experience that pain. Because being mortal is difficult, see? You're always losing the ones you love. And I wanted to protect you from that hurt. . . . I just got it wrong."

"You did?" I said, blinking away falling tears.

She nodded. "All kinds of wrong. First of all, I'd completely forgotten that even if you lose someone Above, you find them down here."

"That's true," I said, wiping away one falling tear as I smiled a little.

"But mostly, I remembered this," she said. "The people we love aren't weaknesses. They are our strengths. After all, if I didn't have you and your parents and Adam in my life, I wouldn't know joy. I'd only know loneliness. And that's worse than being locked in a demon cage."

"Oh, Babi. I love you."

"I love you too. More than anything else. And I'm so sorry you've carried this guilt with you over our fight all this time. Don't cling to it for another second, my darling. Do you know how special you are to me?"

"You rule an underworld kingdom," I argued, brushing away another tear. "Compared to all the bizarre things in Hereafter, I'm not that special. You can flick your wrist and make fire, Babi."

She shook her head. "Do you not see? I left all this just to bring you into existence. You and your father are my most treasured and wondrous creations. No other beings in all the realms could be *more* special."

A warmth filled my chest. And for the first time in my life, I really did believe it.

She grabbed something that was floating on the surface of the water near my arm. The photo of us. Its edges were singed. "This is a terrible picture."

"Babi!"

"I like your drawings better. Keep bringing those to the grave."

"To the grave? But—"

"You need to go back home," she said as we kicked in the water and floated higher, almost to the top of the room where the walls ended. "You can't stay here, or you'll be stuck with me."

"What if I want to be stuck with you?"

"Ben needs you. And you need him. He is very special. So is Yemoja."

"Granny Booker?"

"I didn't come to Forlorn for no good reason, you know. They are a very old family."

"Wait, what?"

"The Bookers are special. Forlorn is special. They need you. And don't you have puppies to take care of? Taking care of animals is important. They depend on you. Don't let them down. You also need to be with your parents."

"What about Wyrm?" I said, filled with worry. "He's still loose."

"Stop this woe-is-me talk. We'll find him. And he'll regret the day he messed with my family—you'd better believe that."

I laughed a little, sniffling. "Okay, I believed that before, but I really do now."

"Besides, there are a lot of great things Above. Why do you think I wanted to travel up there in the first place? You have the Great Pyramid of Giza, bagel delivery, and all those pretty K-pop idols. It's nice. So go back home. But tell your father to stop making pizza. Your mother is right. Enough is enough."

How could she talk like this? About silly things? "Babi, I can't leave you. I need you. We're a team!"

"We'll always be a team, my brouček. And stubbornness runs in the family, so I won't say you'll never be able to visit here again. You might. But you see what happens when a demon turns up. My kingdom needs repairs after all the damage he caused. Doors will be closed. It may be a while before balance can be restored in Hereafter."

"How long? And how do I get back?"

"Have patience. Whatever you do, don't do it alone. No one does anything important alone. You'll have Miss Neja, and you'll have Ben."

She didn't know that. What if Ben wasn't okay?

And on top of that, it sounded like she was telling me goodbye, but I still needed to ask her so much. To *tell* her so much. About everything I'd done.

About my time with Grumbones. Would she ever find him again?

"Be at peace, my little beetle. You freed me from Wyrm's trap, and that's what's important. Go home. Rest. Be alert. And if you need help, know that we can communicate now, whenever you want to talk."

"Because you're a queen of the underworld?"

"Because I love you."

"Together before . . . ," I said.

"Together again," she finished.

A wave crashed and popped her magic bubble, breaking us apart.

"Ba—" I tried to shout, but I was pulled under the water.

I struggled to breathe, panicked. Broke the surface, gasping for air. I couldn't see. It was so dark, and the wind was howling. Water sprayed in my face. I couldn't stop coughing up wine-flavored water. I could see people swimming around me, but I couldn't make out Babi. Something floated past my shoulder—part of a wine cask. I grabbed it and clung to it like a raft. Made it easier to stay above the surface.

But I still couldn't find Babi. I couldn't see anything but the spires of the buildings and lightning. Trees. Water everywhere!

How could the entire city flood? Was it the Lake of Sighs?

The water was choppy and moving *way too* swiftly. Something clawed the back of my head: Donk, clinging on.

Debris rushed past. Tree limbs. Wine barrels.

I'm moving too fast, I thought as a fresh burst of fear shot through me. How could Babi send me into this mess? It was dangerous!

As I roughly drifted, picking up speed, I could only just make out the top of the bridge with the gargoyles. They were flying away, and the bridge itself . . . The water had risen so high that there wasn't room for me to float under it.

I was going to have to get underwater or I'd hit it.

I couldn't—

It was coming so fast.

Pain rocketed through my shoulder, and I went under.

Down.

I couldn't breathe again. My lungs filled up. Felt like they would explode.

Something was in the water. Something white. Moving.

Coming toward me.

I couldn't swim away. Couldn't scream.

A long serpentine shape curled around my body, and I tried to thrash my feet and push myself in another direction, but it was fruitless. In the dark water, I saw flashes of white scales. Fins. And monstrous appendages. It was every description of the Forlorn Worm come to life, and it was winding around me like an anaconda.

An apparition of Wyrm's skeleton face appeared in front of mine. In my bleary eyes, it looked as if he were smiling.

He spoke to me inside my head as his serpent body wrapped around mine. "*LITTLE ASSASSIN! FUNNY RUNNING INTO YOU HERE. HOW ABOUT WE STRIKE A BARGAIN? I NEED A NEW MINION, SEEING AS HOW MY LOYAL SIR KRAK HAS GONE AND GOTTEN HIMSELF HARROWED. YOU COULD BE HIS REPLACE-MENT.*"

I'd rather be locked in a demon cage. Instead I'd probably just drown to death here in the underworld. I guess the plus side was that I'd get to be with Babi.

But.

She was right. I had things to do Above.

I had people.

"*COME NOW. I CAN TELL THAT YOU ARE A LONER LIKE ME. TOGETHER WE CAN TAKE OVER ANOTHER KINGDOM. I*

CAN TEACH YOU SO MANY THINGS. WANT TO LEARN HOW TO MAKE YOUR ENEMIES FEAR YOU AND PEOPLE COWER AT YOUR VERY NAME?"

Already had that, too.

I wanted nothing from him except revenge for what he'd done to my Babi.

Feeling a fresh outpouring of anger and desperation, I struggled inside his coiled form and managed to get my hand into one of my storm jacket pockets. The only thing I had left was my Whispering Pines Cemetery pen. My favorite pen with the skeletons floating in blue liquid.

Clicking the pen's button, I pulled it out of my pocket and jammed it as hard as I could into the flesh of the sea serpent.

His scream inside my head was bright and sharp.

But he didn't release me.

"THAT HURT. NOW YOU'VE MADE ME MAD. THE DEAL IS OFF. HOW ABOUT INSTEAD I JUST KILL YOU HERE IN THE LIMINAL LANDS, WHERE YOUR LONELY SOUL WILL DROWN ETERNALLY—YOU KNOW, JUST AS ONE LAST INSULT TO THE QUEEN?"

Was that possible? I could be stuck here?

In a surge of panic, I flailed and thrashed inside his powerful grip. Kicking. Bashing with my head. He didn't let go. The squeezing only intensified. The pressure in my chest was unbearable. He was going to crush me!

But as I despaired, just *there* in my blurred vision, something new swam toward us in the water. Something dark and big. A creature worse than Wyrm? Or one of his companions . . .

Whatever the thing was, it had arms and legs. Humanoid,

from how it swam—and fast. And as it plunged toward us, I felt all of Wyrm's muscles shift. Terror seized me in that moment.

Dark water billowed around us, and in a rush, the approaching creature launched itself at Wyrm and attacked.

Pain rocketed down my ribs. But it was brief.

Quick as a whip, Wyrm's body loosened and unfurled from around me. His attacker had stolen all his attention.

As I floated backward, I watched them wrestle and grapple in the foam, two shapes angrily intertwined and wildly battling. The humanoid creature slammed its hand on Wyrm's head, and then—

An explosion of bright blue light! Blindingly bright. I lost them for a moment, unable to see or hear anything but a dull buzzing noise.

But when I recovered, I spotted them again. The humanoid creature, still swimming.

It had defeated Wyrm.

Who limply fell through the dark water.

Down, down . . .

Until I couldn't see him anymore.

If I hadn't been drowning, I'd have been ecstatic. But watching him go took all I had left inside me. A black tunnel began shrinking the edges of my vision, smaller and smaller, and I felt myself giving in to the water.

I was going to lose consciousness. My lungs were not going to make it much longer.

It was over.

But just as the light was going out, the humanoid creature who'd defeated Wyrm swam toward me. It quickly grabbed me with arms like two vises.

And it held me tightly. Firmly. Confidently.

It carried me and swam us both upward.

A body that felt like it was just muscle on bones. Long beard. Leather duster coat wrapping around my legs.

But then . . . he let me go.

Before I could tell him goodbye. Before I could thank him for saving my life. Before I could tell him that Babi had her powers back. Before I could tell him that he was the grandfather I'd always wanted.

Another hand clamped around my arm and pulled me upward, out of the water.

I stared into the face of a creature made of smooth black skin and bug eyes.

My father in his diving suit.

"Helena!" My mom cried behind him on our tugboat as tsunami warning sirens sounded in the distance. "Is she breathing? What is happening? Get her up, Adam. It's okay, baby. We got you. Everything's okay now."

CHAPTER 22

The Shadow

After my parents pulled me out of the Forlorn harbor, I was in the hospital for five days. Something was wrong with one of my lungs for a little while, from being underwater, and I then had a kind of chemical imbalance. All I know is that my parents talked about me in whispers when the doctors left, and that they didn't understand how I had gotten from the cemetery to the marina, where they'd been docking the tugboat after a tsunami had hit the coast. Most of Forlorn had been able to evacuate; they'd had an hour's notice. My parents didn't because they'd been out on the tugboat.

It was as if someone was looking out for me.

I'd like to think so, anyway.

My parents settled on a sensible theory to explain how I'd ended up in the water: because the cemetery had flooded in the tsunami, I had gotten swept away in the floodwater and had gone over the seawall. That's what they decided. My dad told my mom that he'd seen something in the water when he was diving and had had . . . a funny feeling. I even heard him say that he *thought* he'd spotted someone else in the water with me, but they had disappeared.

They still don't understand how I got my grandfather's dog tags. But now they're convinced that the wreckage of his ship from Vietnam was stirred up by the storm.

I'm a miracle, they say.

I'd never seen my dad cry that much before. Not even at Babi's funeral.

So I didn't have the heart to tell them that I had met—and harrowed—Grandpa.

And that Babi is a queen of the underworld.

Parents can only handle so much.

Ben was in the hospital in a different wing the first day I was there. That's what my mom told me after I ranted and raved about sewer meeks, and she discreetly told the doctor she was worried I'd suffered a brain injury. They wouldn't let Ben into my room because I was so sick, but I did finally find out that he was recovering nicely from an "unidentified bite" after the cemetery caretaker brought him in. Eventually my parents got me a new phone, so we could text again. A little. In our old Junior Coastal Rangers secret SOS code from back in the day when we had been earning our explorer's badges . . . just in case our parents were spying on us.

I was just relieved he was okay.

And relieved that there was no sign of any white worm.

A week after our trip to Hereafter, I was resting at home and feeling much better. Back to my old self, almost. When I trotted downstairs Saturday evening after a nap and smelled dinner—greeted by Big, Little, Tiny, and Ike the Third wagging their tails—I felt content. The foggy twilight view outside the big window in our living room reminded me of Hereafter, so I double-checked to make sure the streetlamp was modern.

All good. No gargoyles. No creepy birds.

Just the usual nighttime Grum rolling into Forlorn.

The house across the street had suffered some damage from the tsunami, and one of the big oaks next door had smashed our mean neighbor Mrs. Whitehouse's new car. But otherwise, things looked exactly the same as they had before I'd descended into the underworld and rescued my grandmother from a crafty demon.

"There she is, the wonder girl. Got color in your cheeks," Mom said as she smiled at me, padding into the dining room with a stack of plates and a piece of chipped pottery filled with cutlery. "Bet you're good enough to go back to school on Monday."

"Awoof, I don't know about that. My lung," I moaned, gripping my ribs dramatically.

Mom just rolled her eyes and set the table. "The Bookers should be here any minute for dinner. Dad could probably use some help carrying in pizza. He's got a production line set up in front of Hades in the backyard, if you want to check on him—now, where are the cloth napkins?" She hunted around on the shelves of the hutch behind our dining table. "I know I just washed, like, a dozen of them."

I opened the drawer below the shelf. "Napkins. In the napkin drawer. Who woulda thunk it?"

She slung an arm around my shoulder and kissed my head. "Have I told you lately how great you are?"

"Not since this morning."

"Really glad we were searching that wreck when that storm came up," she whispered, suddenly emotional as she touched the dog tags beneath my shirt. "You're the most valuable thing we've salvaged."

"More than . . . pirate's gold?" I whispered back.

"More than all the pirate's gold in the Pacific," she said with a soft smile.

Headlights flashed through our living room window as a silver SUV pulled up to the curb outside our house. The Bookers. Ben's long legs were the first out of the car. He strode up the front steps wearing his blue peacoat, carrying a covered cake pan in both hands. When I opened the door, his smile made my shoulders sag in relief.

"High."

"Low."

Standing on tiptoes, I reached up and hugged him over the cake pan. I didn't care what people said at school. We'd survived the underworld together. Who else could say that? Not many people, I'd bet.

He hugged me back with one arm, and we held on to each other for a little bit.

"Are you really okay?" he whispered.

"I think so," I whispered back.

Then we finally let go of each other, and he nearly dropped the cake. I was a little embarrassed to have hugged so long. But not sorry.

"You, uh, look better," he told me, clearing his throat. "Less . . . drowned."

"And you look less poisoned."

"Ha! Yep." He flexed his wrist while juggling the cake pan and showed me his bandaged finger. "Scars. Probably for life," he said, waggling his brows. "I'm an anomaly. They are studying me for science, baby." He was proud.

I hadn't told him what Babi had said about him being special. That might go to his head. I wasn't sure if I should now, as much as he was glowing over surviving this sewer meek bite. "Guess that was worth nearly dying over?" I teased.

"Bragging rights for years," he said, one corner of his mouth turning upward. He glanced over my shoulder and blinked rapidly. "Oh, uh, hello, Mrs. Novak. Pineapple upside-down cake. My granny made it. Extra brown sugar and butter."

"Excellent!" Mom said.

"Nom, nom, nom," I said appreciatively. "My favorite."

That's one thing they don't tell you about the underworld when you visit it unexpectedly: the lack of food during your entire journey. Ever since I'd gotten back, I'd been starving all the time. I could have scarfed down the entire cake.

"The pineapple's still warm," Ben confirmed. "Granny's sorting side dishes with my parents at the trunk. They brought, like, way too much food. Could probably use more hands." Ike the Third was already aware, lifting his nose to appreciate the food smells.

"On it," Mom said, lightly squeezing the back of Ben's neck affectionately as she passed by, heading down our front stairs. "Set that on the kitchen counter, hon. Then you kids go help Mr. Novak at the pizza oven before he sets himself on fire."

I took the cake pan from Ben and set it on the kitchen counter, waiting until my mom was definitely out of earshot. "Heard anything from Miss Neja yet?"

"Not since the hospital." He greeted the Shag Pack with scratches behind their ears. "Like I told you in our texts, it was kind of a blur. One minute I was seeing spots, and the next, we were riding through a dark tunnel. Then I woke up on a bed in the hospital, and she was arguing with the nurse about medical insurance and snakes."

"Whoa."

"What about Babi Morana? Your texts were confusing."

It was hard to report everything that had happened in the castle using secret code. Hard to tell him exactly what I had done to Grumbones, though I tried my best now to explain. About our former guide. About what happened in Rime Castle.

Who he really was.

Part of the problem in explaining all this to Ben, I thought, was that there were so many unknowns, with the state of Hereafter and what happened to all those harrowed souls when the husks were destroyed. Because one of those husks was my grandfather.

That was a lot. Whenever I thought about it, I got overwhelmed.

Ben puffed out his cheeks. "You know what? I think we need to work on a new private texting code. For underworld affairs. Like, a good one, just for us."

"Really? I'd like that," I said, feeling hopeful about this idea.

Maybe Ben understood more than I realized. I guess best friends did.

I gestured toward the kitchen door, and as the dogs followed us out, I briefly filled him in on a few more things as he asked me questions and we ambled down the back steps. Dad gave us a wave from the brick pizza oven. My father looked frazzled when he was cooking, but in a good way. Patio lights lit up a wooden table that was covered with flour and toppings on one side and cooked pizzas on the other. Woodsmoke floated into the air.

"So . . . ," Ben said. "You and Babi. Ghost chats."

I shook my head. "Still haven't tried it yet."

"Dang," he mumbled.

"Hey!"

He held up both hands in surrender. "No judgement. You'll talk to her again when you're ready."

And I would. I wasn't worried that she wouldn't answer a summons this time. Well, when it came to the underworld, there was always a little unknown in the equation. But. I just hadn't talked to her yet because first, I'd been in the hospital. And then I'd been busy with family stuff at home. Then I'd just decided to wait.

I guess I wanted to get grounded here first.

To stand on my own two feet.

That was the thing about being a good team member. You had to know when to trust the other person. Just because you weren't together didn't mean you abandoned your goals and gave up on everything. I had things to do. Episodes of *Real Housewives* to catch up on. Cemeteries to explore.

Besides, I knew I didn't have to worry about her anymore. She was the Rime Queen with a crown full of power. Babi could take care of herself now.

And I had my people here.

"So Babi Morana is for sure stuck in Hereafter?" Ben said.

"She's not like Miss Neja? She can't travel back and forth from Above to Below?"

"Nope."

"And we can't get back Below through the cemetery. Or so Miss Neja says. I mean, I haven't been back to Whispering Pines. Granny's watching me like a hawk. Plus, it's closed to the public right now, you know?"

"It is?" I stopped in the middle of the yard, still out of earshot from Dad. "Why?"

"Tsunami damage. They have state inspectors checking to make sure there aren't any graves disturbed. You know. For health reasons."

"You mean, to check that there aren't zombies rising from the earth?"

He laughed. "I think maybe they don't want anyone stepping on a grave and falling into a gruesome sinkhole, or whatever. They're making sure it's all stable."

Not as exciting. "What about the gift shop?"

"Think that's fine," he said, glancing at the workshop that sat across the yard from the pizza oven. The workshop is the place where I'd electrocuted myself with Dad when he had been putting power inside. It's shabby, made of metal, originally built for mechanic work—an "eyesore," our neighbors have said—but my parents use it to store some of their larger salvage from the dives and some of my dad's diving equipment. Boat parts. Old floral display material from Babi's former shop.

"Thought I saw something," Ben said, shaking his shoulders. "My eyes have been messed up since we got back. Probably a side effect of that mushroom salve."

I squinted into the shadows. The workshop's sliding door was open, but no light was on. My dad must have been inside earlier, working. He stored wood for the pizza oven in there. Probably forgot to close it. Seemed fine. I picked up a stick and tossed it in that direction, and Big chased after it without issue.

Ben and I both relaxed and continued our conversation.

"Since we got back, I've been doing a lot of thinking about everything we've experienced," Ben said. "And I'm convinced there's got to be more stuff out there than we know about. So I'm thinking about turning the Bigfoot club into a local paranormal club. You know, expanding it. What do you think?"

I frowned. "You're planning on telling all your Bigfooters where we've been?"

"I haven't yet. But we might need some help if we run into any tricky situations. And they're open to things that aren't so-called normal. If anyone's going to listen to us with an open mind, it's them."

He could be right. None of this was normal. Maybe some help would be a good idea.

And I didn't want to be the school loner anymore.

Haunted Helena, absolutely.

Lonely Helena, no.

I knew it wasn't going to be easy to convince a lot of people in school that I wasn't putting death curses on our classmates and didn't command a legion of hellhounds, but with Ben's help, maybe I'd have a shot. Especially if I could stay out of detention. Putting a nix on all occult-book reading in class would be a good start, I supposed.

But most important, I just wanted to spend more time with

Ben. Any friend cool enough to brave the underworld with you is worth it.

"Let's do it," I told him.

"Yeah?" he said, excitement in his eyes. "We can change the name to the Paranormal Enthusiasts Club."

"How about . . . the Onionheads."

He grinned. I could tell he liked that one a lot, but he diplomatically said, "How about . . . we ask the members and put it to a vote?"

"Sounds fair," I agreed. "After all, rules are important."

He groaned and then laughed. "Never ask the ferryman questions."

"Do not stick your finger in front of a sewer meek."

"Or talk to creepy girls throwing dolls down wells."

We both giggled.

"Hey, pizza's almost ready," my dad shouted from across the lawn.

I sighed. "Guess we'd better give him a hand."

Neither of us was in a hurry. I wanted to keep talking. That's the thing about best friends. You never get tired of being around them. I was really glad to have mine back.

We both lingered as Big trotted back from his game of fetch, but when I reached out to take the stick from his shaggy mouth, I was surprised to find something metal instead of wood.

"What's this?" I asked the dog. "You found something?"

The dog dropped a metal bottle into my waiting palm. My heart started beating faster. That was no bottle. It was a flask, missing its cap.

"If I didn't know better," Ben said, picking it up, "I'd say this looks just like Grumbones's flask. Remember?"

I remembered, all right. The one that had kept his identity hidden and smelled like cherry cough syrup. Was it just me, or did I detect the faintest scent of cherries now, wafting from its empty insides?

Impossible! I slowly turned my head. My heart raced as I peered across the lawn, into the workshop's darkened doorway. Nothing.

Or was there . . . ?

My throat tightened.

"The dog brought it from over there," I told Ben in a low voice, pointing.

"From the workshop," he whispered.

We both stared into the shadowed doorway together. Ben drew in a sharp breath.

"What?" I asked, gripping his arm.

He squinted harder, then whispered, "Could have sworn I saw a shadow. Of a person . . . and a large rat?"

A chill skittered down my spine.

I hadn't told Ben about Donk yet.

Miss Neja's words to Ben inside the Phantom Carriage popped up inside my head. *You will be alive but death-kissed. You will see things you didn't see before you journeyed through the underworld.*

Was it possible . . . ? Could it be?

Was Grumbones *right here in my backyard?!*

Hope vaulted inside me.

How could it be? I considered the possibility that this was the fate of harrowed souls after the Nightmare had been destroyed— that they were returning to earth as ghosts.

Laughter spilled from the back door of the house. My mom

was leading the Bookers to the pizza oven, and Granny Booker was craning her neck, looking for us.

"Where's that girl?" she said. "Helena? Let me see you, child."

Ben waved at her as he turned away from the workshop, unconcerned about whatever he might have seen. And maybe with good reason. This could have been an old flask that my parents had found on one of their dives in the harbor.

Probably just getting worked up over nothing all over again.

Because, you know.

I never seriously thought my backyard might be haunted.

Now I *hoped* it was.

ABOUT THE AUTHOR

Jenn Bennett is an award-winning author of young adult books, including *Alex, Approximately*; *Starry Eyes*; *The Lady Rogue*; and *Always Jane*. She also writes romance and fantasy for adults. Her books have earned multiple starred reviews, won the Romance Writers of America's RITA® Award, and been included on *Publishers Weekly*'s annual Best Books list. She lives in a haunted historic home near Birmingham, Alabama, with one husband, two dogs, and several friendly ghosts.